What the critics are saying...

Recommended Read! 5 Angels! "Each tale grabs you and takes you on an extremely explicit roller coaster ride filled with great passion." ~ *Contessa, Fallen Angel Reviews*

4 Stars! "Get ready for some heat and sizzle with this anthology!" ~ *Sarah Paige, Romantic Times BOOKClub*

Sizzlingly sexy romantic tales...If you like reading menage stories, then you won't want to miss these!"~ *Christine, eCataRomance Reviews*

"*Two Men and a Lady* offers up three delightful, sinful, and sexy tales of love, passion and the value of sharing." ~ *Terry Figueroa, Romance Reviews Today*

4.5 Flames! "Unique and ... engaging tales. I really enjoyed this anthology."~ *Crystal, Sizzling Romance Reviews*

5 Cupids! "Hot and steamy romance at its best. An absolutely must read!"~ *Tina, Cupid's Library Reviews*

TWO MEN and *A Lady*

CRICKET STARR
LYNN LAFLEUR
MICHELE R. BARDSLEY

ELLORA'S CAVE
ROMANTICA PUBLISHING

An Ellora's Cave Romantica Publication

www.ellorascave.com

Two Men and a Lady

ISBN # 1419952641
ALL RIGHTS RESERVED.
Lady's Choice Copyright © 2004 Cricket Starr
And Best Friend Makes Three Copyright © 2004 Lynn LaFleur
Saving Sarah Copyright © 2004 Michele R. Bardsley
Edited by: Raelene Gorlinsky
Cover art by: Syneca

Electronic book Publication: November, 2004
Trade paperback Publication: October, 2005

Warning:

The following material contains graphic sexual content meant for mature readers. *Two Men and a Lady* has been rated *E-rotic* by a minimum of three independent reviewers.

Ellora's Cave Publishing offers three levels of Romantica™ reading entertainment: S (S-ensuous), E (E-rotic), and X (X-treme).

S-*ensuous* love scenes are explicit and leave nothing to the imagination.

E-*rotic* love scenes are explicit, leave nothing to the imagination, and are high in volume per the overall word count. In addition, some E-rated titles might contain fantasy material that some readers find objectionable, such as bondage, submission, same sex encounters, forced seductions, etc. E-rated titles are the most graphic titles we carry; it is common, for instance, for an author to use words such as "fucking", "cock", "pussy", etc., within their work of literature.

X-*treme* titles differ from E-rated titles only in plot premise and storyline execution. Unlike E-rated titles, stories designated with the letter X tend to contain controversial subject matter not for the faint of heart.

Contents

Lady's Choice

Cricket Starr

Chapter One

"It's my turn to buy."

"No, it's mine."

Gehon Avermoe — Zelion warrior, interstellar trader, and half-owner in the space-trader *The Traveler* — narrowed his eyes at his partner and best friend. "You bought the last round at the bar on Sedion Seven. Don't you remember?"

"No I don't. You know I can't remember past the sixth round," Jackon said.

"That isn't my fault. I do remember and this one is my turn."

Jackon shook his head and held up his fist. "Let's settle this properly."

Eyes mere slits, Gehon's fist went up as well. "If you insist."

The bartender cringed at the impending fight, no doubt wishing the oversized men would take their argument outside. But instead of the pair pounding each other, they pounded their fists on the bar chanting "Ti, To, Te" in unison.

Jackon's index finger went out while Gehon's hand stayed a fist.

"Hammer smashes Sword. I win," the redhead said with a grin. Digging his credit chips out, he paid for their drinks.

The bartender took the money with relief and headed for the other end of the bar, wondering if the warriors would remain on good behavior the entire time they were there.

Both men drank deep. "Good ale," Gehon said. His gaze darted around the interior of the Lost Time Lounge. Not the most reputable bar in port, but they didn"t water the ale and the chairs and tables were clean for the most part. The floor...well, you normally didn't want to look too close at a tavern floor anyway.

Jackon set down his beer mug and nudged Gehon in the side. "Check out the babe at the table over there." His jaw dropped in open admiration. "She"s perfect!"

Gehon sighed and put his own drink down. As always his best friend had women on the brain. As an unmarried Zelion, that was to be expected, but Jackon was forever finding the perfect babe, the lady of his dreams. Every woman he met he was certain was going to turn out to be his Zelion match.

Of course, not one of those women had been his friend's true mate. While fun in bed, they'd lacked the deeper connection that permitted conception and every time Jackon had been disappointed. After spending a little time loving them, he'd kissed them and said goodbye, and then come back swearing he'd never fall for another pretty face again.

Sometimes just days later he'd find another perfect woman and the whole thing would start again.

Occasionally Gehon thought Jackon was enjoying the search for his mate far too much. It wasn't that he himself didn't enjoy taking a woman to bed, but he didn't do it with any illusion that she'd turn out to be his true. He'd always believed that a Zelion man knew when the woman was right, well before bedding her.

Jackon was convinced every woman was right until bedding her and finding out he was wrong.

Resisting the urge to put sarcastic thoughts into words, Gehon turned to examine his friend's "current future true". "Which table?"

"In the corner. Near the back door." Jackon's voice hushed, deepening into a near purr. He took a deep breath through his nose, his eyes glazing in appreciation. "Gehon, I can SMELL her."

Smell? Gehon straitened and searched the room. If Jackon could catch this woman's scent from this distance, she might very well be his friend's true.

There she was at the corner table, a mug of ale in front of her. She was a medium-sized woman with pale skin that contrasted with her jet-black hair cut close to her shoulders, except for one slender braid that reached to her waist. Even from here, he could see how voluptuous she was, her breasts heavy inside her simple spacewear.

Her features were sharp, angular, her mouth wide with rich red lips. She looked...aristocratic, that was the word. Whoever this woman was, she appeared distinctly out of place in the Lost Time Lounge, in spite of her nondescript spacer fatigues. With that face she should be wearing crystal jewels and sipping wine from a goblet studded with gems, not hoisting a plastic-steel mug of cheap ale. She should be dressed in fine synthsilk...or nothing at all.

Gehon startled at that last thought, sucking air deep through his nostrils. A scent like honey and citrus filled his nose and inside his trousers his cock hardened for immediate action.

He gasped. *Space above and beyond.* The woman was *his* true mate, he knew it!

"Stars below, Gehon. My cock's so hard I could cut arcrystals. She's got to be the one." Jackon jumped to his feet. "I'm going to talk to her."

Wait a zesecond. Gehon glared as his friend rushed across the room to the woman's table. She was his true, not Jackon's, and he'd been looking for her just as long as his friend had. There was only one true mate for any Zelion man—and this woman was his! Grabbing their mugs, he followed.

Lija stared up at the two men flanking her table, twirled the end of her maiden's braid, and tossed it over her shoulder. She should have cut it off long ago, but what Daddy didn't know wouldn't hurt him. So she'd experimented a little...okay, more than a little, but that was a good thing. Experimentation could keep a girl from making mistakes. Suppose she had wrapped her braid around the wrists of the first guy who'd talked her into sex? Daddy wouldn't have been happy about having a lowly mechanic as a son-in-law, even if the guy had had the most beautiful muscles she'd ever seen.

Not that either of the two men in front of her were slouches in the muscle department—or the height, face, and hair departments, either! Either one of the pair appeared capable of bench-pressing her microshuttle, and looking real good while doing it.

The first one to arrive was blond, with eyes like blue light crystals. He was taller than his buddy by maybe three centimeters, even though both men had to be well over two meters tall. His face was lean, with a sexy smile that took her breath away.

The shorter man had hair nearly the red of a summer sunset, and his eyes were the deep brown of fertile earth, set in a round ruddy face. His shoulders were broader than his friend's, but his waist narrowed into slender hips. Without seeing it, she'd bet his rear was round like his face, and that he had plump ass-cheeks just perfect for wrapping a girl's legs around.

Funny, she'd never really been interested in two men at the same time, but both these guys made her mouth water. More than her mouth, actually. The crotch of her spacer suit dampened with her arousal and she crossed her legs, hoping they wouldn't notice.

Both men's gaze riveted below her belt and they sniffed the air, their eyes glazing for a moment. Her eyes widened at their reaction. *Oh, yeah, they'd noticed.* They must have superb senses of smell.

The front of both men's trousers tightened into a pair of impressive packages. In the back of her mind, Lija took in their sizes and did the math. Yep, either of them would do nicely for her last fling of freedom before buckling under to her fate.

Too bad she only needed one. Choosing was going to be tough.

She waved her hand at the chairs next to her at the round table. "Would you gentlemen like to sit down?"

The pair exchanged nearly angry looks as they took their positions, one on each side of her. The redheaded man carrying the mugs slammed them down on the table hard enough to spill some of the contents.

His companion glared at him. "I don't need your help."

"I'm not offering help. You forgot your drink."

"I didn't need a drink, either."

Lija put up her hands. "Gentlemen, please. Here I was feeling lonely and now I have two lovely men to keep me company." She waved to the bartender. "Please, a pitcher for my new friends."

Both men had their credit chips out. "You won't be paying," the blond one told her.

"I'll buy," the redhead said at the same time.

Blue eyes narrowed into slits. "No, I'll buy."

"Not on your life."

"Don't tempt me."

The pair glared at each other then both men's right fists came up.

"Now just a zeminute…" she said, wishing to stop the fight, but to her surprise they chanted in unison, pounding their fists on the table.

"Ti, To, Te."

Red's fist had one finger sticking out, Blondie's had turned into an open palm.

"Sword slices Ax. I win," the red-haired man said smugly.

Blondie glared and folded his arms, but allowed his buddy to pass over the credit chips for the pitcher.

Lija smiled. These hulking he-men played a children's game to settle disputes? *This was going to be fun.* "So, may I ask my companions for their names?"

Red spoke first. "I'm Gehon Avermoe. This is my friend, Jackon Overton."

She extended her hand. "My name is Lija. And I'm pleased to meet you."

Jackon's hand slashed out first, barely beating Gehon's. His palm covered hers possessively. "Not nearly as pleased as I am to meet you, my lady." Pulling her hand to his lips, he kissed it gently. His lips tingled the back of her hand and between her legs the dampness grew.

Lija gulped. At this rate she'd soon need padded undergarments.

Gehon captured her other hand and pulled it to his lips. "I cannot speak of how wonderful it is to meet you, Lady Lija."

Caught between the two of them nibbling her hands, Lija wondered that she was able to breathe. Hot and cold flushes ran up and down her spine, pooling in her dampened groin.

She seriously needed one of these men to bed her. Trouble was, which one? What a delicious dilemma for one woman to have.

Jackon's blue eyes glared over her hand at his friend. "Her taste is for me, Gehon."

Brown eyes narrowed into a matching glare. "Her taste is mine, Jackon."

They stared at each other, then suddenly both men sat up, eyes widening and jaws dropping in unison. Gehon licked the back of the hand he held, Jackon doing the same with his. Lija shivered under their tongues.

"What do you taste?" the redhead asked.

The blond licked his lips relishing the flavor there. "Sweet. Like honeybeets."

"Sweeter than that. Caramallow."

"Mellowdrops."

"Chocoberries."

They both dropped her hands and Lija pulled them back to her side of the table as the men stared at each other, and then at her.

"The same for both of us?" Jackon said, his voice heavy with disbelief.

"So it seems. A cosmic joke," Gehon replied.

Jackon snorted, Gehon snickered, then both men laughed heartily until there were tears in their eyes.

Unsure of what was going on, Lija reached for the pitcher to refill her mug. "One of you want to let me in on the joke?"

Wiping his eyes, Gehon took the pitcher from her and poured for all three of them. "Well, my Lady Lija, it's all about Zelion biology."

Halfway through the second pitcher, she still didn't quite understand the pair's explanation. "So, while you can have lovers before marriage, each Zelion man can only really mate with one woman. This is what you call a "true mate"."

Both men nodded.

"This woman doesn't have to be a Zelion and in fact often isn't. Somehow this was bred into the race to keep it strong."

Jackon hoisted his mug. "Hybrid vigor."

"No hereditary diseases," Gehon added, sipping in agreement.

Lija drank from her mug, wondering at how heavy it seemed. She'd have to be careful. She was getting a little tipsy. "While a Zelion man can have sex with any number of women, he's only fertile with his true mate."

"A Zelion man searches the universe for his mate, one woman at a time," Jackon said.

"Or, in your case, two or three at a time," Gehon snickered.

"Never three, and only once two. The twins, remember?"

"Ah, yes. They were twins, weren't they."

"Well, I had to test both of them. Why not do them at once?"

"There was an efficiency to your decision, I must admit."

Lija stared at Jackon, piqued at this description of his conquests. "You took two women to bed while looking for your true? How many other women have you been with?"

Her jealousy must have been obvious. The blond man held up his hands. "Not that many and it was all in looking for my one true." He glared over at Gehon, who still snickered. "It's not like you've been a Balamari monk for the past many years. You've had your share of women."

Gehon nodded. "My share was somewhat less than yours. But point taken." He turned to Lija. "Zelion men aren't celibate by nature, but we are each faithful to our true once we find her. With our true we can have children and no Zelion man will give that up."

It was becoming hard to lift her mug. How much had she drunk already? "So you believe that I'm your true."

Both men nodded.

"The same woman for both of you?"

They looked at each other and shrugged.

"We've always been close," one told her. It was becoming hard to tell which was which. They were turning a bit blurry around the edges.

"Since we were kids, similar tastes in everything," the other answered. Oh, wait, that was Jackon, she could see his pale hair.

"So how do you know that I'm the right one?"

"You smell like a true to both of us," a blurry Gehon said.

"And you taste like a true," added the Jackon blur.

"Therefore you must be our true," they finished together.

"You can't be serious about my marrying both of you."

The two blurs looked at each other, and for the first time since the pitcher battle, she sensed serious antagonism between them.

The red-topped blur answered her. "No, Lady Lija, we don't expect that. It will have to be our lady's choice as to which of us you marry."

Lija laughed. It was becoming harder and harder to take these two seriously. She'd heard plenty of lines in the past, but this one defied gravity. These guys almost had her believing that she was their one and only hope for having kids, and that she was destined to marry one of them.

Under the circumstances a fine joke that would be.

What a shame. Her original plan had been to come into the bar, have some ale, and find a decent man to take to bed. She'd hit the jackpot on the man front, but unfortunately she'd had too much to drink to take advantage of it.

Time she got back to her microshuttle. A couple hours of sleep in the cockpit and she'd be able to fly home. Lija staggered to her feet. "It's been fun talking to you gentlemen, but I must be going."

The two blurs stood at once.

"Where are you heading for, Lady Lija?" one asked.

She had trouble staying vertical, but fortunately one of the men was close enough to lean against. Strong arms held her close to a massive, manly chest. She looked up and saw his red hair and warm brown eyes. Gehon, that was the name.

"I need to go to my ship. Time to go."

"But…" the man holding her started to say.

The blond blur took her arm. "I think you need some help getting to your ship."

What a wonderful idea. It was harder to walk than she'd expected. What kind of ale did they serve in this bar, anyway?

She summoned her dignity and answered him with her most regal voice. "You may be right. I accept your assistance, Lord Jackon."

"It's Warrior Jackon and Warrior Gehon, but we're happy to help," the man holding her said. "Just put your arm around my neck."

"Hey, I get to carry her," Jackon butted in.

Through her fuzziness he heard them argue back and forth. Finally she heard, "Ti, To, Te" followed by "Ax chops hammer."

She faded out for a moment and when she opened her eyes again, the man holding her had changed to having blond hair surrounding a narrow face. Jackon carried her out of the bar, Gehon walking behind, grumbling under his breath, "I had her first."

Two gorgeous men to guard her on the way to her ship—how delightful! The darkness outside made her sleepy and she snuggled deeper into Jackon's arms. He really did smell delicious…not that Gehon didn't smell fabulous as well.

Truth was, both of these men were just too delectable for words. Too bad she wouldn't be able to spend more time with them. The last thing she noted was when they turned into the spaceport, then she didn't notice anything more.

* * * * *

Lija woke to softness and warmth, not the stiff plastic seat of her microshuttle. She must have made it back home after all. Either that or it had been a dream, her encounter with the men in the Lost Time Lounge.

And what an incredible dream it had been. She'd dreamed she'd headed out in her microshuttle for one last chance to be herself, and met the two most wonderful men, each of whom wanted to be her husband. They were hunky alien warriors, with bulging muscles and bulging pants, and the funniest way of solving disputes with a children's game.

She stretched her arms. *Daddy would never believe this story – even if she could tell him about it.*

Her side itched, and Lija tried to scratch it, only to find that she couldn't move her arm lower than her shoulder. Startled full awake, Lija opened her eyes to see the bare metal walls of a spaceship cabin and a bunk beneath her, a bunk to which she'd been tied by the arms and legs.

Lija didn't recognize the bunk or the cabin, but did the soft sound of the propulsion engines. She was on a ship, a freighter from the engine sounds, and somewhere out in space.

Space be damned. She'd been kidnapped!

Chapter Two

Jackon looked nervously at the video image of their "guest", now awake and struggling with her bonds. She didn't look nearly as cute as she had last night when he'd placed her on the bed, all rumpled, cuddly, and smelling so inviting. It had been all he could do to not join her under the blanket…the same blanket she'd just tossed to the floor. "Do you think she's angry, Gehon?"

Gehon turned up the sound to hear better the indelicate curses coming from their true's delicate lips. "I think she's very angry."

Jackon chewed on his lower lip. "Maybe we shouldn't have tied her down."

"We didn't want her falling out of the bunk when we took off, or leaving the cabin, and there wasn't a lock on the door. We had to secure her."

Lija managed to get one of her wrists to her mouth and was gnawing on the strap around it. Jackon watched her efforts and worried. "That's plastisteel rope. She could break a tooth doing that. We should do something."

Nodding, his partner checked their position in space, switching the controls to automatic. "The ship's secure for now, I guess we better get in there and explain."

Freed from her bonds and sitting up on the bunk, Lija listened to them but obviously did not like their explanation. She glared at them, every delectable ounce of her trembling with fury. "You abducted me, warriors. I'll see you punished for this."

"We didn't want to bring you without your permission, but you weren't in any condition to give it last night," Gehon told her.

"I don't understand how I could have gotten so drunk on three mugs of ale."

Jackon squirmed. Time to come clean about that at least. "Well, that last pitcher wasn't ale, sweetling. We'd moved to Aldean brandy. The taste isn't that different but it's a little stronger."

She froze in place, eyes wide with shock. "You switched my drink to brandy without telling me?"

"Not at all. I'm sure we told you." Desperate, Jackon glanced over at Gehon. "We did tell her, didn't we?"

"I thought you mentioned it. I know we discussed it. The ale was a little weak and we were wanting something stronger."

Jackon snapped his fingers. "Oh, it might have been when she was using the sanitary."

Gehon nodded. "That was it. We did discuss it, but you were in the sanitary."

Lija was livid with fury. "So you switched drinks, got me drunk, then hauled me onto your ship and took off with me. Where is my microshuttle?"

He shrugged. "Back at the spaceport. You fell asleep before telling us which one it was."

"I passed out, you mean!"

Their true looked close to attacking them, and Jackon decided that it had been a good thing that they'd searched her while she was unconscious and removed the hidden weapons in her clothing. He'd hated to get stuck with one of the deadly looking knives they'd found.

There was far more to their little true than met the eye. Not that that would keep him away from her, or Gehon either. Zelion men were used to their women being fighters.

Maybe he could diffuse the situation. "You were adorably tipsy," Jackon told her. "It was delightful carrying you to the ship." He tried a friendly smile that she didn't return. In fact, if her glare could kill, Jackon would be incinerated.

Gehon held up his hands. "You were somewhat the better—that is, the worse—for drink. We couldn't very well leave you there. When we got back to the ship we had an urgent request to deliver some cargo to Brasia. That's why we took off instead of waiting for you to sober up."

Jackon broke in. "Please, Lady Lija. Listen to us. We don't intend any harm to you."

"Nothing other than kidnapping, rape…"

"That's enough of that!"

To Jackon's surprise, Gehon's temper flared. He stared as his buddy's face reddened to a shade he'd only seen once before, when a client had tried to stiff them after a delivery. Unsuccessfully, he remembered. A well-thrust energy sword had disabused the man from not paying them what they were due.

But still, for Gehon to speak that way to a woman? Never would he have predicted that. Having their true so close was making them behave abnormally.

"You are not kidnapped, nor will there be any rape," Gehon told her. "You're a guest on our ship while we discuss matrimony with you."

Her jaw dropped. "Discuss matrimony?" She looked at both of them in disbelief. "You frelling space-cadets really think I'm going to marry one of you?"

That hurt. "We only want to discuss it with you," Jackon told her. "There's no reason to start calling us names."

"You get me drunk…"

"We joined you in a few drinks," Jackon told her firmly.

"…kidnapped me…"

"…invited you to stay on our ship," Gehon added.

"…tied me to a bunk…"

"…secured you against falling out during takeoff," Jackon finished.

"…and now you expect me to marry you? You're right, you aren't the space cadets — I'd be one if I listened to you!"

Gehon folded his arms and leaned toward her, causing Lija to move back on the bed. Even Jackon had to admit that his friend was impressive when he did that.

"How would you like to have a husband who would worship the ground you walk on, who would always be there for you, and who would never betray you? That's what Zelion men are like for their trues."

She rolled her eyes and muttered. "Oh, really."

"Yes really. Anything that happens will be your choice. All we ask is the chance to show you how good it can be."

Staring at the tall redheaded man, Lija couldn't help but see the honesty in his face. Gehon really did believe that he and his buddy would be the best choices for a husband for her. Given her alternatives to date, she had to admit he had a point. Either man, Gehon or Jackon, would be better than the choice her father had come up with for her.

Too bad Prince Brentan wasn't one of these men. But he wasn't and that was that.

On the other hand, she'd been looking for a last fling, a sexual adventure and here she was, abducted right into one. Even if her father found out about it, she could always claim coercion. Which it was — almost.

The situation was practically perfect. They were even going to Brasia where Axona had an embassy. Once she'd gotten to their destination, she'd have no trouble getting away from them. All she'd have to do is give her name to the authorities and she'd be free.

Lija's anger faded into sexual interest. Why not let these guys show her a good time? The worst that would happen would be that she'd enjoy herself.

That wouldn't be so bad, would it?

"So what you're asking is to make love to me? Both of you." She shook her head. "I've got to warn you, I've been told I'm difficult to please during sex."

Blond Jackon grinned at her, oozing sexiness. "Oh I think we can meet any challenge you come up with. No woman has ever left my bed unsatisfied."

"Nor mine," redheaded Gehon answered, eyes narrowing at his rival. The two glared at each other, and Lija was reminded of a pair of bull-deer she'd once seen on Axona, vying for the same female.

Axonian bull-deer were relentless in their pursuit of a doe and Lija could see how these men had more than rampant sexuality in common with them. Just being around them for the next few days would be torture unless she got some sort of satisfaction, soon.

Would it be a mistake to let them make love to her? She'd had lovers in the past who'd had a real problem taking no for an answer once they'd heard yes. Sure, Gehon had assured her that neither he nor Jackon would force her to be their mate, but how often had a man told her one thing then done the complete opposite? If she chose one of them now, she could have a real problem getting rid of him when the time came.

On the other hand...suppose she didn't choose one of them? Suppose she bedded both of them and played one off the other? That could solve any number of problems. She'd get laid, something she was beginning to want very badly, they'd be kept busy trying to win her favor, and when the time came to say goodbye, she'd simply tell them she couldn't possibly choose between them. She was current with her anticonception shots, so there wasn't any way she'd get pregnant. They were certainly healthy...

Lija glanced over at the two men watching her intently, waiting for her decision. Yep, very healthy. Both were so yummy...how could she decide which to marry, even if she could marry one of them? Which she couldn't.

But bed them both? Sure, why not. It was a perfect plan and no time like the present to get started.

She folded her hands on her thighs, rubbing them beneath the fabric of her spacer pants. Both men's eyes widened and their breathing picked up. Lija had to resist smiling at their obvious interest.

"Maybe you're right." Lija moved her hands to the gap between her legs, massaging the upper muscles as if she had a cramp. Sharp intakes of breaths told her the guys had noticed. She glanced up at their now-straining crotches and could barely resist a gasp of her own. These two were fueled and ready for takeoff.

"You've both told me how talented you are in bed. I was thinking I'd give each of you a chance to show me just how good you are."

The guys glanced at each other and then at her. Two pairs of eyes, brown and blue, stared at her.

"Is there any harm in my bedding both of you?" she asked.

"No, not exactly." Gehon hesitated. "But no man wants to share his woman."

Just as she expected. This would work out fine. Once they realized she couldn't choose between them, they'd be happy to let her go. Lija was almost disappointed as to how easy it was going to be.

"It will be like a competition," Jackon broke in eagerly. "A loving competition." He nudged Gehon with a grin. "You've always said that you were better than I was."

Hostility radiated off the red-haired man. "I am better. Quality more than makes up for quantity."

"Well then, now you can prove it. We'll both bed her and she will pick the one she likes best." He licked his sensuous lips as he returned to stare at her. Lija grew warm under his passionate gaze. "Winner gets to marry you."

That wouldn't happen. There would be no "winner", she'd see to that. "It will be my choice, correct?"

Both Gehon and Jackon nodded.

"Very well. How long until we get to Brasia?"

"About four days."

"So, that should give us plenty of time. Everything should be settled by the time we reach their space."

She gave each man a long look-over. Jackon perched on the edge of the single chair in the cabin while Gehon leaned against the wall. For all the nonchalance in their stances they looked ready to pounce.

"Now there is only one question," she said deliberately, knowing the reaction they would have. "Who goes first?"

Hostility radiated off the men and they glared at each other. Their fists slowly came up. "Ti, To…"

"NO!" Shouting and jumping up on the bed, Lija jerked their attention back to her. She gave them her best glare and they sheepishly dropped their fists to their sides. "Not this time. MY choice, remember?"

After exchanging uneasy glances, both men nodded. "Yes, Lady Lija," they said, one after the other.

Buoyed by her first success at seizing control, Lija leaned back, considering her options. She had to pick one of them to make love to her…but which one? Eyeing each of the gorgeous men in front of her, she couldn't help but wonder how she'd fallen into this fate.

All she'd been looking for was a quick last grab at sexual freedom with a man of her choice. Instead she'd hit the jackpot and gotten two.

Which one should she choose to go first? *Space be damned*, the inside of her pants dampened under their gazes, both men watching her with predatory need. How was she ever going to pick one of them?

Another old children's rhyme came to her. Okay, it was silly, but given these guys and their penchant for games, maybe it was appropriate.

She closed her eyes, letting a mental finger do the picking for her. *Eiani, meani, mickey, moe.* When she opened them, she was looking at Jackon.

"You," she said. "You go first."

Gehon frowned, but he nodded slowly, acknowledging her choice. "Very well. Jackon can have today. I'll get tomorrow. We'll see about the rest of the time."

Lija's eyes followed him, but he didn't meet her gaze as he turned to leave the room. "I'll be on the bridge," he mumbled as he slipped through the door.

With an unaccustomed pang of regret, she watched him leave.

Once the door slid shut, Jackon leaned over her, eagerness in his stance. "So, let's get started." His gaze raked her body up and down. "What do you want to do first?"

Delighted as she was with his enthusiasm, Lija couldn't ignore the other demands of her body any longer. Her stomach grumbled, reminding her of how long it had been since her last real meal. Lunch the day before, she realized.

She put one hand on his arm. "Before we do anything, do you suppose I could get something to eat?"

"Of course!" Jackon pulled her onto her feet and toward him. "I'll take you to the galley and you can choose anything your heart desires for breakfast. Sweet rolls, convi buns, cocoabean cake. Juices from any fruit you can name. We have real Earth coffee and Zelion tea. Anything you want I can get you. Just one thing first."

"Oh, what's that?"

"This." He lowered his face opened his mouth over hers, claiming a kiss. It was warm, hard, and everything she could have expected, plus a great deal more. Many men had kissed her before, but not this way. Not possessively, not like she was the only woman in the world for him.

Jackon was claiming her, with his kiss, with his hard body that he pressed tight against her. He wanted her, and he wanted her to know it. He was telling her with his kiss that she was his, for now, for always—if that was her choice. If it wasn't then he'd be alone forever.

Lija broke away from him, leaning back to stare into his face, so wanting, so intense. He breathed heavily, only slightly less than her. As they stared at each other, their breathing synchronized, combining. Becoming one.

He smiled. "You feel it, don't you? The joining. That's what there is between true mates. We become one."

Shaking, Lija pulled away from him. This was the last thing she needed, to find herself bound to one of these men. It wasn't like she could take one to be her husband. She'd have to be very careful.

"But there are two of you," she reminded him. That was her edge, that they wouldn't be able to convince her to choose between them.

Jackon's smile faded. "True, Gehon says he feels as I feel." A look of almost pain crossed his face. "I would be sorry if that is so. I know you are my mate. It would be...difficult if you are also his."

Some of his good humor returned. "But we need not talk of that now. For today and tonight, you are mine to court and love. First we shall see to your breakfast, and then to my quarters." He kissed her hand. "My bed is large and very soft...not that I expect you'll be wanting to sleep much. Come."

Wondering just what she'd gotten herself in for, Lija followed him from the room.

Chapter Three

Breakfast was everything Jackon had promised. Lija ate the last of her fruit roll, washing it down with Zelion tea. Excellent tea, best she'd ever had. The Zelions were noted for their tea, grown in the high mountains of their rugged world.

They were known for their warriors, too, fighting men without compare. Persuading or hiring Zelion men to fight had won more than one war. They were said to be impossible to defeat in battle.

Lija glanced over at Jackon, drinking his own tea, keeping watch on her. He was a prime specimen of a Zelion man, and she began to wonder if she might need to rethink her strategy.

He'd as much as told her that Zelion men were also known to be undefeatable in love as well.

The Zelion man on the other side of the table grinned at her. "Had enough to eat?"

"Yes." There wasn't much else to say. She'd eaten her fill and couldn't manage another bite. No point in putting things off further.

He shoved his still half-full mug away. "Then maybe you'll come to my room now?"

"Maybe that wouldn't such a good idea. I'm supposed to judge you both fairly. What about a neutral location?"

Jackon frowned. "You mean like the cabin you're in now?" He didn't seem to like that suggestion much. "It isn't very decorative. For my first time with my true, I was hoping for something a little more romantic."

Lija seized on that idea. "Maybe we could make it that way."

He nodded, his expression dubious. "I suppose." He seemed to think for a moment and then grinned at her. "Sure. We've got a consignment of material in the hold that would do nicely. I can borrow some of it."

An hour later, Lija stared at her refurbished room. Who would have guessed that inside Jackon's warrior exterior beat the heart of an interior decorator?

A thick rug now cushioned the floor and he'd brought in lighting rods that simulated the soft glow of candlelight to fill each corner. In the new lighting, the formerly bare walls sported soft hangings of pastel colors fading to a deep mauve, the same color of the quilt that covered the bed. It turned out the bunk was a convertible that pulled out into a good three meters width.

Big enough for three, a little voice in her head said. Lija ignored that, instead turning to the one man who would be sharing the bunk with her this day at least.

Jackon grinned.

"It hardly looks like the same room. How is it you had all this stuff?" Lija waved her hand around, indicating the new contents.

Jackon shrugged. "We're traders — that's what we do, buy and sell goods, particularly luxury items. We picked up the fabric on Remas. Some of it is destined for a palace remodel on Brasia."

She gaped. "Remanian fabric needed for a palace remodel? This stuff is worth a fortune!"

"The cost isn't important if it makes you happy. You're my true, Lija. Nothing is too good for you."

"What would Gehon say to that?"

"The same thing. No Zelion man would say different." He put his finger on her lips. "But we won't talk of Gehon now. His time with you will come later. This is just for you and me, my lady."

He ran a practiced estimating gaze down her frame, evaluating her garment. "You could use some new clothes. I'll see what I can find...later."

"Later?"

His grin grew wider. "Now is not the time for finding new clothes. Now we take clothes off."

She was going to argue, but Jackon grabbed the bottom of his shirt and pulled it up and off over his head. One look at his broad shoulders, sculpted pecs and tight abs, and she lost track of any arguments she had. Jackon had the best body she'd ever seen, and she'd seen more than a few.

Well, maybe not that many more, but still, wow!

His grin turned into a chuckle and she realized she'd spoken that last aloud. "I'm glad you approve." Stepping forward, he took hold of her shoulder, pulling her unresisting body into his arms. "Let's see what else you like."

Again his lips captured hers and they merged together. Warm lips, his lips, the only lips in the world, demanding yet gentle. Then there was his tongue...even better...testing and tasting the inside of her mouth with practiced skill.

Practiced...but something else. There was something in the way he groaned, the way he clutched at her. It was like he'd been looking for something for so long and had finally found it. Her taste. Her smell, and the feel of her skin as he stroked her cheek when he came up for air. That's what he'd said Zelion men looked for and how they knew when they'd found their mates.

Their senses told them when they found a woman who matched them and could bear their children. Jackon's were telling him that she was the one. Her senses told her the same thing.

Hers also told her that Jackon was going to be fabulous in bed.

Jackon was shaking as he pulled back, a fine sheen of sweat dotting his brow. His gaze darted around her face as if he didn't know where to look first. His breaths came in gasps, leaving gaps between his words.

"I'd always heard...that it was like this...when I'd found her. I mean you. When I found YOU. Gehon told me it would be unlike anything I'd ever experienced. He was right."

She put one finger on his lips. "You said we weren't to talk of him."

"You're right, I did." He crushed her into another kiss, a claiming kiss that left her as breathless as he was, and swept her off her feet. Lija's world became nothing more than this man's lips on hers, his hard body holding her close. She barely noticed the soft surface of the bed beneath her when he laid her down, kneeling beside her on the bed. Still kissing her, he slipped open the fastenings of her suit, pulling it off her. The cooler air in the room felt wonderful against her superheated skin as he slid his hands up to cup her breasts.

His thumbs found her nipples and ran across them. One thing about it, Jackon was an experienced lover. Lija moaned as he trailed kisses down her neck, his hands doing a sensuous massage across her chest. When his mouth found her nipple, she whimpered. Then his hand moved further down her body and found the dampness between her thighs and she groaned.

How long had it been since she'd been with a man? Too long, obviously, if she was reacting so fast to this one's skilled hands. She never gotten this hot this fast.

The little voice in her head woke up again. Maybe it wasn't that he was so skilled, or that it had been so long since her last time in bed. Maybe there was something to this business of being with a true that made every kiss of the lips, every stroke of a hand, an erotic dream?

No. She couldn't think that. Neither of the Zelion warriors could become her permanent mate. This was just for fun, sex for its own sake, to relieve the tension she'd been under at home.

Tension—tension that was rapidly melting away under Jackon's skilled hands. It was amazing how good his long fingers felt. He slipped one of them into her folds, seeking her clitoris and finding the sensitive nubbin with uncanny speed. He stroked it once, twice… So good—so very, very good. Her legs tensed, along with her belly, and she raised her hips to meet his gentle strokes. Desire like quicksilver ran along her limbs, seeking her core.

His voice caressed her ears. "Like that? Of course you do. Your body has been crying out for my touch. You were made for me to pleasure." Leaning closer, he whispered, "Give me your passion, my true lady. Let yourself go."

She did. With a shattering cry, Lija threw her head back and let her climax rocket through her, claiming her and leaving her shaking. Jackon pulled her close and held her as she sobbed her release. He patted her back and smoothed her hair from her face, whispering endearments into her ears. When she regained control he smiled into her eyes, his pleasure in her climax obvious.

"You've wanted that for some time. It was best to get some of your stored-up need out of the way, so that we can enjoy the rest more."

Still shaking, Lija stared into Jackon's handsome face. All he'd had to do was touch her and she'd exploded. Never had an orgasm come that easily to her before. Or that fast. Or that hard.

Axonian women were notorious for being difficult to satisfy. She'd been told this many times by previous lovers who'd had to work extra hard to bring her to completion. Obviously what Axonian women really needed was to find a few good Zelion men.

Jackon's expression was tender as he stroked the skin of her neck. With his crotch pressed tight against her thigh, she could feel his erection, hard and imperative, yet there was nothing demanding in how he touched her. He wanted her, that was obvious, but he waited for her to recover before proceeding.

She let her gaze travel to the tightness of his black trousers and wondered that the seam held under the strain. Lija put her hand on the thick bulge under the fabric and stroked him.

He purred, then covered her hand with his, halting it in place. "Let me get out of these."

Lija sat up and watched as the tall blond tugged his pants down, freeing his cock from confinement. It sprang out, hard and ready, the tip weeping for joy. Her mouth watered at the sight.

Jackon might very well have the prettiest cock she'd ever seen. Absolutely straight with just the slightest bow upwards, otherwise completely symmetrical. No blemishes along the shaft, the head like a purple plum, ripe for the picking. Simply beautiful, and all for her!

Moving forward on her knees, Lija bent to kiss it, grasping the shaft with her hands. Jackon shuddered under her touch, but remained still as she gently explored his width and length. His chest heaved as he kept control, his fists clutching the bed covering beneath him.

Lija fondled the heavy balls beneath his shaft. Again, sheer perfection. His smell filled her nostrils, heady and rich, exquisitely masculine. The sexual tension he'd worked so hard to dispel her of returned with a vengeance, maybe twice what she'd felt before. Her clit throbbed and she pressed her legs together, trying to give it some relief.

Opening her mouth, Lija took in the head of his cock, stopping short of his shaft. Jackon groaned. She let her tongue slip into the narrow opening in the tip, tasting the flavor of him. Wonderful, just wonderful. She could eat him all day.

Jackon grabbed her head and pushed himself further into her mouth. "Please, more," he groaned. "Your mouth feels so good."

Lija went on a cock-eating spree, enthusiastically sucking the head in and out of her mouth, letting her teeth catch the edges of the glans on the upswing. Her hand worked along his shaft while it swelled to fill and overfill it, making her use both palms to cover his width.

Jackon's fingers anchored in her hair, directing but not forcing her actions. His words became halting then completely indistinct as passion drew him closer to completion. Abruptly he stiffened and his eyes flew open.

"My lady, stop, please. I want my first seed to be spent in you."

Lija lifted her head but didn't release his cock or stop stroking it. "Jackon, if we're to be friends, I want you to use my name."

"But lady…"

She pulled extra hard and he had to struggle to keep from coming. When he recovered control, there was a dangerous look in his eyes. "You did that on purpose," he said accusingly.

She grinned. "You planning on using my name?"

He gave a short laugh. "I better. You're a dangerous woman to disobey. I should have known that when I found those knives of yours."

"So *you* took them. I'll want them back, later."

"Absolutely. Whatever the lady…I mean whatever you want, Lija. Can I have my cock back now? I really want to put it inside you."

Lija licked the end of it, tasting more of his essence, sensing how close he was to coming. The ache between her legs intensified. She wanted him inside her as well.

Releasing him, she sat back as Jackon moved to his knees. He grabbed her and pulled her tight against his chest, his cock poking her in the stomach. He caught her lips in another spellbinding kiss, and this time when it broke she was flat on her back and he hovered over her, weight braced on his hands, his cock between her legs and poised to take possession.

"My turn for control, Lija. This joining is a claiming. You are my true mate."

"Only if that's my choice," she countered.

She had to ignore the quick pain in his eyes before he nodded. "Only if you choose. For me there is no other choice, only you." He surged forward, embedding himself deep inside her. Lija gasped at the force of his entry, then the sweetness of how wonderful he felt. His cock filled and stretched her in ways she couldn't remember being filled before. Was he really that much bigger, or was there something else at work here?

Whatever it was, she couldn't argue with how great it felt.

She could see the struggle in his face, the need for completion. He needed to let go but wanted to make it last for her sake.

The pressure between her legs told her he didn't really need to wait. She was ready to climax again.

"It's okay," she told him. "This is for the claiming. There will be another for fun."

She could hardly miss the gratitude in his face as he pulled back and surged forward again. That was the last thing she recognized as he took up a steady set of thrusts, each one more powerful than the last. Lija wrapped her legs around his waist and gave herself up to him, keeping pace as best she could. Inside her, the pressure grew and she clutched the hard muscles of his upper arms.

It was like an explosion deep within when she climaxed. Lija cried out, barely noticing that Jackon came at the same time, his shaft pulsing in her pussy and sending its seed deep into her womb.

There would be no child from this coupling. Her shots were up to date, protecting her from pregnancy. If the Zelion men were to be believed, she was their only hope for children, in spite of how much seed they spilt in other women. In the seconds after her climax, that realization hurt. Without her, this man would never have a child of his own.

Lija imagined such a child, with her violet eyes and his blond hair. Or maybe her black hair and his eyes like a summer sky, it wouldn't matter. Just so long as he or she had Jackon's smile, the one he was favoring her with right now, the one full of joy and caring.

Her maiden's braid fell against her chest, and Jackon lifted it, putting it on the bed behind her. He didn't comment on it. Probably didn't know what it was.

"That was fantastic, Lija, but all too brief. I promise to make up for it later."

She managed to smile at him. There was no point in telling him how useless all promises were because she'd already been promised to another. No reason to do more than enjoy their interlude. It would be all they had.

This was the last time she'd be able to choose who her lover would be.

She had to say something. "I'm not sure anything could be more satisfying than that was, Jackon."

His smile turned into a grin. "Be very careful of what you say. That sounds very much like a challenge. Sounds like I'll have to work extra hard if I'm to impress you now."

No he didn't, but she didn't need to tell him that either. Lija let her fingers slip through his blond hair, enjoying its texture, enjoying the feel of this man, on her and around her. His cock still felt hard inside her. He nuzzled her neck, breathing deeply of her scent.

The scent that told him she was special to him, his "true." It was nice to be special to someone for a change.

His eyes glazed over and inside her his cock twitched.

"So, what shall we do now?"

Jackon opened his eyes. "Now we do it again. This time for fun."

Pulling her up into his arms, he began to move and again Lija lost track of the world.

* * * * *

Jackon moaned deeply as he came for the third time in the past hour. Or was it the fourth? Hard to say, all he knew was that after the claiming they'd gone on to making love for fun. Fun, fun, and more fun.

Oh, yes, it was fun, but it was also a lot more than that. Sex had always been enjoyable, but now...

Stars below, this was a whole other universe of enjoyment. Sex with his true wasn't just fun, it was...was...wonderful. Marvelous. He'd never believed before how different it could be.

Right now he couldn't imagine any other woman than Lija in his arms or his life. If only she'd belong to him permanently, he'd be in heaven right now. As it was he was closer to paradise than he'd ever been in his life.

From the look on her face, she felt the same way.

He stared down into her eyes, wide with passion, a hint of astonishment coloring their purple depths. "Isn't this wonderful, Lija? Have you ever felt anything like it before? I feel like I could make love to you for always and never get tired of it."

"Never?" She seemed to scoff at his words. "Men are always promising more than they can give."

"Not me. Not any Zelion man. When we find our true mate, she's it, the last woman we'll ever make love to. For me, that's you. You're my true, Lija, now and always."

"But suppose I don't pick you to be my husband, Jackon. Suppose I choose Gehon instead?"

Sudden jealousy raged through him at the idea of his friend winning Lija, but he managed to control it. The only outward sign he allowed was a tightening of his arms around her.

He couldn't be angry at Gehon, much as he wanted to be. After all, it wasn't his best friend's fault that she'd turned out to be the only one for both of them. He kept his voice steady. "Whichever of us you pick will be the best husband he can be for you. You won't be sorry to have either of us."

Chapter Four

Lija met Gehon in the galley the next morning, Jackon's arm still protectively around her waist. Jackon stared at his friend then at Lija, longing in his eyes. He clearly wanted her to tell the other man that she'd made her choice, and that he'd be her husband.

She couldn't tell him that. After being so close to him she didn't want to continue this farce, but what was she to do? Admit to them that she was only using them for sex, a last bit of freedom?

There was a lie in that now, though. That hadn't been just sex that she'd had with Jackon. It had been something much sweeter, much more precious. She'd made love with him, maybe the first time she'd made love with anyone.

But she couldn't *be* in love with him. She couldn't love either of them and therefore she had to fulfill the bargain and give Gehon his time with her.

The redheaded man didn't look happy. He probably resented having to go second. For a moment Lija wondered if he would refuse to have anything to do with her now that she'd been with Jackon, but as soon as she was close enough, he breathed in deeply through his nose. His eyes glazed over and his breathing grew ragged, and when he looked at her again there was desire in his eyes.

"Have you made a choice, Lady Lija? Are you Jackon's now?" he asked, obviously willing her to say no.

Lija shook her head. "I promised I'd give you both a chance. It's your turn today."

Jackon stiffened and released her, the action showing his reluctance. Anger was in his posture, but he didn't say anything, just turned and headed for the bridge. Lija watched him leave, regretting everything. They'd been so close...how could she have hurt him so badly?

"He'll be fine. Neither of us likes having to share you." Gehon had come up behind her and when she turned she found herself staring up into his face. Handsome, like Jackon, but different as well.

Jackon's face showed his love of fun and laughter. They'd played all day yesterday, sex games as well as other more mundane pastimes. Lija couldn't remember another time she'd laughed so hard or for so long.

There was no laughter in Gehon's eyes, but a wary watchfulness and sternness in his expression. Lija felt like he could see into her soul, and know the game she was playing. He'd accuse her now of not taking them seriously and lock her into her room for the rest of the trip. Her mad adventure would be over, both men would hate her, and she'd go to her upcoming wedding with only bitter memories…

Abruptly Gehon smiled and it softened his features. "You needn't fear me, Lady Lija. I understand how difficult this must be for you, as well as us."

"It is…difficult. I don't know how I could choose between you."

He chuckled. "Since you were in Jackon's arms all day yesterday, I'm surprised, but pleased to hear it anyway." He glanced around at the ship's walls. "This place isn't soundproof, you know."

Heat flushed through her cheeks. "You could hear us…"

"I heard nothing I haven't heard before. I've been working with Jackon a long time," he said dryly. Gehon waved at the food prep machines. "Why don't you get something to eat?"

He sat opposite her with a cup of Earth coffee, apparently his favorite wake-up drink, while she helped herself to a plateful of what seemed to be freshly sliced fruit and sweetened rolls. His attitude was so similar to the way Jackon had watched her the day before that she almost forgot he wasn't the same man. Only the reminder of his red hair kept her from mistaking the men for each other.

When she'd emptied her plate, Lija lingered over her tea, reluctant to admit to being finished. She stole a glance at Gehon, who seemed content to sip his drink.

Finally she noticed his lips twitching. "This is awkward, isn't it?" he told her.

"Yes." She hesitated. "I'm not sure why. I didn't know either of you that well yesterday."

Leaning back he pushed his mug away. "Yesterday was easier because you really needed one of us to make love to you. Today you don't."

Again she felt heat in her face. "I wasn't…"

Gehon gave a short bark of a laugh. "My lady, you broadcasted sexual need like a beacon. You might as well have been wearing a light-sign saying "take me now". If it is one thing a Zelion man knows how to read, it is his woman when she's in heat."

Furious, Lija jumped to her feet. "I was *not* in heat. It had just been a long time between lovers."

"Between proficient lovers, you mean. More than that, you've never had anyone like Jackon before. No one has ever made you scream like that," he said wryly.

Lija eyes widened. "You can tell that, too?"

Gehon held up his hands as if trying to calm her down. "I meant no disrespect, my lady. You're my true mate and there are many things I can tell from the way you smell and the look in your eyes. I know that yesterday was the best sexual experience you ever had." He sighed. "Jackon is very likely the best man when it comes to sexual athletics."

Returning to her seat, she couldn't help the bite in her tone when she spoke next. "In that case, how do you expect to compete with him?"

"I don't, exactly. Yesterday I had time to think about what the best approach would be. I'm going to give you something that Jackon didn't yesterday."

"What is that?"

Gehon smiled, a warm funny smile that lit up his face. "Jackon gave you sex. Great sex, I'm sure, so I've got to go beyond what he did." He took a deep breath. "I'm going to offer you more than sex. I'm going to offer you romance."

In spite of herself she laughed. "Romance? Like hearts and flowers?" She glanced around the comfortable but spare surroundings of *The Traveler*'s galley. "This isn't the most romantic environment to work in."

Gehon leaned forward and reached out to touch her face. Lija startled at the gentleness in his fingers and the trail of sparks they left as they caressed her.

"Any place can be romantic when you're in love, my lady."

She pulled away. "You aren't in love with me."

Again he had a smile she couldn't read. "I might be. I know I could be, given any time at all. But you're right—this is not the place to discuss romance. I have someplace else in mind."

In spite of herself she was curious. "What are you going to do?"

"It is what *we're* going to do." Gehon took her hand and held it to his lips, breathing the scent of it deep into his nostrils. He chuckled. "First thing we need to do is wash my partner off you."

Lija snatched her hand back. "I did clean up." She sniffed her hand. "I don't smell anything."

Gehon shook his head. "Zelions have strong senses of smell, particularly where their mates are concerned. Anyway, I think you'll enjoy what I have in mind."

He rose to his feet and held out his hand. "Come, Lady Lija. Our romance awaits."

She stopped him. "Only if you call me Lija. You don't want me to do to you what I did to your partner to make him use my name."

Gehon broke out into a grin. "I can just imagine. Jackon can be stubborn when it comes to protocol. Very well, as you wish. Will you come with me, Lija?"

She put her hand in his and let him lead her to another part of the ship. He opened the door, and they stepped into warmth and moisture and the heavy smell of growing things. The harsh lighting from the ceiling panels was dimmed and gentled by tall wide-leafed plants that surrounded them as soon as they stepped inside.

Lija breathed appreciatively of the fresher air. "You have a ship's garden? I thought that was something more on larger ships."

"It's just a small one and serves many purposes. We're in space for long periods sometimes and this place helps with the air and water purification, and we can grow some food like the fresh fruit you had this morning."

He pulled her over to a corner, nearly hidden by the towering plants, some of which she now saw bore fruit in various states of ripeness. "It is also a good excuse for this."

Lija halted and stared in astonishment. In the corner was a sonic shower, similar to the one in the private sanitary she had off her cabin. The waterless cleaning stall wasn't that strange a sight, except for its location. What was unusual was the large wooden tub that stood next to it, big enough to fit two people. The waterproof lid that was used to keep the contents in place during low gravity times had been removed, and she could see steam rising from the surface.

She turned to the tall redheaded man beside her. "You have a hot tub?"

Gehon shrugged. "As I mentioned before, Zelions have very good senses of smell and we need more than sonic showers to feel clean. A good soak is just the thing." He nodded at the surrounding plants. "Besides, it holds the water needed to keep the plants healthy." He sighed. "Sometimes at the end of a long journey, we can't use it because too much water has been used. Fortunately that's not the case today."

Excitement filled her. While she'd heard about the supposed benefits of soaking in hot water, she'd never experienced it before. This was a new adventure. "What do we do to use it?"

"First you clean up in the shower. We don't want contaminants in the tub. Then you just climb in and soak. It'll relax you and…" he hesitated. "It will ease any soreness you have."

Lija tried not to blush again at Gehon's indirect reminder of Jackon and her activities the day before. Now that he mentioned it, she was a little tender in places that hadn't gotten that much of a workout in the past, and there was a nagging ache in the small of her back.

Going to bed with a sexual athlete put a strain on muscles, as well as wear and tear on delicate tissues.

She went to unfasten the top of the simple gown that Jackon had found for her, some sort of Zelion woman's dress with long sleeves and a skirt that fell to mid-calf. Abruptly she realized that Gehon was watching her, and turned from him, embarrassed. She didn't have anything on underneath.

Again she heard his chuckle. He placed his hands on her shoulders and turned her toward him. "Lija, I plan on being lovers with you within the next few hours, but if it makes you feel better, I'll turn my back while you get undressed."

Now she felt silly. Of course he'd be seeing her naked soon. She might as well get it over with. Her hands flew to the fastenings, but he stopped them, holding them with his.

"I would rather you be comfortable with me, Lija." He raised her hands to his lips, kissing the backs of them. As light as his touch was, it still sent thrills through her body. She lifted her face to his.

Gehon hesitated, but only for a moment. Then he swooped down to claim her lips in a burning kiss. It was like being kissed by Jackon, but different. Lija felt the same swoon as his mouth moved over hers, his tongue sweeping inside to taste her.

His body where it touched hers was hard, and as he pressed closer, became harder still. Lija thrilled at his hardness. Obviously

Gehon was just as well endowed as Jackon and she looked forward to becoming acquainted with his equipment.

She wondered at that. How could she be intimate with two men in so short a timespan? Still, somehow there didn't seem to be anything wrong with kissing Gehon. His touch, his kiss, the faint scent of him as he held her to him...it was all just as arousing as it had been with Jackon.

Had she become some sort of glutton for sex, now that she was with these two? In the past she'd fantasized about being with other men, but the reality was that it had been rare for her to feel this good with even one. Gehon had said it right, that never before had she had sex like she'd had with Jackon. After him all other men would seem wanting.

Except maybe for this one. Without thinking about it, Lija let Gehon hold her as close as he wanted, even when his hands wandered to her ass to lift it and press her closer to his massive erection.

Was his cock as pretty as Jackon's had been? Hard to believe but she was certain to find out pretty soon.

He pulled away. "Let me undress you, Lija, then you can get into the shower." His hands undid the simple fastenings that held her garment up at the shoulders, with practiced fingers that told her he'd undone this kind of dress countless times before.

A flicker of jealousy slid through her at that thought. Jackon, too, had had experience, and not just with the clips on a dress. How many women had been with these men before? They might not like sharing, but then again neither did she.

Jackon let the gown fall to the floor and gazed with rapt admiration. "Lija, you're so beautiful." His breath seemed to catch in his throat.

She tried to twist from his hold. "I'm sure you've seen many women more beautiful than I."

A firm hand caught her chin, turning her face to his. In his eyes she read his sincerity. "No woman could possibly be as beautiful to me. You are my mate, Lija, the woman with whom I could have a family. Tell me you believe that, please."

She couldn't help but believe him, not with the way he was looking at her. Tamping down her insecurity, Lija nodded her answer. Gehon rewarded her with one of his rare smiles. "Good then." He pushed her toward the shower. "I've already been in there. Clean up and I'll see you in the tub."

The sonic "spray" prickled along her skin, leaving it tingling for some time after she turned it off. The dry cleaning removed impurities from her skin using highly focused sound waves. It was efficient as a cleansing device, but left something to be desired when it came to relaxation.

She stepped out of the stall to see her dress and Gehon's pants and shirt folded neatly on a nearby bench, along with what looked to be a pair of heavy towels.

He was already in the large tub, only his head bobbing above the surface of the water, his features partially obscured by the rising mist. As she stepped closer, Gehon's eyes riveted onto her, watching her cross the short distance with anticipation in his face.

Lija was happy to notice that while he glanced at her breasts and the triangle of hair that covered her woman's mound, it was her face he looked at the longest. He smiled as she reached the short step she needed to climb to get into the tub.

"You might want to put your hair up before you get in, to keep it dry."

Lija noticed he'd made a queue from his shoulder-length hair and pinned it up. She did the same, wrapping her maiden's braid into a circlet on her head, the way she'd done the few times she'd been in water before. Hers was a dry planet and open pools of water simply didn't exist, so bathing or swimming didn't happen that often.

Eager for this new experience, she dipped one foot, then the other into the water. It was a perfect temperature, just a little on the hot side, and she slipped the rest of the way in with an appreciative groan, only at the last moment realizing that she couldn't feel the bottom. The tub must continue well below the floor of the room to be so deep. Clutching the side, she managed to keep from going underwater completely, only getting a little of her hair wet in the process.

She found a seat on a narrow shelf jutting out from the inside of the tub, just opposite Gehon, whose face still bore a slight smile. Big as the tub was, he could touch her if he reached out with those long arms of his, but for the moment he seemed content to watch her.

His watching was almost as arousing as his touch had been. Lija sighed. Both these men were far more expert in lovemaking than she was, and it showed. She shouldn't be getting excited just because a man was looking at her.

She felt completely out of her depth here, and not just because the tub was taller than she was.

"Are you enjoying yourself?" Gehon's voice had a soft purr to it that drove her libido even crazier. As relaxing as the water was, it wasn't just its warmth that was making her hot.

Trying to keep her voice level, she answered him. "It feels really nice."

He moved slowly along the edge of tub until he was just inches from her. The ledge was at a height that the top of his broad shoulders could be seen above the water. Their width made her curious about the rest of him. She knew Gehon was shorter than Jackon, but from here he seemed more muscular.

She looked down and realized that like her he was completely naked in the tub. She could see reddish brown hair covering his broad chest and trailing down his flat stomach all the way to...oh, yes, the hair down there was red, too. She could see his penis, the pale organ waving stiffly at her from its surrounding reddish cluster of curls. The image reminded her of a holovid she'd seen once about Earth's oceans. His cock could have been an undersea creature resting on its bed of seaweed.

A really large undersea creature.

One hand came out of the water to rest on her shoulder, drawing her attention away from his waving cock. "Would you like me to rub your back?"

It sounded harmless enough, although she doubted anything this man did would be completely harmless. He'd promised her romance, and she had to admit, this was romantic, with the warm water and ship's lighting muted by the surrounding plants. From the corner of her eye she saw a flicker of fire and realized he'd lit a candle on a shelf next to the tub, some sort of incense fragrance that was the source of the rich spicy smell surrounding them.

She nodded, and allowed him to turn her away from him. His large hands worked her shoulders, wringing one moan after the other from her. Continuing down her back, Gehon found every tight muscle she had, every knot along her spine, and with gentle force, relaxed them.

By the time he was done, her mind and body was so tranquil she could have floated away.

"Gehon, that feels so good," she said, her voice barely more than a whisper.

He moved closer, cradling her back into his front. In the small of her back she felt the length of his erection as his arms surrounded her. He leaned forward to whisper in her ear, his breath warm against her cheek. "I'm glad, Lija. I only want you to feel good with me."

"Because I'm your true, your hope for children?"

"That's part of it. Zelion warriors are trained in two things—fighting, and the need to reproduce. The first is far easier than the second. To reproduce we must find that one woman who complements us. For me, that's you, so of course I want you to want to be with me."

He stopped to kiss her neck, the sensation of his lips against her skin a delight. She almost missed the rest of his speech.

"The rest is that I really like you...and I suspect I'm more than a little in love with you. I know that's hard to believe with as little time as we've spent together, but that's the way it is when we meet the right woman. Our true mate. You're my match for more than how our bodies fit together. It's because our minds fit together as well, our hearts and our souls."

He turned her face and she saw the sincerity in his eyes. "When I mate with you for the first time, Lija, I will use the claiming words. That isn't binding on you, but it is for me. I do it, not to sway your decision, but because I must. I know already how it will be between us. It will be wonderful, unique." A shadow crossed his face. "I suspect you already know that, since you've been with Jackon already. You're his true as well, so making love with him would be the same. You could pick either one of us and be assured a good life with a husband who will always love you.

"I can hope you pick me..." his voice trailed off and he looked away from her. "Whomever you pick, we will always be friends, Lija. Jackon and I have been together too long to stop that."

"Wouldn't that be awkward, being around me if I choose your friend?" She couldn't help her question.

Gehon nodded. "It would be difficult, at first. Seeing you and him together, knowing what I am missing. But perhaps I could be like an uncle to your children. A second father."

He ran a finger down her face. "I'd rather they were mine, though. I'd rather you want them to be mine."

What could she say to that? She couldn't, wouldn't have either of these men's children. It was impossible…and she was beginning to wish that wasn't the case. In spite of everything an image entered her mind…

…of a young child…no, two children, boys, one with hair the flame of a sunset sky, the other hair like a summer sun. They both had violet eyes. They played together along the wooded bank of a stream, open water dancing and rippling under the light of two suns in the sky overhead.

Her two sons…

Along the pathway came a third child, a daughter, younger than the others, her dark hair short, with one braid reaching her shoulder. She laughed as the boys welcomed their little sister, and Lija could see that her eyes were brown…

Lija startled. That had felt like a vision of the future…or at least one future. Her people weren't prone to imaginings but sometimes at critical points in their lives others had reported having daydreams like this vision. Sometimes those dreams turned out to be a prediction of the future.

Space knows this was a critical point in her life. But no, that's not what this was. It was just her imagination working overtime after Gehon's speech, conjuring up a family that could never be.

He turned her in his arms to face him. "Are you all right?" Gehon said concern in his deep brown eyes. "You look like you saw something."

"I'm fine. It was nothing." He didn't seem convinced and Lija didn't want to answer any more questions just then. Unlike his friend, Gehon was far too perceptive. She felt like he could see right through her with those knowing eyes of his. They narrowed at her even now, and she could see his mouth working on another question.

Time for a distraction.

Lija threw her arms around his neck and kissed him, long and hard. His surprise lasted only as long as it took for her to slip her tongue into his mouth and after that it would have been impossible to determine who'd started their kiss.

He pulled her closer and wrapped his arms tight around her. Her breasts pressed tight against his chest and the hardness of his cock dug into her belly. Breaking off, Gehon groaned indistinct words that she could find no meaning in. Not that she was looking for much meaning at the moment. It was too wonderful to be held this way by him.

Her desperate ruse had worked too well. She was as distracted as he was and once again all she wanted to do was bed a Zelion man.

Gehon tasted the side of her neck, seemingly overcome by the flavor of her skin. He breathed deeply, sometimes through his nose as if trying to be certain of her scent. His strong hands slipped under her bottom, lifting her higher in his arms. Before she realized what he intended, she felt the hard tip of his cock at the entrance to her core.

Startled, Lija tensed, waiting to feel that hard thickness drive into her. She wasn't prepared, and after yesterday even a little tender. It would hurt. Not that she'd stop him. Part of her wanted him in her, deep and hard. She wanted his cock in her, pounded away, filling her.

Instead Gehon froze in place, his breath coming hard against her shoulder. His whole body shook with the effort to maintain control. Finally he lifted her higher, resting her in his lap, his erection safely beneath her.

He chuckled, but the sound was ragged without much amusement in it. "First time I ever did that. I've never had a problem with control before." Leaning back he stared into her face. "I won't take you like this, unprepared for me. Sometime else, maybe. When we're comfortable with each other."

Now his arms softened, still holding her, but not as tightly. He nibbled on her lips for a moment.

"I want our first time to be memorable, but not because it hurt, or you didn't expect it. I want it to be..."

His voice trailed off as if not sure how to say what he meant. Remembering what he'd said before in the galley, Lija filled it in for him. "You want it to be romantic when we make love for the first time."

Now his chuckle did have humor in it. "Yes, that was it. I'm glad you're my true, Lija. I like a woman with brains in her head."

It was her turn to laugh. "I'm glad you like me for more than my body."

"Of course I do. You are my exact match, and that means more than just your body to me." He laughed. "There is only so much time that can be spent in bed. Although," he said meaningfully, rubbing his hard length against the cleft of her bottom, "spending a little time in bed sounds pretty good right now."

"So what do we do?"

"First thing I think we should do is get out of this water. I have plans for you that don't involve aquatic sports."

Gehon climbed out of the tub and made his way to the bench where their clothes were. Lija admired the strong lines of his back and his firm buttocks as he walked. While Jackon could claim a somewhat better torso, Gehon's ass was far superior to his friend's.

She almost sighed when he grabbed one of the towels and proceeded to dry himself, covering his lower body before she could see his cock. So far she'd only gotten glimpses of it when it had been underwater. From what she'd felt, he was a big man, but she wanted to see for herself.

He tied the fabric length in place and grabbed the second towel before returning to help her out the water. "Take it easy, you don't want to slip."

Gehon's gaze as it skimmed down her nude body was hot enough that she was almost surprised the water covering her didn't turn to steam. Still his hands were gentle as he carefully wiped the moisture away, leaving her skin warm and dry.

Finished, he laid the towel on the floor, which was covered in some kind of absorbent material that was soft underfoot. Then he had her sit on the towel.

"Lie on your stomach and I'll continue your massage. I want you relaxed, Lija."

Relaxation wasn't high on her list of interests, but she did as he asked. His talented fingers again started on her shoulders, working the last of the kinks out before moving to caress her lower back. By the time he was massaging her buttocks, she was openly moaning her appreciation.

Keeping one hand on her bottom, Gehon slipped the other between her legs, giving the lightest strokes to the folds there. Eager for his touch, Lija spread her legs in open invitation to continue. The hand on her ass gripped the cheek harder while the other began a slow exploration of her sensitive folds. When she tried to move, he pressed down on her bottom, keeping her in place.

"You like to be in control, don't you?" she gasped out when it was clear his hold on her was deliberate.

He answered without interrupting his sensuous assault. "When I can be. Right now I do. I want to control how you respond to me."

She turned her head to look back up at him. "Why is that?"

He laughed wryly. "Because I very much doubt I'll be able to do it very often in the future, Lija. You aren't someone who likes to be controlled." He slapped her bottom lightly. "Now lie back down and let me pleasure you."

She did and he did. His fingers delved deeply into the cleft between her legs, finding her clit where her crotch touched the floor. He twirled it between two fingers while his thumb found the entrance to her pussy. Since she'd stopped moving around he was able to use his free hand to stroke her back, then slip around to find her nipple.

Lija stiffened, then groaned as he manipulated her most sensitive places.

Has she thought she was too tired for more sex? Apparently not. Her body thrilled at his actions and screamed for his touch. Everything he did to her left her wanting more and more of the same.

Or more and more different. It didn't matter. So long as Gehon was touching her, Lija was happy.

In fact the way he was caressing her was making her a lot more than happy. She moaned under his hands, letting his touch drive her to a place she hadn't expected to see again quite so soon.

Lija climaxed with a loud cry of fulfillment and joy.

Chapter Five

Gehon watched Lija's face as she recovered, letting his fingers trail across her sweet ass. He'd told her before that he could only see her as beautiful because she was his true mate. That couldn't be denied, but in addition he knew she was lovely for her own sake.

He lay on the towel next to her, just allowing one arm to rest against her back. With his body aching to be inside her, too much contact wouldn't be wise. It would only take a moment to roll her onto her back and plunge into her. Just the thought of doing so made his cock throb in happy anticipation.

He wasn't going to do that, though. He'd promised her romance, and riding her hard wasn't terribly romantic. With her soft body beneath him and those long legs of hers wrapped around his waist, it was really appealing though.

She turned her face and he could see her violet eyes, luminous with passion, her cheeks flushed from her orgasm. There was surprise in her face as well, as if she hadn't expected to climax. She'd said she was hard to satisfy but he hadn't found that to be so. If anything she was hypersensitive to his touch. Every stroke provoked a reaction.

Just like a true should be in the arms of her match.

And yet he could feel her resistance. She wanted to give in to him, but didn't want to at the same time. Inside her was a battle as her body tried to tell her what her mind did not want to hear.

"What shall we do now, Gehon?" Her soft voice had a suggestiveness to it that made his hardness harder, and certainly more difficult to ignore.

"What do you want to do, Lija?" he answered. Now that he'd made her come, he wanted to give her control over their activities.

Some of her hair had loosened and fallen across her face. He brushed it out of her eyes, tucking it under her long braid. A flicker of curiosity whipped through him. It was such an unusual hairstyle and he knew so little about her people. Did the braid have some significance? He opened his mouth to ask her.

"I think you should make love to me, Gehon."

Question forgotten, he gaped at her. "What?"

Lija rolled onto her back, her breasts high in the air. "I said I think it's time. I want you to make love to me."

Hardly an invitation to not take seriously.

Her hands skimmed his upper body until they landed on the towel he'd wrapped around his waist. Tugging on it, she made it clear she wanted it off. "I want to see what you look like."

How could he refuse? He sat up on his knees and slowly untied the cloth, pulling it open. Lija's eyes widened as she took in the size of him particularly his width, which he knew was bigger than Jackon. His rival for their true might have a longer staff, but no one could deny his was larger around. Besides, size didn't matter as much as knowing what to do with it.

He knew what to do…and now he was going to prove it.

Lija's hand moved to touch him, her gentle fingers like fire against his skin. His cock throbbed as she wrapped her hand around him, as if measuring his size for certain. Her movements were tentative and it took all his control not to take matters into his own hand and direct her as she stroked him. She wanted to touch him and that was good enough.

Then she sat up and took him into her mouth, and that was far more than good enough. In fact being in her mouth was pretty great. It was hot and wet, and he had to hold himself firm to keep from releasing right away. She pulled his cock out to smile at him, and he groaned at the loss.

Her expression was pure tease. "So, now do you want to make love to me?"

As if there'd been any doubt. Gehon pushed her onto her back and spread her knees wide, fitting himself to her. It felt so good, so right, like he was coming home. All his instincts and senses told him she was his perfect match—her smell, her touch, the feel of her skin, and the taste of her lips. He leaned forward to kiss her, reveling in how good just kissing her was, holding off entering her.

Lija squirmed under him, and he knew he better not hold off any longer.

Breaking off the kiss, he supported himself on his arms, staring down into her face. "This is for claiming, Lija. You are my true mate." With the last words he thrust forward, embedding himself to the hilt.

Stars below, she felt like heaven. It *was* like coming home, being inside her. Her body welcomed him, her pussy encasing his cock with tight heat. It was enough to make a man sob, knowing how good it was and how uncertain their future remained. She hadn't committed to being his mate.

Once claimed, he couldn't revoke his relationship to her. Even if Lija moved on, he was forever bound to her and no woman would ever be able to replace her.

He only wished that she understood that. Maybe it would make a difference.

He stared down into her beautiful eyes, wide with combined passion and pleasure. His woman…Lija couldn't look more like his mate than she did at this moment.

Gehon closed his eyes. It didn't matter about later, or tomorrow. It didn't matter that she was temporarily sterile, and thus this mating would never produce children.

It didn't even matter that he very much doubted Lija was seriously considering either Jackon or himself as a husband.

Nothing mattered but that now, at very long last, he'd found his true mate and she was under him and he was inside her. No matter what the future held, he held her.

At least for the moment.

Was it enough? No. Not really. But it was likely all he would ever get, and therefore would have to do. One time with the woman who could make him the happiest man in the universe, if only she'd agree to be his wife. Even if she didn't agree, he had her now.

It would have to do.

He pulled back and surged forward again. Lija whimpered, the first sign she'd made that she wasn't completely comfortable with his bulk in her tightness.

So be it. It wasn't like he could make himself smaller. He pulled back and surged forward again, this time harder.

Lija moaned. Well, at the very least, she wouldn't forget him, Gehon told himself. He repeated his action, again and again, setting up a rhythm. In and out, in and out. He'd done it before, many times before, but never had it felt like this. This was his mate, his true mate. No one would ever be like her. No one could.

Lija's hands fell on his back and then on his ass, her fingernails digging into his flesh. As if spurred, he picked up the pace, and she clung to him, legs wrapped tight around his waist, her hand clutching him as if for dear life. She gasped out odd words, sometimes barely more than syllables, passion-driven and meaningless, except for what they meant to him.

They meant that whether or not she wanted it so, she reacted to him. He, Gehon, warrior of Zelion, was her match. He could give her physical pleasure when others had failed. Lija wanted him and she did it in spite of her reservations.

They were having sex, pure and simple, but there was nothing simple about this coupling. He drove into her, giving her no mercy. It might be the only time he'd have her...but he didn't care about that. Better to fuck her in a flame of glory than to be a small flicker of passion in the thread of her life.

Inwardly he vowed that he, at least, would be remembered.

He wanted her to know. It would be with her always what she'd given up when she refused him, tomorrow or the day after. She would always remember what it was like to lie with a man who was her match.

Tension built in him, and in spite of how much he wanted to continue, his orgasm came closer. Gehon worked faster, feeling in Lija a corresponding move toward completion.

Of course. They were matched, after all. Why wouldn't they climax at the same time?

In and out and driving onward. One more thrust.

A scream built up in the back of his throat and he lost track of how Lija was reacting to their coupling. Instead he felt his own climax flash through him until it couldn't be denied any longer.

Throwing back his head, he cried out, feeling the pulsing of his cock at the same time, sending his seed deep into her womb. Lija finished with him, shuddering under him.

Gehon lowered himself on top of her, enjoying the softness of her breasts against his chest and the warmth of her arms holding him close. For the moment he felt cherished and loved. She'd accepted him...for now.

Gehon nuzzled her neck, enjoying the texture of her skin beneath his lips. She was perfect for him. Probably perfect for Jackon, as well, although he hadn't been able to ask his friend about it.

Not that he really needed to ask. Jackon's jealousy when he left this morning spoke volumes about how he felt about Lija. Never had his friend shown the slightest concern for keeping a woman once he'd had her. With Lija he had, and that said in no uncertain terms that she was his mate, just as she was Gehon's.

That should have been the problem — that they both wanted her — but Gehon knew it wasn't. He knew there was more going on than two men wanting the same woman.

Having sex with Jackon hadn't convinced Lija to stay as his mate. If she'd been amenable to being a true mate, Gehon shouldn't have had a chance once his friend had gone first.

That hadn't happened and it worried him more than he liked. Lija didn't behave like a woman who needed convincing of her status as one of their true. Instead she acted like a woman who couldn't — or wouldn't — be convinced.

There was something she wasn't telling him or Jackon. Something she was hiding.

"That was fantastic."

Even as she said the words, Gehon could feel her slipping away from him. Stars below, why couldn't she see how good things were between them and how good they would be in the future? All she had to do was say yes to their marriage.

How hard could that be?

* * * * *

What was she going to do? More and more it got harder to not give in to this man. Only the fact that his friend held an equal appeal for her kept her from doing just that.

Lija groaned. Suppose she really did have the right to take one of these men to be her husband? Which one would she choose?

Jackon with his striking good looks and stamina, his love of fun? Or Gehon, warm and stable, equally good in bed, but more romantic?

Too bad she couldn't just marry both of them, but she doubted either man would accept that solution…would they?

Lija resisted a sigh. Irrelevant anyway with Brentan around. She tensed at the thought of the Natarn prince, overbearing and obnoxious as well. She'd bet he wasn't even a very good lover.

"Lija, what is it?" Gehon was watching, his expression mobile and showing his concern. "What troubles you?"

"Nothing..."

"Not nothing. Nothing wouldn't make your eyebrow twitch like that."

Lija's hand flew to her face. He'd uncovered the trick her eyebrow did, that fast? "How did you know?"

"That your eyebrow twitches when you're upset?" The big man shrugged. "Lija, I've done little else but watch you for a while. I know your moods, what you like and dislike. You don't have many secrets from me."

Except one really big one. Alarmed Lija changed the subject back to sex. "Is that why we're so good in bed, because you know me so well?"

He nuzzled her neck, his face hidden from her. "That's one reason. It also helps that I love you."

"What?" Grabbing his head by the hair, Lija pulled it back so she could see his eyes. "What did you say?"

Warm, honest brown eyes gazed down at her and she saw the truth in them, before he repeated the words. "I love you, Lija. You're my true, and that's part of it. But I'm glad you are my true because you are such a woman deserving of love. You have mine."

He laughed, the sound ironic. "I can see I'm the first to tell you, as well. No one before has told you he loved you, not even Jackon. At least that was one thing I did first."

"Maybe he doesn't..." her voice trailed off at the emphatic shaking of his head.

"Oh, Jackon is in love...trust me on that. He's a bit shyer when it comes to his feelings, that's all." His hand caressed her hair, including the long braid still wound around her head. "He claimed you, didn't he?"

"Claimed?"

"When you made love the first time. He did it for the claiming."

She remembered the words when Jackon had first entered her, the same words Gehon had said. "Yes..."

"Then he's bound to you, the same as I am. He wouldn't have done that if he hadn't been in love already."

"Bound, how?"

Gehon leaned back and gathered her into his arms. "Just that, bound. From now on you're the only woman either of us will want. No other woman will appeal to us," he glanced down at his relaxed cock, "or even make us hard. Eventually you'd feel the same about one of us, or so I'm told. That's the way it's been with outsider women in the past."

Not even get hard? Her guilt over her deception grew to mountainous proportions. "What if I don't? What if I can't commit to either of you?" Had she thought she felt bad before? Now she felt a hundred times worse. She'd let them claim her, and now these guys were going to be practically eunuchs for the rest of their lives?

"Why didn't you tell me this before?"

His expression was wistful. "It wouldn't have made any difference, Lija. Once we find our true, we're committed to her even if she isn't to us."

Overwhelmed by his revelation, she pushed on Gehon until he let her go. Standing, she tried to pull herself together, failing to stop the tears trickling down her cheeks. "It isn't fair, Gehon. Not to me, or you, or Jackon. You should have told me."

"And you would have done what? Not had sex with us? What good would that have done?"

She pointed to his cock. "At least that would have worked. You could have found someone else eventually."

He shook his head sadly. "You really don't understand, Lija. There isn't anyone but you for me—or Jackon—to love, and having sex without love isn't something I want anymore. Not now that I've been with you." He took a deep breath. "I wouldn't have traded these past two hours with you for anything, not even a lifetime of meaningless sex."

Lija stared at him. He meant it, too. Every instinct she had told her that Gehon was telling the honest truth, that making love with her once was worth giving up any future sexual encounters with other women. No one had ever said anything like that to her before. No one had told her he loved her before.

She'd known how different it had been to make love with Gehon and with Jackon. Now she knew just what that difference was. It had actually been making love, not just a sexual encounter with a partner who cared more for the act than her. These men cared for her and it was tearing her apart. All she wanted right then was to commit to them.

And she couldn't. Even if she were free to do so, selecting one would doom the other to a life without love. How could she make a choice like that? How could they ask her to do so?

Unable to say anything, Lija rose and grabbed her gown from the bench. She pulled it on and headed out of the ship's garden.

"Lija, where are you going?" Gehon's soft voice stopped her, although he made no move to rise from his position on the floor.

She gathered her courage and turned to face him. His face showed no condemnation or regret. He watched her the way he always did, with quiet understanding.

"I'm sorry if what I said upset you. I figured you better know the truth."

Of all the things she expected, an apology wasn't one of them. What would he say if he knew the truth, that she hadn't really been free to take them up on their offer? Guilt flooded her.

"I need some time, Gehon. To think. I'll be in my room." Turning she fled as if he chased her, although she knew he wouldn't move from his position on the floor.

Chapter Six

Jackon cornered Gehon in the ship's galley. "What did you do to Lija?" he asked, glaring at his partner.

Morosely the redheaded man stared down into his coffee, which had likely lost its steam hours ago. He lifted the cup to his lips and sipped, grimacing at the stale taste. "I didn't do anything to her that you didn't do."

Jackon wasn't buying any of that. "She spends the morning with you, then locks herself in her room. She hasn't come out for anything including food, and we know she's a woman who likes to eat. When I asked if there was something I could bring her, she said no, but there were tears in her voice." Folding his arms he stared menacingly. "I at least made her laugh when it was my turn. What did you do to make her cry?"

"She's been crying?" Pushing the cup away, Gehon looked up, worry in his face. He sighed. "All I did was tell her the truth."

"What truth?"

"About the claiming and how she was the only one now for both of us."

Jackon groaned. "You told her we'd be impotent with other women? Oh great. Don't you see how that might make her feel guilty?"

"It's the truth…"

"Which she wasn't ready to handle yet. Lija is an outsider, Gehon, she doesn't understand the things we take for granted. She didn't need to know about the results of claiming, since it isn't her fault. All she needed to do was select one of us, not worry about what would happen to the other. Now you've got her all confused."

Gehon folded his hands under his chin. "She wasn't going to select one of us anyway."

Jackon's heart sank. "What? How do you know that?"

He shrugged. "Stuff she said. Mostly what she didn't say. When I told her that we both loved her, she became upset. A woman isn't supposed to become upset when you tell her that."

"You told her I loved her?" As if he needed another reason to be angry. "That was something I was going to do!"

"When, Jackon? After all, you spent the entire day with her. I only had a couple of hours…"

"In which you upset things for both of us!"

Gehon held up his hands. "You're right, you're right. I shouldn't have told her what the claiming meant. I didn't realize it would make such a difference to her."

Gehon so rarely admitted to being wrong about anything, his agreement mollified Jackon somewhat. Of course some of that was that he wasn't wrong often. He still shouldn't have said that Jackon was in love with Lija…a man liked to speak for himself.

"And I'm sorry I spoke for you about loving her. You should have had the right to tell her yourself."

Jackon shook his head at his partner's insight. It was scary sometimes how Gehon could read people. "So why don't you think she'd pick one of us? Why come with us if that was the case?"

"We didn't give her a lot of choice in the coming, remember? We abducted her from the bar. She wanted to make love with us, so she agreed to give us a chance to court her, but I don't think she took it seriously…until what I said this morning."

Jackon's jaw dropped. "You mean she was just using us for sex? That's…that's…"

"Just what one of us would have done before we met her." Gehon leveled his steady gaze. "How many women have you bedded never intending to get serious about?"

Hard to argue with that, Jackon admitted to himself. "So she was using us for sex, and now finds herself with both of us committed to her and that upsets her. Why?"

"Because she does care about us. I think she's even a little in love with us, but something is stopping her from admitting it. I think her plan is to declare that she can't make up her mind and we'll both be out a wife."

That was a gloomy prognosis. Jackon went to the drink dispenser and got fresh mugs of coffee and tea. Putting the coffee in front of

Gehon, he sat down on the opposite side of the table. "So what do we do? Right now she won't even talk to us."

Sipping his drink, Gehon nodded. "We have a few things to try. First is that you're right, she isn't one to go hungry for long. Second is that she does enjoy sex and really does want us both." He stared at his partner. "You willing to work together on this?"

"She wants both of us. You're suggesting…" Jackon felt his eyes widen. "You mean at the same time?"

At Gehon's nod, Jackon tamped down his instinctive jealousy and nodded in return. "I say we should give the lady what she wants." He held out his hand. "Partners?"

Gehon took it. "Partners," he replied and they shook firmly.

Chapter Seven

There was a knock at the door. "Lija, are you in there?" she heard Gehon ask.

Lija lifted her face from the dampened pillow that had been its home for the past hour. "Go away."

"Please let us come in. We brought you some food."

"We? You mean both of you are out there?"

Jackon answered her. "Gehon and I just want to talk to you while you eat."

She buried her head back into the pillow. "I'm not hungry."

"Are you sure? It's been hours since you ate anything. I put some of those little shellfish you like so much on a tray. And some really nice cheese, and fruit. We brought some tea as well."

Her traitorous stomach growled. Even guilty misery couldn't shut it up for long. Jackon had fed her a dozen of the delectable fishy morsels yesterday during an extended picnic lunch on the bed. She'd probably choke on them if she tried to eat them now, but the tea did sound good. And maybe some fruit...a little cheese. Some pickles.

They hadn't mentioned pickles but she bet they'd go back for them if she asked. They'd do anything if she asked, if only for the chance to win her. Not much she could do about that except try not to take advantage of it.

It sounded like they'd gone to so much trouble. The least she could do was show gratitude for bringing food to her.

Rubbing the rest of her tears from her face she sat up on the bed. "You can come in."

Both men had wary looks as they came through the door. As promised, Jackon had a tray with a variety of goodies on it, which he promptly placed on the bed in front of her. She almost started to cry again when she saw the collection of puckered green rods nestled next to the pile of pink-flecked shellfish.

He'd remembered the pickles.

Gehon carried a hotpot and a set of mugs, which he placed on the table near the door. Pouring tea into one, he handed it to her. "I suspect you need this."

She drank the spicy hot tea and felt its bracing effect on her tattered emotions. Neither man spoke as she nibbled her way through the platter, sitting on the chairs opposite the door and sipping their own tea, occasionally helping themselves to something from the plate. Finally she'd finished, both the platter and her tea, although she played with the mug rather than putting it down.

Finally she raised her head to meet the eyes of the men across from her. "What did you want to talk to me about?"

They exchanged glances then Gehon spoke. "We want you to make love to us again."

Bluntly put. Lija sighed and tried to explain. "It isn't that I don't want to, but I can't. I can't choose between you."

"Then don't choose."

"Don't choose?" Lija stared at him. "I don't understand."

Jackon cleared his throat. "You want both of us, Lija, and we both want you. So…"

"…why not have us both. Right now," Gehon finished for him.

"You both want to make love with me? At the same time?" Her disbelief at their suggestion almost outstripped her intrigue at the idea. She could have both of these strong virile men at the same time, in the same bed, both of those lovely cocks at her disposal?

Oh my. Her body flooded with liquid heat even as her cheeks burned. Her arousal didn't go unnoticed; both men lifted their noses, catching her scent in the stillness of the small room.

"I think she likes the idea, Gehon," Jackon said, a relieved grin on his face.

"So it seems." While not smiling, some of the tension slid from the redhead's stance. "Do *you* like the idea?" he asked, emphasizing the word you. "Will you let us both find pleasure with you?"

Even in her wildest dreams she'd never dreamed anything this wild. How could she say no? It was the chance of a lifetime, a memory to take with her into the future and her arranged marriage.

"Well, if you really want to…"

Both men advanced at once, shoulders colliding in their eagerness. They glared at each other then Jackon stepped aside with a courtly bow, letting Gehon slip onto the bed next to her. "Only fair you go first this time."

"Thank you," Gehon replied with exaggerated courtesy. Lija wondered if this was going to be such a good idea, if they were going to be competing for her attention. Suppose they got into a fight over her...

Gehon put his arm around her shoulders and captured her mouth, erasing all questions from her mind. Without a doubt the man was the best kisser. Well, except for maybe Jackon who'd moved onto the bed behind her, sliding up to wrap his arms around her waist. He nibbled along the back of her neck.

"Tell us what you want, Lija," Jackon told her. "We'll follow your lead."

What they were doing right now was just fine for a start. Gehon continued to kiss her while Jackon moved his hands up and down her body. He cupped her breasts and gave them a gentle massage through her gown. She moaned into Gehon's mouth as Jackon's fingers found her nipples, pinching them just enough to fire them into pointed sensitivity.

"I think we have too many clothes on," she gasped when Gehon gave her the opportunity to breathe.

With a laugh, Jackon pulled her back into his arms, while Gehon stood and slipped out of his shirt and trousers. Then Gehon held her while Jackon stripped, his cock hard and heavy against her back.

Both men helped pull her gown over her head, their four hands getting in the way as often as accomplishing the task. One thing about it, if they were going to do this kind of thing often, the guys would have to learn to work better together.

Lija startled at that last thought. Did she really think they had a future together, the three of them?

Her lovers knelt next to her, their cocks straight out before them. As she remembered, Jackon's was perfectly formed without a curve to speak of. Gehon's wasn't as regularly shaped, but she now noticed the finest collection of freckles along its length. Her fingers reached for it, wanting to connect the dots. Of course if she was fondling Gehon's cock she might as well play with Jackon's, too. Soon she had both men well in hand.

"Lija, perhaps you could settle a bet we have," Jackon managed to get out, his breaths coming in heavy bursts.

"Not now," Gehon said through clenched teeth.

"Why not? You couldn't possible be any more erect."

Amused, Lija dropped both cocks which fell forlornly onto the bed and crossed her arms. "What do you want from me?"

Gehon glared as Jackon explained. "We have a bet as to who is bigger. I say I am because of my length, but Gehon is clearly thicker…"

Lija giggled. She'd actually wondered about that herself. "You want me to measure you?"

"If you don't mind…" Jackon's words were wasted as Lija jumped up to fetch a measuring tool from the desk.

She carefully measured each one, length and circumference and using the built in p-tab of the tool had the answer in minutes, ignoring Gehon's mutterings about wasting good lovemaking time.

Clutching the measuring tool to her chest, she turned to them. "If you don't mind my asking, what is the prize of the bet?"

They exchanged guilty looks.

"Well," Jackon said. "Winner gets to sleep with you tonight rather than go on watch."

Lips twitching, Lija showed them the figures on the tablet. After reading the numbers, the men stared at each other in astonishment.

"We're the same size?"

"In volume to five decimal points." She grinned at them. "I guess it will have to be my choice again."

Ever playful, Jackon slid closer to her on the bed. "And how do you expect to make that decision?"

Gehon moved in from the other side. "Maybe it will be the one who makes you come first."

"Or the one who comes last."

"Or the one who does it best."

Lija laughed. Both men were so eager, and now that they weren't fighting with each other all their attention was turned on her. She loved being the center of attention.

"Maybe we'll just have to decide when the time comes. In the meantime…"

This time she kissed Jackon while Gehon moved behind her and nuzzled her neck, playing with her hair and the long braid that fell down her back. Jackon"s lips moved possessively over hers, his tongue masterfully engaging hers with long strokes. Lija thrilled under his mouth's possession.

The talented hands of Gehon, which had massaged her muscles into limp relaxation earlier by the hot tub, now seemed determined to stimulate her body to an equal state of excitement. One hand took turns tweaking her nipples while the other traced sensual lines down her stomach, leading to but not quite touching the soft hair of her woman's mound. She moaned into Jackon's mouth as Gehon's teasing finally settled into the cleft between her legs and caressed her already aware clit. It throbbed into full arousal under his gentle persuasion and Lija's moans became louder and longer.

He could do that all day, she thought.

Gehon's thick cock moved in rhythm with his finger against her clit and she felt her dampness flood his hand, just as his cock wept against her back in a narrow trail. She leaned back into it, giving it a hard surface to rub against.

Jackon's cock lay on her thigh, a warm, solid presence. Lija collected it with her hand, caressing him with long strokes that had him gasping instead of kissing her.

"Stars below, Lija, that feels good!"

Gehon's chuckle tickled her ear. "Figures. I make you moan and he gets the hand job."

"We'll…just…have to…take…turns." Jackon gasped out.

Arching her back, she used the cleft of her ass to stroke Gehon's cock. He groaned and hissed something unintelligible but no longer complained about being neglected. He grabbed her waist and held her in place as he took advantage of her back cleavage.

Lija smiled—no one was going to come away from this encounter unsatisfied, particularly not her. She had a cock in the hand and another sliding along her rear end, and two pairs of mouths and hands playing with her. She lifted her ass higher and Gehon's hand slipped between her legs, delving deeply into the folds of her pussy. Two fingers slid into her sheath while his thumb found her clit. Fingers and thumb moved in unison, the first probing while the other moved in narrow circles that brought her close to ecstasy. She gasped out her appreciation.

Jackon dipped his head and his lips latched onto each of her nipples in turn, suckling them into hardened points. Between his lips and Gehon's hand, she gave herself over to an orgasm of planet-shattering dimensions.

When she recovered, Jackon's face was in her field of vision, a grin on his face. "I guess we'll have to call that a draw since both Gehon and I worked together."

Her answering laugh was shaky. "You can work together like that anytime you want. I don't mind."

His eyes lit up and she realized she'd given him hope of their continuing relationship. Before she could say more, he'd pulled her into a kiss. Meanwhile, Gehon lifted her rear end and slid his head underneath, his tongue probing in place of his hand. Lija moaned aloud at his talented mouth's efforts.

Leaning forward, she gave herself over to Gehon's tongue. Jackon's perfect cock dangled before her. She gave it a single lick, tasting his delicious flavor, and then took him full in her mouth, sucking him deep inside. Now it was Jackon's turn to groan as she worked his cock with her lips and tongue.

"Oh Lija, yes. Like that. You're so good with your mouth."

Gehon's mouth was good as well and Lija quickly found herself coming again. She let go of Jackon's cock, not wanting to bite him accidentally, then shuddered and moaned her release. Gehon slid out from under her, pulled her back into his arms and cuddled her close.

"I want to be in you Lija."

She looked at Jackon whose lips smiled, but his eyes seemed cautious. "Sure, he can be first this time. I'll take more of your mouth right now."

Still shaking from two glorious climaxes, better than anything she'd felt before, all Lija could do was to nod her assent. Again she leaned forward and felt Gehon's cock probing her from behind. Slowly he entered her, inch by careful inch, his thickness stretching her in ways she hadn't felt before. From behind he seemed longer, maybe even as long as Jackon, and hit new places in her inner pussy walls. She moaned as Gehon filled her, his hands grasping her hips, holding her steady.

When he was fully impaled, he rested for a moment. Jackon moved closer, supporting her shoulders, and letting one hand stroke her back. Lija couldn't see their faces, but she'd bet they were staring at each other. Gehon's face would show his pleasure at the possession of her pussy, Jackon would be jealous that she'd allowed his friend to fuck her first.

She could feel the tension between them, even through her pleasure. Jackon had said he wanted more of her mouth on his cock. Maybe it would be better if she acted on that.

Fortunately his cock was just within her reach. Lija took hold of it, running her hand along its length, stopping to finger the skin around its tip. Jackon groaned and his hand came up to cup the back of her head.

"Please, yes, more of your mouth."

She closed her lips around him and he moved fully inside her mouth, fucking her there while Gehon moved in her from behind, making her ready to scream with each push into her. Had any woman ever had two lovers like this, so hard and ready for her? She'd be surprised if the answer was yes.

Behind her Gehon set a fast rhythm, very unlike what he'd done before, his steady groans telling her how much he was enjoying it. Jackon's hands held her head, supporting but not directing. Gehon's thrusts worked to drive her against his friend's cock, his pulls on her hips setting the rhythm.

In her mouth, Jackon's cock pulsed, his orgasm close. "I'm going to come, Lija," he muttered through clenched lips."

Her answer was to step up her efforts, and soon he cried out and her mouth flooded with his cum, salty-sweet, which Lija swallowed as fast as she could. Her own orgasm was too close for her to be too careful, and some leaked from her mouth to coat her chin.

Once he'd recovered from his orgasm, Jackon dropped his head to find her lips and lick her face clean.

Behind her, Gehon groaned and she knew he'd finish soon. Jackon's fingers delved into her folds and gently stroked her clit, driving her past the point of no return. Her pussy contracted with this orgasm, clutching at Gehon's cock and milking it as he emptied into her.

When they were done they collapsed on the bed, the two men's arms crossing as they both held her, Jackon in front, Gehon from behind. Two men and Lija in the middle, warm, safe, secure...and loved.

Loved. It was something she'd never expected to feel, but she felt it with these men, in their arms. They loved her, both of them.

"That was really amazing."

Of course it was Jackon who'd spoken. He kissed her gently, still tasting slightly of his cum. Turning, Lija found Gehon, who also kissed her, his lips saying what he couldn't express.

Two men, both wonderful, both wonderful in bed. What was a woman to do? Nothing at the moment. She was too tired.

Yawning Lija patted the bed. "This is pretty big. It should fit all of us."

Above her the guys exchanged looks then Jackon shrugged. It really was Gehon's turn. "Maybe some other time. I'm not sure I'm quite ready to share a bed with Gehon. Besides, someone should be on the bridge in case something gets too close. The proximity alarm barely gives us enough time to take evasive action."

Resolutely he pulled away from her. "I got to sleep with you last night, it's only fair that Gehon takes tonight."

Jackon climbed off the bed and put on his clothes. Gehon took advantage of his absence by moving into the space next to Lija, who already looked half asleep. Just before leaving, Jackon turned to smile at them. For the first time, he didn't feel jealous over Gehon's possessive arm around their woman's shoulder. How could he when Gehon actually looked happy for the first time in years?

He opened his mouth to wish them a good rest—then the proximity alarm blared and all hell broke loose!

Chapter Eight

Jackon sped for the bridge closely followed by Gehon, still struggling into his clothes. Lija followed at a distance, fastening her spacer fatigues as she went. Under the bulky fabric she secured the knife she'd insisted Jackon return to her yesterday as a sign of good faith.

She just felt naked without self-protection of some sort.

It only took a few moments before they reached the bridge, alarms blaring around them. Lija hadn't seen the ship's control center before so she took a good look. It was larger than she'd expected, plenty of room for three people, with seats to spare. She took advantage of one near the outside wall, where she could see the forward viewscreen and the image on it.

That image wasn't terribly encouraging. A much larger ship stood before them, its bulk blocking out the stars that should have been there. At the alarm the ship's engines had slowed automatically, a normal action in a two-man ship where often both crew were absent from the bridge, forcing *The Traveler* to come to a halt on its own.

Gehon took the captain's seat in the middle while Jackon covered the secondary controls to one side. He hit a button and the alarm shut off, the silence a welcome relief to her ears.

Both men could control the ship from their location, but in general whoever sat in the central seat assumed command. Since they hadn't exchanged any words on the subject, Lija realized that Gehon normally took command in situations like this.

Jackon flipped a few controls and before them the viewscreen shimmered and cleared. Where space and the ship had been a face appeared, dark eyes dominating a thin pale face surrounded by short dark hair, lips nothing more than a grim slash frowning at them.

In the shadows of *The Traveler*'s bridge, Lija cringed and wished herself anywhere but where she was. Back on Dingalus Three would be good, or Axona, where she should have been in the first place.

Any place but on the Zelions' ship. *Maybe this has nothing to do with me*, she prayed.

The man on the screen narrowed his eyes and seemed to search the room around Gehon, although Lija knew it was unlikely he could see much more than shadows around whoever sat in the captain's chair. Visual communication protocols demanded that one person be visible but no more and she doubted the Zelions would be different. Why tell potential adversaries how few people you had on your ship?

"Opening comm-links now," Jackon said, his voice businesslike. He barely sounded like the man who'd been in her bed just minutes before, whispering endearments into her ears.

Neither did Gehon when he spoke into the open link to the other ship. "This is *The Traveler* out of Zelion. Captain Gehon Avermoe speaking. Who are you and what is your business?"

The dark-haired man glared into the screen. "I am Prince Brentan Ab Natarn and my business is with you, Zelion."

Leaning back in his chair, Gehon folded his arms across his chest and returned the Prince's glare. "What business does a Natarn prince have with me? Have we some contract I know nothing about?"

"You have something that belongs to me. Manalija L'Lautgiga of Axona."

One of Gehon's eyebrows went up. "And how would such a lady belong to you?"

Brentan growled. "She's mine because she is my wife."

In her corner Lija involuntarily gasped. Gehon stiffened but didn't turn to look at her, although Jackon stared openly from his position. He mouthed at her, "You're married?"

She shook her head "no", and clutched her braid. Not so long as she had that, was she any man's wife. What was Brentan up to, making such a claim?

"I know you have her, Zelion. There were witnesses to your abducting her from a bar on Dingalus Three."

Gehon's eyes widened with mock surprise. "Dingalus Three? What would your wife be doing in a bar there? I thought the Natarns kept close watch over their women."

"Why she was there is no business of yours!" Brentan's fury radiated over the comm-link. "The point is that she's on your ship and I want her back!"

Gehon shook his head. "One thing I know is that we don't have your wife on board this ship, Prince Brentan, nor have we any unwilling passengers."

"Then you won't mind if we board and check for ourselves."

The red-haired man leaned forward in his chair and practically hissed his next words. "I would not suggest that. *The Traveler* is Zelion territory and we do not take kindly to boardings without our permission."

Brentan's face set in an expression Lija knew well and it struck fear deep into her heart. She reached for the blade she'd hidden and patted it for reassurance.

"If that's your answer, then I have nothing further to say to you, Zelion." He waved his hand and the transmission died immediately.

Both men turned to face her. "Is there something you want to explain to us, Lija?" Gehon asked. "Do you know this man?"

"I know him, but he's not my husband. Not yet, anyway," she said. From their questioning looks she knew she better explain more. "Natarn and my planet, Axona, are neighboring planets. Not quite at war, although the possibility is always there. They aren't exactly the most peaceful of neighbors."

"I can see how that might be possible," Jackon said with a grimace.

"I met Brentan a few years ago. I didn't much like him, but apparently he liked me. At least he wanted me. The Natarn disputed our hold on some common territory and he offered to run interference for us if I agreed to be his wife. Since I hadn't taken a husband yet..." she fingered her braid, "...my father tentatively agreed to his proposal, but only if I was willing. I said I'd think about it."

"You were going to say yes?" Jackon's voice was quiet.

"Before I met you I was. It wasn't like I had found a man I that I wanted to be with and...after a while..."

"You were tired of being alone," Gehon finished for her. He and Jackon exchanged looks. "I think we both know how that is."

"So you'd made up your mind to marry this Prince B. Had you told him that?" Jackon asked.

"No, but I told my father. He must have told Brentan I was willing. I wanted some time to think before I committed myself."

"So you went to the Lost Time Lounge on Dingalus Three," Gehon said. "To think about marrying a man you not only didn't love, but didn't even like. And—maybe also to find someone to have a last wild night of inconsequential sex with?"

Lija blushed what she sure was crimson red. "Something like that. I just got lucky and got you two instead."

Jackon chuckled and even Gehon smiled. He moved to her side and picked up the end of her braid. "What is the significance of this, Lija?"

Time to tell the truth. "It's called a maiden's braid, a lock of hair that never gets cut, only braided from the time an Axonian girl is a small child. Tradition is that when it's long enough, she can marry. Prior to the marriage ceremony she cuts it off, binds her husband's wrist with it, and leads him to her father." Lija clutched hers tightly and clenched her jaw. "It will be a rainy day on Axona before I cut it for Brentan."

"Perhaps then you'll cut it for one of us?" Gehon asked softly.

"Well, no one is going to cut anything unless we get out of here soon," Jackon interjected grimly. "It looks like your "husband" has us surrounded."

Gehon returned his station and activated a holo-display of the space around them. "I see what you mean." He pointed to a couple of smaller blips just meters away from them. They seemed to be moving away from the freighter. "What do you suppose those are?"

"Fighters most likely. But what are they doing?"

The answer came in moments, when a shudder shook the ship around them and the alarms blared again.

"Hull breach! Those frelling bastards broke our skin." Jackon's fingers flew along the ship's controls, determining the locations and selecting remedies. "Pinpoints in sections two, three. I've got those sealed. There's another one…near the oxygen tanks." He halted, as if unsure what to do. "That doesn't look like a pin."

Lija knew that pinpoint hull breaches were a common space pirate tactic, putting tiny holes in a ship's skin that let the air escape in small amounts. Do it right and you could take over a ship, either by killing the crew or isolating them in the unbroken parts of the ship. Pinpoints were easy to fix as well so the ship was usable without suits afterward.

Lija stared at the screen as well. A non-pinpoint could mean…

"Invaders," she cried. "We've been boarded." She pointed to the telltale heat signatures of human bodies near their air supply.

"They could put something into the tanks…" Gehon ran to the bridge ventilation controls to cut off the flow, but it was too late. A sickly sweet smell filled the atmosphere of the small bridge and a wave of dizziness overwhelmed her.

Jackon took two steps toward her before collapsing. Gehon managed to grab her and they tumbled to the floor together, his chest cushioning her head when they fell. The room spun for a few seconds more then Lija knew nothing more.

Chapter Nine

Lija woke to softness underneath her, warmth on top, and a fluffy pillow cushioning her aching head. Aching? That didn't go nearly far enough. She had a splitting headache, no doubt due to whatever the Natarns had used to knock them out.

Well, it could be worse. From the feel of the bed, at least Brentan hadn't thrown her into the dungeons.

She reached up to rub her temple only to feel a tug on her wrist. Opening her eyes she saw the thin ropes binding her wrists to the bed. A quick check revealed that her knife was gone as well. *What was it with men disarming women and tying them up?*

As best she could she sat up in the bed, fighting the pain in her head. A quick look around confirmed that she was in some sort of personal quarters on the Natarn ship. Luxurious quarters with a masculine touch, highly visible viewscreens, images of half-dressed women, and exotic weapons secured to the wall. She lay back down and stifled a groan. No doubt she was in Brentan's rooms, tied to his bed, and awaiting his pleasure.

She eyed one of the sharpened blades near her on the wall and smiled grimly. It was out of reach now, but if she could get to it, Brentan would experience something from her other than pleasure.

"Oh good. You're awake."

The familiar voice forced Lija's gaze away from the knife to glare at her captor. Two meters tall, black hair, and a brutally handsome face. Once she'd thought he was at least somewhat attractive. Now her stomach roiled at the idea of him being too close to her.

Her sick look must have registered with him. A look that could have actually been concern crossed his face. "How are you feeling? When we found you one of your captors was restraining you. Did he hurt you?"

Lija narrowed her eyes at him. Gehon had been trying to protect her from falling on her head as she passed out. "I have a splitting headache. And no the Zelion didn't hurt me. Neither of them hurt me. I wasn't their prisoner, Brentan, I was a guest." She nodded her head meaningfully at the rope around her wrist. "Unlike here."

"Oh, yes, the restraints." He moved to unfasten her and then fetched a clear liquid that reduced the pain in her head to a dull roar. As he held it to her lips, she got a strong whiff of the strong body scent he used. Some time ago she would have simply called it unpleasant. Now it was almost sickening and she nearly gagged on the medicine.

"There now," he said when she seemed recovered. "Tell me how you came to be in the clutches of the Zelion ruffians."

She rubbed her wrist with exaggerated concern. No point in letting Brentan know that she wasn't really hurt. He might associate an injured wrist with helplessness. "They aren't ruffians and I wasn't in their clutches."

Brentan frowned. "They took you from Dingalus Three. We found your microshuttle there, so they clearly hadn't planned to let you go."

"My shuttle? Where is it now?"

"It's safe in my hanger bay. I knew you'd want it so I brought it with me."

It was more likely he knew she would be less able to get away from him if he held her shuttle. "What were you doing looking for me on Dingalus Three?"

"After you took off from the negotiations, I got worried about you. That's why we followed you there. Then we discovered you'd been taken onto the Zelion ship and we went after them."

"You had no business stopping *The Traveler*. The Zelions won't take kindly to it."

Brentan took a menacing pose. "I don't take kindly to men raping my woman."

"I'm not your woman and they didn't rape me."

"One of them had sex with you. I had the medic examine you as soon as we got you on board, and he said…"

His voice broke off when she stood up, her fists clenched and fury burning through her. He almost seemed to cower before her. The arrogance of this man. She wasn't his property to poke at.

"You had no right to do that. You don't own me, Brentan, and whatever I did with Gehon and Jackon was my business not yours."

"You're my wife, Lija…"

"That's another thing. I am *not* your wife."

"I posted the banns for us already. According to my people, that makes you my wife."

"According to my people, that's not enough." She held up her braid, "so long as I wear this I'm a free woman. I never said I'd marry you and it's my decision to make."

"Your father…"

"…had no business offering me in the first place!"

Her anger finally shut him up. Brentan took a step back, and she felt his temper rise to match hers. "So, you liked one of the Zelions better than me? Which one?"

Both of them although she doubted she should tell him that. "They each had a different appeal," she said instead.

Brentan leaned against the wall. He looked relaxed, but she knew differently. "I suppose you know that you couldn't marry one of them unless you were his true." He smiled when she stiffened. "Yes, I know about the Zelions and their true mates. So, which one told you that you're his match?"

When she didn't answer, he chuckled. "Won't tell me, huh? Well, I know something else. Once a Zelion has been with his true, he can't make love to another woman." He nodded at her wide-eyed gasp. "I see you've heard that, too. So, I decided to test it out by having your friends entertained."

Crossing to a viewscreen, he activated it, using the remote to switch the scene to what looked to be an interrogation room probably somewhere on the ship. Brentan beckoned to her. "Here, come watch."

Afraid of what she'd see, Lija moved slowly forward. What kind of torture had this monster conjured for her lovers? A familiar sounding groan from the screen pulled her closer.

Two men lay on their backs fastened wrists and ankles by chains to the narrow cots under them. She tried to see their features, but red and blond hair that had fallen across their faces and obscured them. All she could see were their mouths as each man gasped and moaned as if in agony.

Lija gasped herself when she saw the reason. The men moaned because each of them had a woman energetically sucking on his very aroused cock!

She couldn't believe it. Gehon and Jackon had lied to her? So much for the pair being eunuchs without her. Fighting her tears, Lija sat down heavily on a nearby chair. She'd trusted them, believed what they'd told her. It hurt, far worse than she'd expected.

Probably the men had been playing with her, just as she'd done with them. They'd probably intended all along to have a threesome and she'd walked right into it.

"I can see this is quite a shock to you. I was surprised to see how fast they responded, but my ladies are very talented in this area. Surely you can admire their expertise. What man wouldn't enjoy their efforts?"

She glanced up at the screen again. The woman working on Jackon leaned back, exposing his cock to the viewer in the room. Lija froze, watching her stroke the length with her hand.

Standing, Lija moved closer and silently took the remote from Brentan, using it to focus closer.

"Yes, I can see her technique very well. I wonder how the other one is." Under her control, the viewer moved, directed at the other bed and the woman working on Gehon. Again she focused on his cock.

Lija shut off the viewscreen and tossed the remote aside.

Brentan smiled at her. "So, now that you've seen your friends in action, you still want to marry one of them?"

"I've made my mind up about that at least. I couldn't possibly marry a man who'd deceived me." Lija gave Brentan a curious look. "Do you know much about my people's marriage ceremony?"

"I know it has something to do with that braid of yours." He leered at her. "What about it?"

Lija leaned toward him stroking her braid suggestively. "It's part of our traditions. On my wedding day I cut it off and bind my husband's hands with it."

"You'd bind my hands? Kinky." He stared at the long black braid in her hand and licked his lips. "What do you need to do it?"

Lija stepped toward him, letting her hips sway suggestively. "I need you to get on the bed. I'll bind you there."

Brentan scampered over to the bed. "Should I take my clothes off?"

She barely avoided shuddering. "Not necessary. I'll take care of that later."

Interest at that promise firing his eyes, Brentan lay down and stretched his hands over his head. "Do we need a witness? I could use the comm to get someone in here."

"Maybe later." Lija pulled one of the long knives off the wall. At Brentan's startled look, she smiled. "I need it to cut the braid."

He relaxed. "I see. And then you'll be my wife?"

"As soon as I wrap it around your wrist." She kept one hand on the braid and the other on the knife, moving toward him. Reaching the bed, she straddled his chest and gazed down at him. She smiled. "Ready?"

At his nod, Lija dropped her braid and grabbed the ropes that had bound her and wrapped them around Brentan's wrists, securing his arms to the bed. He yelled, but silenced as soon as she put the sharp blade of the knife against his neck.

"What...what's going on?" he stammered.

"I told you I wouldn't marry a man who lied to me."

"What lie?"

"Those weren't the Zelions in that chamber. You put doubles in for them." She pressed harder with the blade and a thin streak of blood bubbled against the edge.

"How did you know?" he gasped.

"Well, it wasn't that hard to tell. Jackon's cock is completely straight, while the double you used had a definite bend to his. And Gehon's has freckles, especially along the shaft."

"How would you recognize..." Realization set in and he stared at her in disgust. "You slept with both of them? You little whore!" he snarled.

"Careful, Brentan. I'm the one with the blade and I don't like being called names." He stilled as the edge cut deeper into his throat.

"What do you want?"

"Freedom, for the Zelions and myself."

"I don't like threats, woman."

"Well, that's at least one thing we have in common."

A sinister snarl crossed his lips. "Perhaps. But you are still on my ship which I control, and if those aren't your friends on the screen, then you might wonder what is happening to them."

Brentan's eyes showed more danger now than she'd seen in them before, and Lija worried about what that meant. If she hadn't already made up her mind to have nothing more to do with him, she would have at that moment. She had no interest in being married to a man whose idea of courting was to hijack a ship she was a passenger on, and threaten harm to her friends.

Besides, if a man like that was in control of Axona...

Behind her the door to Brentan's quarters opened with a near silent snick.

"Your grace?"

Lija tilted her head to see a tall dark-haired woman enter. The newcomer took in Lija's position on top of Brentan and started to back out. "I'm so sorry, I didn't know you were occupied."

"Wait!" Lija said. "Come in here."

Cautiously the woman closed the door behind her and moved slowly to the bed. Her eyes widened when she spied the knife Lija held to Brentan's neck.

"Do you care what happens to him?" Lija asked, hoping the answer would be yes. She cut deeper into his neck for emphasis and a thin trail of blood flowed from the wound, staining the pillow his head rested on.

Staring at the blood, the woman paled, but nodded.

"Very well," Lija said, "come over here. I need to secure him and it's either going to be with ropes, or by cutting his throat."

She ran to the bed and under Lija's direction found additional restraints to use to bind Brentan to the bed. He twisted and complained loudly until she produced a gag from a drawer near the bed and applied it.

Her knowledge and efficiency told Lija a lot about Brentan and how he used his retainers. In particular this woman with her downcast eyes knew much about the prince's desires.

Once he was secured, Lija climbed off Brentan's chest and dragged the woman to a corner. She held the knife under the woman's chin, although something told her that was unnecessary and that this woman would do as she wanted without threats.

"What's your name?"

"Alsia," she said.

"All right, Alsia. All I want is to get off this ship and take my friends with me. Do you know where the Zelions were taken?"

After a quick glance at Brentan who glared at them from the bed, Alsia nodded.

Relief passed through Lija. "Take me to them."

Silently the woman led her into an adjacent sitting room and then into the corridor. Lija followed, the knife hidden in the folds of her fatigues as they passed through the ship. For a moment she wondered why she knew she could trust Alsia. Why would a woman loyal to Brentan help her to escape? Unless...

When they were in a quiet corridor, Lija pulled the dark-haired woman to the wall. "What is your relationship with the prince?"

"I...I'm his pleasure slave." Alsia's voice stammered.

"The Coalition doesn't permit slavery. What would he call you?"

Some inner strength passed through her and she raised her head proudly. "It doesn't matter what Prince Brentan calls me. I know what I am to him."

Lija let her go and relaxed against the wall. "You really do care for him, don't you?"

"He's my prince."

"And your lover," Lija guessed and knew she was right by the blush in the other woman's cheeks. "I suspect you care a great deal for him, too. I doubt you'd want to see him take a wife."

Alsia's eyes turned dark with anger. "He doesn't need someone to be his wife."

Lija could have burst out laughing but restrained herself. So, Brentan's current woman didn't like the idea of the prince marrying. Probably that's why she'd been so cooperative so far in helping her escape. "I agree he doesn't need me. And I don't want to be in his life — or in your way. I just want to go home with my friends. You help us get free, and I can promise Brentan won't even think about marrying me."

After a moment's hesitation Alsia nodded. "I think we understand each other. Once we free your friends I'll take you to where your microshuttle is stored. That would be the fastest way to get back to the Zelion ship." She looked Lija over and smiled. "The way you are dressed, you will stand out too much on the route we need to take. Come with me."

She led the way to the ship's women's quarters.

Chapter Ten

Ten minutes later they were headed toward the ship's brig. Lija was now dressed as Alsia was, in thin pink gauzy pants and a form-fitting maroon top that revealed her cleavage. The Natarn woman had insisted that this was what a woman on Brentan's ship would be expected to wear.

Secretly Lija fumed over the clothes, thanking providence that she'd discovered how incompatible she'd have been with the prince prior to becoming his wife. She'd have hated to have been forced to divorce him—or failing that, arrange an unfortunate but carefully planned death for him.

Lija followed Alsia down a set of darkened corridors. The occasional crewman they met looked the women up and down in a way that left Lija feeling unclean, but they didn't do more than that.

Finally they stopped at a guard station. Alsia leaned over the desk toward the two men on duty, letting them have a good look at her breasts.

"We're here to see the Zelion prisoners," she told them, her voice taking on a husky quality.

The men paid more attention to her cleavage than her words. "There are a couple women in there already. Why not stay out here with us?" one asked.

Alsia chuckled. "I was told they needed some help so they sent us." She shrugged. "Maybe if we have time later, we can work something in," she said suggestively.

With a grin, the guards waved them through, telling them which cell held the prisoners, and giving them the code for the door.

Once outside the cell, Lija nervously waited for Alsia to open the door, using the keypad next to it. What was happening to Gehon and Jackon? Brentan had implied he was having them tortured. Were they all right?

As the door opened she heard a low moan, and rushed inside, reaching for her stolen knife, ready to pull it from its hiding place inside her sleeve.

The scene inside the cell was nearly the same as the one she'd seen in Brentan's room, the two beds in the narrow cell, two men tied to the beds, two women energetically giving them oral sex. Even the groans were similar.

There were two changes. The first was that this time the men were definitely Gehon and Jackon, their faces not hidden by hair or odd viewer angles.

The second was that in spite of the efforts of the women sucking on their cocks, neither man showed even the slightest hint of an erection.

"Stars below, woman," Gehon growled. "Would you leave off with that? I'm getting sore."

The dark-haired beauty at his crotch dropped his flaccid cock and gave him a helpless look. "Perhaps you'd like to suck on my breasts?" she asked hopefully. "Would that help?"

He lay back with a sigh. "Nice of you to offer, but I'd really rather not."

Things weren't going any better on the other bed.

"And to think I used to enjoy this," Jackon moaned. "It's just not the same when you don't want it."

The woman working on him sat back and glared at him. "You could try to be a little more appreciative. I'm one of the best there is at this."

"I'm sure you are, but it isn't you I want."

She played with his limp member. "Maybe you need a man to do this for you. I could see if one of the guards is available."

"Stars, no!" Jackon leaned his head to glare at her and caught sight of the pair at the door. Lija moved toward him and in the smallness of the room, her scent drifted over to him. He breathed deeply, closing his eyes.

Under the woman's hand his cock rose majestically into full mast. She startled and licked her lips.

"That's more like it," she said with obvious enthusiasm, leaning over to take him into her mouth. Jackon moaned again, this time showing some appreciation at her efforts.

The nerve of that hussy! Lija started forward but Alsia caught her arm before she could pull her knife.

"Leave off with that," Alsia said.

For the first time the other women noticed their presence. Immediately they jumped to their feet and bowed. "Lady Alsia!"

She nodded at them. "You are relieved. We'll take care of the prisoners now."

The pair looked at each other, but dipped their heads. "We did our best, Lady, but they just weren't interested," the woman who'd been working on Gehon said.

"Mine was…" the hussy who'd been with Jackon started to say, but was silenced into confusion at Lija's murderous look.

"You did your best, I'm sure." Alsia reassured them. "Sometimes a man just isn't ready for sex." She leaned forward and whispered, "The guards out in the hall are in the mood. Perhaps you could entertain them instead?"

Their eyes widened with appreciation and, all grins, they departed the room. Apparently entertaining the guards was a welcome diversion.

Once they were gone, Lija pulled her knife and began cutting the ropes on Gehon and Jackon's wrists and ankles. As soon as the men were free, they wrapped their long arms around her, hugging her from either side.

"Thank the stars you're all right," Gehon told her.

"I was so worried," Jackon said.

Lija laughed, wiping tears of relief from her eyes. "I was worried, too. Brentan told me he was having you tortured."

"Oh, he was…" both men said at once.

Alsia's lips twitched. "I'll be sure to pass that on to my ladies. They'll be amused at how you regarded their efforts to give you pleasure."

Gehon stood up and fastened his pants, leaving Jackon to pull Lija behind him as if to protect her. Both men took an aggressive posture, prepared to fight, even if the only one to battle was a slender unarmed woman.

"And you would be?" Gehon said in his deepest growl.

The lady met his glare with one of amusement. "Lady Alsia. Head of Brentan's household."

Lija struggled out from behind Jackon. "She's helping us get away, Gehon. No need to take her head off."

He eased some of his belligerence. "You'll help us? Why?"

"Let's just say I have an interest in your lady not being my prince's wife." She looked over their clothing, which did not resemble the gray uniforms of Brentan's forces. "We'll need to go to where the microshuttle is. Hold here for a moment."

When she returned she carried two uniforms and a pair of stun guns. At Lija's questioning gaze she shrugged. "Their owners aren't using them at the moment."

Once the men were dressed, Alsia led the way to the ship's shuttle bay. Their route took them past the now empty guard station, and Lija heard moaning and giggling coming from the adjacent open cells. *So that's where Alsia got the uniforms.* The guards really didn't need their clothes at the moment.

Lija resisted her urge to laugh as they crossed into the main hall.

She kept her hand on her knife, while Jackon and Gehon kept a close hold on their stunners. Each step took them closer to the shuttle bay her ship was in, but also into more occupied territory.

Dressed as they were, the men were given barely any notice, their long hair tucked up under the uniform caps. Lija and Alsia received the most attention, men eyeing their bodies in the revealing costumes, although the fact that one of the women was the Prince's head of household kept anything more than eyes wandering their bodies.

A good thing, Lija realized, as both Jackon and Gehon looked ready to stun any man who'd dare lay a finger on her...then beat the frozen body into a pulp for good measure. Being knocked out, dragged from their ship, and sexually assaulted hadn't done much for their tempers.

Each of the pair was spoiling for a fight and she hoped they could get to her ship without having one. So far their luck was holding.

It ran out when they turned the final corner into the shuttle bay. Prince Brentan stood inside with six armed men, their weapons drawn. He smiled an unpleasant greeting.

"I see you managed to find your way here." Alsia cowered as he raked her with a contemptuous gaze. "What did they promise to get your help?"

"Nothing..." she stammered.

"Really? Not even that they would take you away from here?"

"She only asked that we would go away without hurting anyone," Lija interjected. "She was worried that we might go back to your rooms and slice your throat."

"You were that afraid for me?" His voice changed for a moment and Lija thought he might actually feel something for this woman who obviously cared so much for him. He shook his head. "Never mind. I'll deal with you later."

"As for you." He turned back to Lija, who'd used the distraction to move toward him. She was just a meter or so away. If she could just get close enough and pull her knife...

"Down, Lija," Jackon called, and she dove to the floor. Before the Natarns could react the Zelions pulled their stunners and fired, quickly putting four of the others on the floor. The other two fired, but Jackon and Gehon ducked their shots and with bloodcurdling screams rushed forward, engaging the remaining pair in hand-to-hand combat.

Brentan stared as they battled, his hand reaching for his own weapon. Jumping to her feet, Lija pulled her knife from its concealment and kicked him in the groin, forcing him to his knees. As he moaned, one hand over his injured privates, she held the point of her knife under his chin. "Call off your men, Brentan."

"Too late for that," Jackon said cheerfully. "They're already down."

Glancing to the side, Lija saw that her Zelion warriors had already disabled their opponents, leaving them to lie on the deck. The battle had been good for them, they were now relaxed and much more their old happy selves.

Lija relaxed as well. This hadn't been such a bad thing after all. It was going to be hard enough with the three of them crowding the tiny shuttle. Better that they work some of that excess energy out now.

Jackon and Gehon came over and each grabbed one of Brentan's shoulders. "What do you want us to do with him, Lija?" Gehon asked.

"We could break something," Jackon said in a hopeful tone.

"No breaking," she told them firmly. "I promised Alsia he wouldn't be harmed."

Brentan groaned louder, still clutching his abused balls. The Zelions looked at her quizzically.

"He'll survive," she told them.

Gehon shrugged. "Still, better to make him more comfortable." He aimed the stunner and fired. Brentan went limp on the floor. The sudden silence as his moans stopped was unnerving.

Alsia rushed forward to cradle him in her arms. There were tears in her eyes as she looked up at them. "Your ship is over there," she indicated the direction with a nod of her head. "You better go now."

As they headed away, Lija looked back to see the Natarn woman kiss Brentan's forehead, and she wondered if he'd ever realize what a good thing he had in her.

Her microshuttle was where she'd been told it would be, the sleek craft a welcome sight. Both Zelions stared at it with undisguised admiration.

"Very nice, Lija," Jackon said. "This is one of the latest models. Very expensive, last I looked." He grinned at her. "Our true has riches?"

Gehon gave her a curious glance, but didn't say anything.

With a roll of her eyes, she gestured to the hatch. "Inside, both of you."

It was a close fit inside. Lija took the control seat, leaving the men to share the narrow passenger bench behind her. Before any of the shuttle bay workers could interfere, her fingers flew through the launch procedures.

Firing up the engines took but a moment, and then they took off toward the bay's opening into space. There was crackle as the shuttle's shields briefly merged with the screen across the bay's flyway and then they were out in open space. Lija moved into a series of sharp curves, designed to confuse any trackers they might have. It was hard enough to track a microshuttle given its size, but she was taking no chances. She didn't want any company before heading toward the Zelion ship.

Behind her Jackon laughed, but the sound was forced. "You're quite a pilot, Lija. You always go this fast?"

"Only when I'm escaping Natarn ships." She twisted the controls and directed the ship into another loop.

Jackon gulped. "I'm glad. I'd hate to think you always flew this way."

Gehon punched his friend in the arm. "There is nothing wrong with her flying." He grinned at her, obviously enjoying the ride. "Let's see just how fast you can make it go!"

Who would have expected that staid, quiet Gehon would be the daredevil of the pair? She grinned to herself. One thing about it, life with these two would never be boring.

Lija pushed the shuttles speed to maximum, ignoring the groans and appreciative yells from behind her.

Eventually she circled back to the Zelion ship, coming up on the side away from the Natarn ship. The microshuttle was small enough to not be visible against the bulk of the freighter, but she didn't want to take any chances.

Gehon clapped her on the shoulder. "That was great, Lija," he said, eyes bright with excitement.

"Yeah, great." Jackon looked a little green. "Can't remember a better ride."

She moved to connect the shuttle's doorway with the ship's dock then turned to face them. Taking a deep breath, she prepared herself for the fight she knew was coming.

"Gehon, Jackon this is where we split up. You get on your ship and hide in the hydroponics where your life signs will be hidden."

Both men's jaws dropped, blue and brown eyes wide with shock. "Lija, you're our true," Jackon said.

"I know that but more important to us now is that I'm your decoy." She checked the crono on the ship's console. "Right about now Brentan is waking up and shouting orders to go after us. I can lead them away with the microshuttle and they'll have to push it to keep up with me."

"Fine," Gehon said. "We'll go with you."

She shook her head. "Can't. I'm heading for Axona and this ship won't take three people for that long a trip. Not enough life support. Your ship can"t make the trip at the speed I'm planning, not with it needing repairs. Besides knowing Brentan, he's likely left some people on it to salvage it. He's not above piracy when it suits his purposes. It will take both of you to take care of them."

Both men's eyes glowed at the thought of another battle. Lija suppressed a sigh. Yes, life with these two would definitely not be boring.

"So, the plan is, you get on your ship, hide until the Natarns are gone, take care of any who remain." She paused for a breath. The air was getting stale already. "Try not to kill them, though. If I'm going to break my engagement to Brentan, I'll need all the goodwill I can get with his people and casualties won't help that."

Gehon took her hand. "So you are breaking off with him?"

"I told him I wouldn't marry a man who deceived me. Besides, he has someone who loves him."

Jackon grabbed her other hand. "What about us, Lija? Will you choose one of us?"

She hesitated for a moment her eyes downcast. Then she gazed proudly into both their faces. Two handsome men, either of which would make her an ideal husband. How was she to choose?

"Come to Axona as soon as you get your ship repaired and your delivery on Brasia completed. It will take me that long to settle with the Natarns anyway. I'll give you my answer there."

Chapter Eleven

Jackon paced the floor next to the bench where Gehon seemingly relaxed, leaning against the wall, his legs outstretched, hands folded on his knees. Only the constant twitching of the redhead's thumbs told Jackon that his friend was at least a little bit nervous.

He, on the other hand, was nearly jumping out of his skin.

Lija had promised an answer for them when they reached Axona, but when they'd landed yesterday she hadn't been there to greet them at the port, in spite of their calling ahead to announce their arrival. Instead there'd been a curt message telling them to come to the planet's government palace in the morning.

Stopping for a moment, he tugged on the neckpiece of the formal jacket he'd been provided with and asked to wear upon arriving at the palace that morning. "Why do they always make these things so tight?" he said.

Gehon stopped twitching and glanced up at his friend. "To make us look good, of course," he said a hint of a grin on his face. "It's hard to slouch when you're wearing a tight collar."

Jackon settled onto the bench, doing his best to slouch anyway. "I don't understand why you aren't more nervous. It's been two weeks. Maybe she changed her mind about wanting either of us."

Gehon smoothed the fabric of his jacket with his hands. "I don't think she changed her mind."

He glanced at the hall around them, the smooth marble and tall columns that supported the high roof. "Why do you suppose she wanted us to meet us here?"

"Because if she does choose one of us, she needs to present him to her father, his wrists bound with her braid." Gehon looked around the hall with amusement. "I think he lives here."

"No," Jackon scoffed. "Can't be. This is where the royal family lives..." his voice trailed off as he realized what his friend was saying. "You think she's a-a-a princess?"

"Something like that."

"Oh." He mulled that one over for a while. "That would explain her being engaged to a prince." Something else occurred to him. "You don't suppose she's planning on having us arrested for abducting her, do you?"

Gehon's lips twitched. "Would you waste good clothes on a man you're going to throw into prison?"

"I suppose not." Curious, he looked closer at his too-calm friend. "Aren't you at all nervous?"

"A little, but I think I know what she's going to do."

"What's that?" Jackon asked, jumping with curiosity.

At the end of the hall a single figure appeared, silhouetted against a window. Gehon stood and smoothed his jacket top, his gaze locking on the woman who came toward them, her gait slow and purposeful. "I think she's going to do the right thing," he murmured.

Jackon stood as well, resisting the urge to run forward and capture her with his arms. When she got close enough, he was glad he hadn't. This beauty hardly looked like the young woman who'd sexually cavorted with his partner and himself. Lija's slender frame wore a simple yet elegant gown of silver synthsilk, and her glossy black hair was done up in an elaborate set of swirls. Only her long braid had been left alone, to fall past her breasts and almost to her waist.

Even her face had changed, subtle colors enhancing the edges of her cheeks and those beautiful violet eyes of hers. Her lips were glossier than he remembered them being when she'd taken him into her mouth while Gehon had entered her from behind. Then she'd been a wild woman, insatiable for their touch.

Now she looked cool and aloof, and completely untouchable.

For a moment Jackon wondered if she'd kept the Natarn women's garb that she'd escaped in. He hoped so. She'd looked so sexy in that outfit, even if it had made him want to tear the eyes out of every man who'd looked at her. It would be nice to see her wear it again just for him. Or for Gehon, he reminded himself, his competition for her love. He clenched his hand, for the moment wishing he could strike down the other man and remove that threat to his happiness.

Then he relaxed his hand, forced his mind away from such thoughts. Even if Gehon hadn't been his best friend, he'd promised it would be Lija's choice. Gehon said she'd do the right thing. Now all that remained would be to find out what that was.

Lija smiled as soon as she came close enough, and now Jackon could see the woman who was his true and had brought him such pleasure. She wore some perfume, jasmine he thought, which mixed with her own scent and made him hard as a rock. Thank the stars that his pants were loose and the jacket front long enough to cover his crotch.

They'd played ti-to-te earlier, so Gehon spoke for them. "Lady Lija, it is good to see you again. Or should I say Princess Lija?"

Her smile broadened. "Just Lija will do, Gehon." She turned to Jackon. "Same for you, Jackon. I'm glad to see you both so well."

Some of his tension eased. "Well, the Natarns only left a dozen men on *The Traveler*. Hardly put up much of a struggle. We were careful not to kill any of them, as you asked, and we left them on Brasia in the hands of the authorities."

"So I heard. Well done. I've done my part as well, and my engagement to Prince Brentan is officially nullified."

"So you're free to consider other offers?" Gehon spoke softly, and Jackon was pleased to hear some trembling in his friend's voice.

"I am."

Jackon exchanged anxious glances with Gehon. "How do we ask, Lija?"

She drew her head up proudly. "Do you both wish to become my consort?"

"Yes."

"Yes." Jackon's answer came slightly behind Gehon's. He hoped she hadn't noticed and wouldn't hold it against him.

"Then both of you hold out your arms."

Standing to the left of Gehon, Jackon did as she asked. From a sleeve hidden inside her elegant gown, Lija produced a long thin dagger. Jackon recognized it as similar to the ones he'd taken from her on their ship.

Lija held her braid up away from her face and with a single slice, cut it free. She stepped forward, the long black rope of hair lying across her palm.

"This is my choice, as we all agreed?" Both Gehon and Jackon nodded.

"Very well, I choose both of you!" Lija seized Jackon's right arm and Gehon's left and bound their wrists together. She held the loose end in her hand. "Thank goodness it's long enough."

"Both of us? We'll both be your husbands?" Jackon stared at her while Gehon's face cracked into a smile. "Is that possible?"

"Well, ordinarily no," Lija said. "But as it happens my father isn't king of Axona...up to now he's been the prince regent, waiting for me to reach my majority. Our planet is ruled by a hereditary queen, and as of yesterday that's me. While most of the time an Axonian queen chooses only one consort, there is no law that says she can't have two, or more if she likes."

Hopeful interest entered her eyes. "You don't suppose there could be another Zelion like you who needs a true mate?"

Jackon's howl of protest was broken off by Gehon's laughter. "You really think you'd be able to handle more than two Zelions in your bed, Lija?"

"No, I suppose not. I'll stick with the pair of you," she said, grinning impudently. Then she kissed them both, first Jackon then Gehon. "You're the men I'm in love with."

Jackon used his free hand to stroke her shoulder. "We're in love with you, too."

"I know." She smiled and tugged on the braid. "So, ready to meet Daddy?" Side by side Jackon and Gehon walked behind her, as she led them into the audience room of the palace.

"Lija, honey," Jackon asked just before they went past the curious eyes of the Axona elite. "I was wondering. I don't suppose you kept that Natarn dress?"

-She looked surprised, but Gehon smiled, nodding at the memory.

"I did," she said, "but why are you interested?"

The Zelion men exchanged glances and Jackon knew they'd had the same ideas about that garment. He grinned happily. This was going to be quite a marriage where the men had so much in common. "Gehon and I were thinking about what you might wear on our wedding night..."

Lija gave them both a disgusted look. "Oh, no. It will be a dark day on the sun before I ever wear that thing again!"

* * * * *

With one strong, final pull, Lija fastened the maroon bodice tightly across her breasts. She had to suck in her breath a little for the catches to meet, but the resulting cleavage was worth it. She smiled at her reflection in the mirror, patting her still relatively flat stomach, revealed by the hip-hugging pink gauze pants.

The Natarn dress still fit, even if she wasn't quite as trim as she used to be. Well, after five years of marriage and two children, she had a right to the few extra centimeters she'd acquired, even if it did make her husbands" favorite fantasy garment a little tight.

Not that her men would mind. Once they saw her in this, they'd be ready for action, the first being to get her out of it. Lija grinned at the thought of both their hands vying to unfasten her, taking turns...or not, as the case might be. She fingered the barely visible mend that the pants had required after Jackon had playfully tried to remove them with his teeth. It was a wonder the outfit still survived with all the use it had gotten.

She took one last admiring look at her reflection. And to think she'd once said she'd never wear this outfit again. As it happened, she'd often put it on when the pressures of life as a monarch grew too much and she needed a distraction. Sometimes she liked to surprise the guys, particularly when they were too sidetracked to come to bed on time.

Five years of marriage and they were becoming too comfortable in it. Time to shake things up a bit.

Lija headed for the lounge. From the open door she heard Gehon and Jackon arguing playfully as usual. It was Gehon's turn to stay with her for the month, acting as royal consort and keeping her bed warm while Jackon took *The Traveler* out on the spaceways, accompanied by one of their younger Zelion cousins. This had become the pattern they'd established early in their marriage.

While her duties as queen of Axona weren't too strenuous, it did keep her busy and having at least one man around to share the load helped tremendously. Also, during the past five years Jackon and Gehon's trading business had grown to the point that involving a younger set of men made sense. They were even talking about purchasing an extra ship sometime in the near future and manning it with their plentiful supply of Zelion relatives.

While they'd remained partners as well as good friends, Gehon and Jackon divided their time equally between the ship and her bed. They were just too possessive to share her for long. When she became pregnant, the men had been almost fanatical about knowing just who had made her conceive—not that it hadn't been perfectly clear when each of their sons had been born just who'd fathered whom. Fortunately, in spite of that, it also hadn't made a difference in how they treated the boys, who effectively had two fathers.

The one time the three of them were together for certain was on their wedding anniversary—and that was today. Lija sighed. Five years…the time seemed both longer and shorter. Tonight she had an idea to propose that might make it more common for both men to stay with her and share her bed. She had a plan that could work to keep both her men satisfied for some time to come, not to mention fulfilling one of her little fantasies, the one that had come to mind ever since she realized she had two devoted husbands.

Lija could hear their banter through the open door. "So how is Marlon working out?" Gehon asked. Lija knew that Marlon was the latest young cousin to join *The Traveler*'s crew.

"Pretty good. He did really well in bargaining against the Trowls."

"Oh?" Gehon sounded almost miffed. "As good as me?"

Jackon's loud laugh could have been heard on Zelion itself. "Oh, far better. He didn't get as distracted as you always got by their women. Marlon knows when the time is right to indulge in the flesh…and not before."

"Oh, like you ever were able to ignore a Trowl woman in the old days."

Lija suppressed a snicker. Like any woman could hold either of her husbands" attention the way she did. She glanced into the room where the men traded insults and smiled. On the couch, her son Jaon's pale head rested against Gehon's knee, while Jackon cuddled toddler Gaj, his thin shock of hair a red flame against the man's white shirt. Kept up well past their bedtime in honor of having both their daddies present, the boys' heads nodded sleepily, oblivious to their fathers" conversation.

"Don't you think it's time for everyone to be in bed?" she asked, stepping into the room.

As she predicted, both men's faces lit up at her attire and it took only moments for them to disappear in the direction of the boys" bedroom, only pausing long enough to allow her to give both of her offspring a goodnight kiss.

Returning to the bedroom, Lija moved around the large bed she shared with her men, lighting candles and laying out the special bottle of oil she'd bought for this occasion. In minutes Gehon and Jackon were back, their flushed, eager faces promising her a wedding anniversary long to be remembered.

Both men approached and gathered her into their arms, one on either side. "Happy anniversary, Lija," Gehon told her, as if he hadn't said exactly the same thing that morning when they'd awakened.

As was usual for him on his "off" months, Jackon held back, a tinge of bittersweet in his smile. "Happy anniversary. May we have a hundred more."

"A hundred more at least, my husbands." Lija returned their smiles as well as their kisses. "I've been looking forward to tonight for some time. There is something special I want to try."

Gehon exchanged a wary look with Jackon. "What would that be, our lady?"

She trailed a hand along each of their strongly masculine chests. "Oh, something that occurred to me a long time ago, when I realized I could have both of you at once in my bed. Something that I could only do with two men."

Interest fired in both men's eyes. Jackon, this month's odd man out, seemed especially intrigued. "What did you have in mind, Lija?"

"Join me on the bed and I'll show you."

One look at the bottle of heavy oil on the table and two pairs of male eyebrows went up in unison. Gehon lifted it and examined the contents. "Lija, honey…if you're thinking what I think you're thinking…" His voice trailed off as he swallowed, his concern evident.

Clearly a bold answer was needed. Lija fixed both men with her sexiest stare. "I want to have both of you inside me at once."

"Won't it hurt you to do this?" Jackon asked, equally apprehensive.

She caressed both their worried faces. "It is a fantasy of mine to be able to give you both pleasure. If it is a problem, then we can stop, but

I'd like to try it at least this one time. I read about it in that book you brought me for my birthing day."

Gehon grimaced. The book of erotic tales had been his present to her, brought back from his last trading trip. It had featured a number of stories of trios like theirs in various sexual situations, including the one she had in mind. "I hadn't meant it to be a suggestion, Lija."

Her smile broadened. "I didn't think you did, although I very much enjoyed reading it. And it gave me a few ideas." She shrugged. "If we find we don't care for it, we don't have to do it again."

The men took a little time to think it over, then Jackon nodded and Gehon held out his hands. "If this is your choice, Lija," Gehon said.

At their agreement, Lija tingled all over in sudden sensual awareness. Two strong, ready men, two ever-ready cocks. She grinned. "It always has been my choice — to be with you." She indicated the bed. "Let's move, then."

In moments they were naked on the soft surface, Lija's garments mixing with her husbands" on the floor. The men knelt before her on the bed and she took turns suckling their cocks until both were slick and at full mast.

Gehon uncapped the bottle of oil and the heavy aromatic odor filled the room, sweet and sexy. He poured some in his hand then handed the bottle to Jackon who did the same. Lija lay on her side as they took positions in front and behind her, spreading the oil across her skin in long sensual strokes that served to heighten her need. So good their touch was, she thought. Sexual need coursed through her, particularly when Jackon lifted her leg to rub oil on her clit, pussy and ass.

He'd always had the most talented fingers, Lija thought, lifting her leg higher to give him better access. Then Jackon's hand moved further back while Gehon's took the front and she could have melted on the spot. Someone's free hand tweaked her nipples, and she felt Jackon nibble the back of her neck while Gehon engaged her mouth in a tongue battle.

In the midst of her pleasure, a brief surge of pity coursed through Lija for all those women in the universe who didn't have two husbands to make love to them at once. It was simply so unfair...not that she'd give either of hers up, ever.

But this was just the precursor to what she really wanted. The men were clearly delaying getting to the heart of her request, something rather unusual for them given the hurry they usually were in, to be inside her. Apparently they were still a little uncomfortable with the idea. It was sweet in a way—they wanted to protect her—but it was frustrating as well.

Then she felt Jackon's fingers start to tease her anus in a way they hadn't before, probing and stretching, preparing her for something larger. Lija hid her grin. It was a good thing he was odd-man this month and so he'd get the honor of trying this new kind of entry first. Jackon always had been the more adventuresome of the men when it came to sex.

At the same time, Gehon had rubbed oil on his cock and was now slowly rubbing it along her clit with sensuous movements that nearly drove her insane. With what Gehon was doing, Lija was barely aware of when Jackon's fingers disappeared from her ass, but she knew when they were replaced by the oil-slickened head of his cock. As it pressed slowly into her ass, she couldn't help but notice that!

She tried to control her gasp. Jackon's initial entry was painful, but Gehon's efforts on her clit drove her into a sudden and complete orgasm that took precedence over everything else. When Lija's mind cleared, she could feel Jackon's cock firmly wedged deep inside her.

"Am I hurting you?" he asked into her ear, worry in his voice, but the huskiness of passion as well. He clearly liked being inside all that tightness.

She was finding having him there rather likeable herself. "A little before, but not now. It's...interesting."

"Interesting," Jackon laughed shortly. "Yeah, that it is."

"Let's see how interesting you find this," Gehon said, a touch of jealousy in his voice. He slid his cock along her folds until the tip reached the opening to her slit, and leaned into her, making his presence felt. With one move he surged into her, filling her as completely as Jackon had. Lija moaned as he took possession, driving deep within her.

Filled from before and behind, she couldn't have imagined how intensely pleasurable the reality of it was, both men's cocks in her pussy and ass. It was beyond anything she'd ever imagined.

Each man took a single long stroke and pleasure took on a whole new level of meaning. Lija moaned as the men moved in unison, her body convulsing between them. Orgasms began, small at first, but then longer and more intense, climaxes that came hard and fast, one after another, each one stronger than before. Lija cried out with each one, her voice near raw with the intensity of her screams.

Before and behind her, she felt the hard bodies of her husbands tense, then she heard first Jackon then Gehon give their own shouts of ecstasy as her ass and pussy milked them into completion. Hot cum flowed into her, adding to her sensory overload until she could only lie replete on the bed.

It was fast, hard, and intense…and everything she'd hoped for. She could only hope the men felt the same way about it. From the way they were breathing and kissing whatever skin of hers was within reach, that seemed likely.

Afterward they lay together, arms and legs tangled until it was hard to pinpoint just who had their hand where, but no one cared. Lija saw the future stretched before her, more nights like this one, more times spent in the arms of her lovers, either singularly or together like tonight. A wonderful future for them, filled with love and laughter and incredibly pleasurable sex.

For a moment Lija remembered her vision on the ship when she'd first spent time with Gehon and seen her children, the boys she already had and the daughter still to come. Could she have conceived that child tonight? If so, it would be Gehon's, but she knew that already from the child's eyes. It seemed appropriate that Jackon would have been present as well at her daughter's conception. He was as much her husband as Gehon and deserved to be part of that child's creation.

Lija snuggled closer to her men and hoped she was right about her daughter. What a wonderful night to make a child. When she finally recovered enough to speak she laughed softly.

"You wondered if I knew what I was doing, but I was right—that was a good way for us to make love." She accepted their chuckled agreement before continuing. "After all, I'm queen and I have to do what is best for myself, and my people. Fortunately I've always made excellent choices, the best of which was falling in love with the two of you."

Both men joined in her laughter.

"That's true, Lija, and we love you, too. But how could you have possibly failed to make a good choice?" Jackon told her, pulling her into his arms and kissing one side of her face. "After all, when a lady starts with a pair of Zelion warriors…"

Gehon kissed her other cheek and pulled her even closer. "...any choice she makes is bound to be a good one."

The End

About the author:

Cricket Starr lives in the San Francisco Bay area with her husband of more years than she chooses to count. She loves fantasies, particularly sexual fantasies, and sees her writing as an opportunity to test boundaries. Her driving ambition is to have more fun than anyone should or could have. While published in other venues under her own name, she's found a home for her erotica writing here at Ellora's Cave.

Cricket welcomes mail from readers. You can write to her c/o Ellora's Cave Publishing at 1056 Home Ave. Akron, Oh 44310-3502.

Also by Cricket Starr:

And Best Friend Makes Three

Lynn LaFleur

Chapter One

Brenna West loved spring. She loved to see the flowers blooming, the grass turning green, the trees filling out with leaves. The feel of a gentle breeze on her face always made her smile. With the cool, cloudy weather being the norm for several months, spring came later to the Pacific Northwest than in other parts of the country. That made the unseasonably warm weather with temperatures in the high sixties even more enjoyable. Spring meant a time of rebirth, a fresh start.

A time for love.

Lowering the window of her BMW, she sniffed deeply of the fresh, sun-scented air. This sixteenth day of April was extraordinary for another reason — it meant one year with Eric.

Meeting Eric McFarland was the best thing that ever happened to her.

She'd walked into his real estate office, intent only on looking at listings for houses. Instead, she'd taken one look at Eric and her heart had started pounding. When he offered to show her the houses in her price range, she'd quickly agreed.

By the time they'd toured the third house, she had no doubt she was already falling for him.

Brenna had never imagined she could love a man as much as she loved Eric. His dark, wavy hair, gray eyes and husky body had sent her hormones into a frenzy. His movie star looks naturally drew her attention first, but his caring heart had made her fall so hard for him.

The amazing, wonderful thing about loving Eric was the fact that he loved her, too.

Tonight would be special. Brenna had planned an anniversary dinner for them, including the baked salmon, au gratin potatoes, and spinach salad Eric enjoyed so much. She'd left work early after telling her boss, Carey, that it was her and Eric's special day. She wanted to give herself time to prepare the meal, her house...and herself.

Oh, yes, she had plans for her amazing lover. She glanced at the large sack that she'd picked up from her girlfriend in Tumwater. Once a month, she restocked her candle supply from her friend's boutique. She'd gone a little overboard this time and bought double what she usually did, but she planned to use most of them this weekend. She always burned candles while she and Eric made love, and she intended to make love with him many times over the weekend. Work had taken her out of town for three days. She'd missed being in his arms, feeling him inside her. Tonight, she would start making up for those three days without him.

Her cell phone rang as she pulled into a parking spot at the grocery store. She turned off the ignition and fumbled for her bag. As usual, her phone lay somewhere in the bottom of the large tote she used as a purse.

"Keep ringing," she mumbled. "I'll find you." She pushed aside her calendar, compact, notepad, a tube of mascara, a package of tissues and several pens. "Aha!" Grabbing the phone, she quickly punched the "Yes" button without looking at the display to see the caller's number. "Hello?"

"Is this Ms. Brenna West?" a sexy male asked.

The sound of Eric's voice made Brenna smile. "It is."

"The Brenna West who is an incredible kisser?"

"I do love kissing."

"The Brenna West who has the most amazing brown eyes?"

"The color of chocolate, I've been told."

"The Brenna West who has a cute little birthmark on her left thigh?"

"I do have one of those."

"The Brenna West who has the sexiest body in the world?"

"I don't know if I'd go *that* far."

"The Brenna West who makes love as if she can't get enough?"

Brenna giggled. "I have to say yes to that."

"So everything I've heard about you is true. Well, then, you sound like the perfect woman for me. I think we need to get together."

"That could be arranged."

"There are many advantages to being the boss. One of those advantages includes leaving the office early. I can be at your place in an hour."

"Don't you dare! You can't get there before six. I have plans."

"Aw, come on, sweetheart. Six o'clock is hours away. I don't think I can wait that long to hold you. I haven't felt that luscious body against me for three whole days."

"You'll survive a little while longer."

"You're completely heartless, do you know that?"

Brenna snuggled down in her seat. "I'll make it up to you, I promise."

"How?" His voice dropped to a husky purr. "What will you do to make it up to me?"

"Do you want details?"

"Oh, yeah. *Explicit* details."

Phone sex. In the grocery store parking lot. That would be a first. Brenna glanced around to see if anyone happened to be close to her car. She didn't see anyone, but turned on her key long enough to raise her window, just to be sure no one overheard her.

"We'll start with a candlelit dinner. I'm making baked salmon just the way you like it."

"Mmm, sounds good."

"I'll play my slow, smoky jazz CDs while we eat. After dinner, it'll be cool enough to build a fire. We'll sit on the floor near the fireplace and have coffee. There will be candles lit everywhere, of course."

"Of course. Will there be some kissing in there somewhere?"

"Lots of kissing. First on the lips, then on other body parts."

"What body parts? Remember — specific details."

His voice sounded strangled. Brenna hugged the phone closer to her ear. "On your neck. I love kissing your neck. I'll nip your throat with my teeth, just a bit, then soothe it with my tongue."

"Then what?"

"I'll run my hands under your shirt and comb my fingers through your chest hair. Have I told you how much I love your chest hair?"

"Yeah, you have."

"I'll touch your nipples with my fingertips, then take off your shirt and lick them."

Brenna would swear she heard him swallow. "Then what?"

"I'll push you back on the floor so I can unfasten your pants. By this time, you should have a very nice hard-on."

"There's no doubt about that."

Brenna smiled. Eric never had a problem getting hard. "I'll take your cock in my hands and caress it. Then I'll lick you from your balls to the head, over and over."

"Then what?" he croaked.

"When your cock is nice and wet, I'll take off my blouse and bra and slide it between my breasts."

"Jesus, babe."

"You said you wanted explicit."

"Yeah, I did." He cleared his throat. "Do I get to do something to you?"

"Not until you come in my mouth."

"Okay, that's it. I'll be at your house in fifteen minutes. I can make it in ten if I ignore all the stop signs and red lights."

Brenna laughed. She'd made him crazy, and she loved it. "I'm not at home."

"Where the hell are you?"

"I'm shopping on the Westside."

"Shit," he muttered, then released a heavy breath. "I can't leave now anyway, unless I hold a ream of paper in front of my fly."

"You don't want to shake up the office?"

"Hardly. The people in this office gossip enough as it is."

Brenna giggled. She could imagine Eric sitting behind his desk, unable to do anything about the erection pressing against his zipper.

"I've missed you," he said softly.

His sweet words and gentle voice brought a lump to her throat. "I've missed you, too."

"Are you sure I can't come over before six?"

"Please don't. I have a very special evening planned for us."

"Do you need me to bring anything? Vibrator, lubricant, nipple clamps—"

A bubble of laughter caused her to release an unladylike snort. "No!"

"How about a bottle of wine?"

"That you can bring."

"Dessert?"

"No, I'll take care of that."

"Then I'll see you later. I love you, babe."

"I love you, too. Bye."

Brenna dropped the cell phone back in her tote. She inhaled deeply and released her breath slowly as love swelled up in her heart. It must be illegal to be this happy.

Shaking her head to get her thoughts back on track, Brenna grabbed her tote. She had a few things to buy inside the grocery store before she went to the mall. This special evening called for a sexy new bra and panties set from Victoria's Secret.

* * * * *

Eric replaced the receiver and leaned back in his chair. He tapped his chin with one finger while thinking about his conversation with Brenna. A smile touched his lips. She was incredible. Sexy, beautiful, intelligent, caring...

And surprising.

He tugged on the fly of his pants to adjust his erection. After a year of dating Brenna, Eric would swear he knew her as well as a man could know a woman. Then she would throw him a curve he didn't expect, like the episode of phone sex they'd just had. She'd never done anything like that. While she had no problem telling him what she wanted or needed in the bedroom, she didn't throw around words like "cock" and "balls".

Hearing her talk that way was arousing as hell.

The swelling of his cock made him groan. Remembering the way she'd talked to him wouldn't help his condition one bit.

Contracts, man. Think about contracts and new listings and selling that monstrosity in Lacey that'll bring in a really nice commission.

A rap on his open office door drew his attention. Eric looked up to see Penny Sorenson, his best agent and one of his closest friends, standing in the doorway.

"Got a minute, boss man?"

"Sure."

He scooted his chair back under his desk to hide his condition. Penny walked in with an armload of file folders.

"Six new listings."

"Geez, Penny, do you tackle people on the street and threaten to sing to make them sell their homes?"

"My voice isn't *that* bad." Penny laid the folders on Eric's desk. "I like those fat commission checks. I have a ravenous hunger for books to feed."

"And you like to buy clothes."

"And I like to buy clothes." She sat in one of the cushy chairs before Eric's desk and crossed her legs. "The file on top will interest you."

"Oh?" Eric flipped open the folder. He perused the top sheet, reading the brief description of the house. Two-story Tudor, four bedrooms, three bathrooms, large evergreens, three acres of waterfront land on Eld Inlet...

His heart sped up when he realized which property this could be. He dug through the paperwork, searching for more information. "Where are the pictures?"

"I haven't downloaded them from my digital yet. I just got back a few minutes ago."

His gaze snapped to hers. Only Penny knew about his interest in this property. "This is it. This is the house."

Penny grinned. "It is."

"Download the pictures and send them to me."

"Will do. I'll hurry."

Eric's intercom rang as Penny left his office. "Yes, Allie," he said after punching the button.

"There's a gentleman on line two," Eric's receptionist said. "He says he's a friend of yours, but wouldn't give me his name."

"I'll take it. Thanks, Allie." Eric pressed the button for line two. "This is Eric."

"This is Keith."

Shocked at the sound of the voice on the phone, Eric remained silent a moment before a huge grin covered his face. "Hey, man, what's going on? You haven't called in months, and your e-mails aren't exactly frequent."

"Yeah, I know. With all the mess in the Middle East, my life has been crazy."

"I'll bet." Eric couldn't stop a shiver when he thought about his friend's occupation as a foreign correspondent for CNN. Not an easy job, especially with the unrest in the Middle East. "Where are you?"

"La Guardia. I'm on my way to Atlanta, then on to Dallas, then Phoenix, then I'm heading to Seattle."

"Are you serious?"

"Totally serious. I need a vacation, big time, and who better to go see than my best bud from college?"

"This is great. When will you be here?"

"I'm not sure of the exact date, but within the next two weeks. Will that work with your schedule?"

"I'll *make* it work." Still smiling, Eric slumped in his chair and crossed one ankle over the opposite knee. "I can't wait for you to meet Brenna."

"So you two are still together?"

"One year today."

"That's great, Eric. I'm happy for you." Eric could hear a noise through the phone that sounded like a voice over a loudspeaker. "They just announced my flight. I gotta go."

"Call me when you're on your way. I'll pick you up at Sea-Tac Airport."

"It's a deal."

Eric replaced the receiver. Memories swamped him, memories of his college days with Keith Dillard as his roommate. He chuckled. *Man, we were wild.* Beer parties, all-night study sessions, all-night make out sessions, sex with the same girls…

Eric linked his hands behind his head. Oh, yeah. Some of the best sex he'd ever had had been in college. He'd always been careful to use condoms, but had loved to experiment. When Keith had mentioned trying a *ménage a trois* with Eric and Keith's current girlfriend, Eric had agreed without hesitating.

It'd been fun. Not anything he'd want to do on a regular basis, but it had been fun.

Penny poked her head through the doorway. "I emailed you those pix."

"Thanks." Thoughts of Keith and college quickly disappeared as Eric transferred Penny's pictures from his email to his hard drive. He opened each one, his excitement growing with every new picture.

Eric had met Brenna one year ago when she'd come into his office. She'd seen some of the listings on their website and wanted to see the houses up close, not just on a computer screen. A single look at her and he'd known he had to get to know her better. Not wanting any of his agents to take her away before he got the chance to talk to her, he'd volunteered to drive her by the homes himself.

They'd driven by the Tudor on their way to see a listing in Brenna's quoted price range. She'd fallen in love with the Tudor at first sight. It hadn't been for sale a year ago. Now it was.

Eric picked up his telephone receiver and dialed Penny's extension.

"Yes?"

"I want an appointment with the owners of that house. Will you set it up for me?"

"When?"

"Now, if they can see me."

"I'll give the husband a call."

Eric opened the middle drawer of his desk and removed the small blue ring box. Lifting the lid, he studied the glittering two-carat, round solitaire. He planned to propose to Brenna tonight. That house would be the perfect wedding present.

Chapter Two

Eric stood in the kitchen doorway and watched Brenna move about the spacious room. When she'd visited his office a year ago, she had been adamant about having a large kitchen in the house she purchased. She'd succeeded. For a relatively small house, the kitchen had a sizable floor plan. The numerous cabinets, countertops, and center island gave her plenty of room to cook and create.

Leaning against the doorframe, he smiled as he watched her check something in the oven. A long, black and gray skirt stretched over that luscious ass. He could see the heels of her black boots peeking from beneath the hem. She closed the oven and stood, her back still to him, and touched her hair. How he loved burying his hands in that thick, dark mane while he kissed her. She wore it up tonight, piled on top of her head and held with one of those funny-looking clips that women used in their hair. Soft tendrils caressed her neck.

He wanted to push aside those tendrils and caress her neck with his lips.

She turned at the sink, letting him see her profile in her black sweater. His gaze settled on her breasts. Not too large, not too small, they were the perfect size to fill his hands. Brenna had commented several times that she wished they were bigger. By the time Eric finished touching them, sucking the nipples, running his tongue around the areolas, she would be panting and admitting perhaps they weren't too small after all.

Eric grinned. He enjoyed convincing her how much he loved her breasts...and every other part of her. He loved Brenna for *her*, because she was a caring, sensitive woman with a great sense of humor.

Having a killer body didn't hurt, either.

The timer on the stove drew her back to the oven. Eric was blessed with another glimpse of her ass as she removed the salmon. She set the pan on top of the stove, then turned toward him. She stopped short after one step. The astonishment in her eyes quickly changed to pleasure.

"Hi," she said with a smile.

"Hi."

"How long have you been standing there?"

"Only a few minutes." He walked forward and set his bottle of wine on the island. "I've been enjoying the view."

"You just like to see my bottom in the air."

"That's for sure." He cradled her face in his hands and kissed her softly. "I'll take any opportunity I get to see your bottom in the air, preferable with your legs spread wide apart."

Brenna wrapped her arms around his hips. She slid her hands down, cupped his buttocks, and squeezed. "Well, I kinda like your bottom, too."

Eric nipped her neck. "You like to hold it while I fuck you," he growled into her ear.

"Mmm, I love it when you talk dirty." Brenna tilted her head, giving him easier access to her neck. Eric gently bit her earlobe, then darted his tongue into her ear. A soft moan from Brenna made him tighten his hold on her. Blood rushed to his cock. It wouldn't take more than two kisses for him to have a full-blown erection.

"The salmon will get cold," she whispered.

"I like cold salmon." He kissed her jaw, her cheek, her chin.

Maybe *one* kiss.

"You're being very naughty."

"I like being naughty." He covered her lips with his and kissed her deeply. His tongue stroked her lower lip again and again, asking for entrance into her mouth. She parted her lips just a bit, enough to tease him with her taste.

Yep, one kiss was plenty. He shifted his stance, moving one foot between hers to bring their bodies closer together. They were only a few steps away from the island. He could walk her backward and lift her up to sit on the island, then reach under her skirt and —

"Wouldn't you like to eat first?" Brenna asked after she ended their kiss.

Eric's fantasy still filled his mind, so it took him a moment to respond to her question. "Oh, yeah. How about if I start with a nipple appetizer and work my way down your body?"

Brenna laughed. Standing on her tiptoes, she encircled his neck with her arms. "I made all your favorite foods."

"*You're* my favorite food." Eric ran his hands up and down her sides from her breasts to her hips and back. "I'd gladly eat you three times a day."

"Not very nourishing."

He grinned. "But a lot of fun."

"True." She kissed his lips softly. "Why don't you pour us a glass of wine while I finish the salad?"

Obviously, sex before dinner was out of the question. Eric's erection deflated a bit. "Can I stand behind you and play with your breasts while you finish the salad?"

"Yes."

"Deal."

Eric dropped a kiss on the tip of her nose before crossing the room to the cutlery drawer. Locating the corkscrew, he expertly opened the bottle of Chardonnay he'd brought, then turned toward the cabinet that held Brenna's glassware.

"The wineglasses are on the table in the dining room," Brenna said.

He looked at her, his eyebrows raised in question. They always ate at the island or the small table next to the bay window in the kitchen. The dining room was the perfect size for entertaining, but seemed too large and formal for a simple meal. "We're eating in the dining room?"

"It's our anniversary. Of course we're eating in the dining room."

Brenna remembering the anniversary of the day they met didn't surprise Eric. A woman as sensitive as she would naturally remember all the important dates in her life. Wanting to play with her a bit, he asked, "It's our anniversary? Really?"

The flash of pain in her eyes made him feel like a worm for teasing her about something so important. Eric walked back to her, tipped up her chin, and kissed her. "You didn't honestly think I could forget the day we met, do you?" He kissed her once more. "Meeting you was the best thing that ever happened to me."

"Me too," she whispered.

He caressed her cheek with his thumb. "I'll go get the wineglasses."

Eric took one step into the dining room and stopped. She'd outdone herself. The overhead light was off; the only illumination came from a grouping of tall, white tapers in the middle of the table. She'd placed a vase of fresh flowers next to the tapers. Her best china, crystal, napkins, and placemats graced the glass table. He hadn't noticed the music when he came in the house since he'd been so involved with looking at Brenna. Now he could hear the soft sax coming through the speakers that were hidden throughout the house.

Brenna's romantic streak was turned up to full throttle tonight. Eric smiled. Good. That made his plan to propose even better.

Picking up the wineglasses, Eric returned to the kitchen. He poured the cold Chardonnay into each glass and lifted one to Brenna's mouth. She held his gaze while she took a sip.

"Very good."

Eric turned the glass and drank from the spot her lips had touched. "Yes, it is."

The sultry look that filled her eyes never failed to make his heart pound and blood rush to his cock. Setting the glass on the island, Eric stepped behind her and cupped her breasts in his hands. His erection flared to life again.

Brenna shot him a look over her shoulder. "What are you doing?"

"You said I could play with these while you finished the salad." He rasped his thumbs across her nipples. "I *love* playing with these." Stepping closer, he nestled his cock in the cleft of her ass.

Brenna dropped her salad tongs. "I can't concentrate when you do that."

"How much concentration does it take to toss a salad?"

"You're incorrigible, do you know that?"

"Yeah, but you love me."

Brenna smiled at him. "Yes, I do." She turned and placed the salad bowl in his hands. "Tell your "friend" to calm down until after dinner. Make yourself useful and take this to the table. Then you can come back for the rolls."

Sometimes she could be a bossy little thing. The trait only made him love her more. "Yes, ma'am."

* * * * *

Brenna shut the refrigerator after placing the last of the leftovers inside it. Leaning against the door, she watched Eric close the dishwasher. He always insisted on helping her clean up after a meal. They worked together in the kitchen, more often than not taking much longer than necessary for they took a kiss break whenever possible.

She loved taking kiss breaks.

They'd already taken several while cleaning the kitchen, leaving her breathless, hot, and damp between her thighs. Her breasts felt full and butterflies danced around in her tummy. Three days without being in Eric's arms was much too long.

He walked toward her. That sexy swagger of his heated her blood even more. "Why don't you make the coffee and I'll build a fire?"

"Okay."

The desire in her throat made her voice come out as a husky whisper. A satisfied male gleam lit his eyes. He knew exactly the kind of effect he had on her. Tipping up her chin, he kissed her gently, then left the room.

Brenna had to fan her face a moment to bring her hormones back under control before she could start the coffee.

She found Eric seated on the floor in front of the fireplace. He had turned off the lamps on either side of the L-shaped couch, so the room was lit only with the glow of the fire and the many candles on the mantle and tables. He watched her approach, his gaze traveling over her breasts and hips.

Those butterflies started beating inside her tummy again. A year with him should have dampened her desire for him. It hadn't. If anything, it increased more with each day. Every kiss, every look, every touch, only made her want him more.

She wanted a lifetime with him.

Brenna handed one mug of coffee to Eric and sat on the floor beside him. She sipped the strong brew, but he didn't taste his. Instead, he held his mug in one hand and looked at her. She took another sip before facing him.

"You're staring at me."

"Yes, I am. I enjoy staring at you." He touched her jaw with his free hand. His thumb coasted over her lips. "You're so beautiful, Brenna," he whispered.

His words of praise brought heat to her cheeks. Brenna's reflection didn't break any mirrors, but she knew she wasn't the beauty Eric claimed. "When's the last time you had your eyes checked?"

"I see just fine. You *are* beautiful and talented and intelligent and—"

"Okay, now you're embarrassing me big-time."

"I don't understand why. My God, you design multimillion dollar lighting programs. That takes an incredible amount of talent and intelligence."

Brenna's job took time and patience as well as intelligence. She earned a very nice living because she did her job well. But accepting Eric's—or *anyone's*—compliments had never been easy.

Eric cupped her chin and caressed it with his thumb. "What can I do to convince you how special you are?"

Brenna nipped his thumb lightly with her teeth. "Kiss me?"

He smiled. "With pleasure."

His lips covered hers in a tender, loving kiss. Brenna sighed into his mouth. Each time he kissed her was better than the last. She parted her lips when she felt the soft touch of his tongue. He ventured a fraction of an inch into her mouth, withdrew, then ventured a bit farther. Over and over, he repeated the action. Brenna's bones melted and she had to clutch his upper arms to remain upright.

Eric pulled back enough to look into her eyes. "You, Brenna West, are an excellent kisser."

"I've taken lessons from a master."

"Master, huh?" He grinned devilishly. "I like the sound of that."

"Don't let it go to your head, buster."

"Speaking of heads, I believe there was some talk on the phone today about kissing body parts."

Brenna had to bite her lower lip to keep from smiling. "I seem to recall a conversation something like that."

"So when does all that kissing of body parts start?"

"How about right now?"

Chapter Three

Brenna rose to her knees between his legs. Grasping the hem of his sweater, she pulled it over his head and tossed it aside. Her gaze moved over his broad shoulders, strong arms, and hair-dusted chest. Eric wasn't her first lover. She'd seen other men's chests, and she'd seen pictures of well-built men. None of them could compare to Eric. His father's family came from Ireland, but there was also Mediterranean blood from his mother's family running through his veins. She wouldn't call his skin olive, but he always had the appearance of a tan.

It made him look deliciously sexy.

So did the well-defined muscles in his arms. Eric liked working out, and it definitely showed. He gave himself one day a week to be lazy, but the rest of the week included a regular exercise program.

The exercise program certainly paid off.

Brenna ran her fingernails lightly down his firm chest and flat stomach, then back up again. She did it once more while leaning closer and nibbling the pounding vein in his neck.

He drew in a sharp breath. "Careful, my little vampire."

"Did that hurt? I'm sorry." She swiped her tongue across the bite, hoping to relieve the sting. "Better?"

"Yeah," he said, his voice thick. "Much better."

Brenna shifted so she could nibble the other side of his neck. Eric cupped her buttocks and massaged them as she feasted on his skin. A light sheen of sweat made him taste salty.

Scrumptious, but she wanted more. She pushed on his shoulders until he reclined on the carpet.

Anticipation of what Brenna would do to him sent blood rushing back to Eric's cock, making him hard in seconds.

No other woman had ever affected him the way Brenna did.

She tugged her skirt up to her thighs and straddled his hips. A smug, feminine smile turned up her lips when she settled her pussy over his groin. "Hard already? And I haven't even done anything yet."

"I have a vivid imagination."

"Apparently."

She wiggled her hips, settling herself more firmly over his groin. Eric could feel the heat from her pussy through his slacks and shorts and her panties. He groaned and lifted his hips, gently grinding his cock against her. "That feels good."

"I've only just begun to make you feel good." Starting at his stomach, she ran her fingertips up his body to his shoulders the way she had a moment earlier. Goose bumps erupted on his skin at the feathery touch. She made the return journey with her fingernails. Eric groaned again when she lightly scratched his nipples.

"Like that?" she asked.

"You know I do."

Brenna scratched his nipples again, then leaned forward and soothed the scratches with her tongue. Over and over, she licked his nipples until they were firm nubs. Eric clenched his fists to keep from grabbing her head. The feel of her soft tongue, her warm breath, made him want to throw her to her back and thrust deep inside her.

Moving back on his thighs, she bit and licked a path across his chest and down his stomach. The tip of her tongue dipped inside his navel. Eric closed his eyes to better savor the sensations. He drew in a breath and held it when she unfastened his belt. The button on his pants loosened. He released his breath in a *whoosh* as she slowly lowered his zipper.

Eric opened his eyes again. Brenna looked at his face as she reached inside his shorts. Her gaze fell to his groin when she freed his cock. She wrapped both hands around it and caressed it from head to balls and back again.

Eric sucked in a breath between his teeth. "That's nice, babe."

"It certainly is. I love touching you." She released him long enough to tug his shorts and slacks past his hips. Returning her hands to him, she palmed his balls with one hand while rubbing her thumb over the head with the other. "I love your size. You're big, but not *too* big. You fit inside me just right." She bent forward. "I love your scent, your taste," she whispered.

Her mouth enveloped the head. Eric automatically lifted his hips, trying to drive his cock farther into her mouth.

Brenna pulled away from him. "Uh-uh. No rushing. Lie still and let me love you."

"*Lie still?* You're asking a lot of a man."

She squeezed his cock. "You have a lot to give," she said with a grin. She scooted down his legs, taking his shorts and pants with her. When she reached his feet, she grabbed his socks and shoes too, and pulled them off. The rest of his clothes joined his sweater in a pile next to the loveseat.

Sitting back on her heels, she looked at his body. "This is the way I like you. You are so gorgeous and sexy."

"I feel the same way about you. So how come I'm naked and you're still dressed?"

"Because I'm in charge tonight."

"Oh, you are?" Eric cleared his throat to keep from grinning. He hooked his hands behind his head. "Does that mean I'm at your mercy for whatever evil thing you decide to do?"

"It certainly does." She pushed his legs apart and moved between them. "I get to do *anything* I want to you tonight."

"Like some of that stuff you talked about on the phone?"

"Yes."

Eric couldn't stop his grin this time. "Goody."

Brenna laughed. "I love a man who's so easy." Her expression once more lust-filled, she ran her hands up and down his thighs. "You *are* easy, right?"

"Extremely."

She scooted farther between his legs. Bending over, she took his cock in her mouth again.

This time, Eric did grab her head. He couldn't help himself. The warmth and moisture of her mouth felt so good. He lifted his hips just a bit, silently encouraging her to take him deeper. She slid her mouth slowly down his length, until her lips touched his balls.

"God, babe," he rasped.

Holding him with one hand, Brenna swirled her tongue around and over the head. "Do you like this?"

"Yesssss."

She caressed the slit with the tip of her tongue, then licked the head again. She ran her tongue down each side and over the head before engulfing him once more. His cock grew harder and wetter with each pass of her lips over the velvety skin.

Drawing closer and closer to orgasm, Eric dropped back to earth with a thump when Brenna removed her mouth.

"Don't stop!"

"I had to. You were about to come, and I'm not ready for you to do that."

"*You're* not ready?" She was going to kill him. "Jesus, Brenna—"

"My rules, remember?"

Her rules could only go so far before he had to take over. Throwing her to her back and fucking her until she couldn't walk was sounding better and better.

That thought intensified when Brenna pulled her sweater over her head. She wore a lacy black bra that barely covered her nipples. It pushed her creamy breasts together and upward, making her look far more busty than usual.

Eric swallowed. Hard. He wanted to be inside her more than he wanted to see the sun tomorrow.

Brenna ran her fingers over her breasts. "Do you like my new bra?"

"Very much." His voice sounded strained to his own ears, but he couldn't talk normally with desire clogging his throat.

"I bought it today." She dipped the fingers of one hand into her cleavage. "I'm also wearing skimpy little panties to match it."

"When do I get to see them?"

"Soon." Unfastening the front clasp of her bra, she slowly peeled back the cups. Those perfect, rose-tipped breasts came into view. Eric's mouth watered with the desire to have her hard nipples in his mouth. Brenna slid the straps down her arms and pitched the bra to land on the pile of Eric's clothes. "I have some other things in mind first."

Leaning forward, Brenna surrounded his wet cock with her breasts. Eric growled low in his throat and hooked his hands behind his head again so he could see her better. He watched her cup her breasts and push them together to hold him in place. He pumped his hips once, shoving his cock more firmly between her breasts. The sensation felt so good, he pumped again. And again.

Brenna moved her hands until her fingertips touched her nipples. Eric stilled a moment to watch her pluck at them with her middle and forefingers. His breathing deepened at the sight of her pleasuring herself. The only thing better than watching her play with her nipples was watching her rub her clit.

The thought of that made him begin pumping his hips again. Every time his cock appeared at the top of her breasts, she licked the head. Each pump, each lick, brought him closer to orgasm.

"Tell me when you're going to come," Brenna said.

"I'm close."

"Tell me."

Eric closed his eyes and pumped three more times. "Now!"

Brenna took him in her mouth. Eric grabbed her head, squeezed his eyes shut, and muttered a soft curse as his seed shot down her throat.

He didn't know how much time passed before he was able to think clearly again. When he finally managed to open his eyes, he saw Brenna standing over him, one foot on each side of his waist. She wore nothing but a very tiny pair of black lace panties.

"I hope you don't think we're through."

Eric slid his hands up her smooth legs, as far as he could reach. "No, ma'am. I was just trying to remember how to breathe."

"Good." She reached up and released the clip from her hair. The dark curls fell in a cascade to her nipples. Pushing it aside, she cradled her breasts in her hands and caressed them. "You like to watch me touch myself, don't you?"

"Yes. Very much."

"Which do you like to watch the most me touching my breasts or between my legs?"

"Either one works for me." He squeezed her calves. "Is it my turn to tell you what to do?"

"I think that's only fair."

"Squeeze your nipples."

Eyes closed, she tilted her head back while rolling her nipples between her thumbs and forefingers. Her pelvis shifted as she touched herself. She was obviously enjoying the sensations in her body.

He wanted her to enjoy so much more.

"Now slide your hand inside your panties."

Brenna looked him in the eyes. She slowly slid her right hand down her stomach and past the waistband of her panties.

"Push a finger inside you."

Her panties hid her hand from him, but he could tell by her movements that she'd obeyed his command. He squeezed her calves again. "Add another finger."

More movement, this time accompanied by a moan and more pelvis shifting.

"Now lick them."

Brenna pulled her hand from her panties and dragged her tongue up her fingers. That action pushed Eric over the edge. He grabbed her free hand and tugged hard. She released a surprised yelp as she fell on top of him. Eric caught her so she wouldn't hurt herself, then quickly flipped them so she lay on her back with him looming over her.

"Now we play by *my* rules."

Chapter Four

A shiver danced up Brenna's spine, but not one of fear. The fierce look in Eric's eyes made her clit throb and her pussy moisten even more. Before she had the chance to draw a breath, he slid his hand inside her panties and covered her mouth with his in a voracious kiss.

He pushed two fingers inside her. Brenna gasped from the sensation, and his tongue filled her mouth. A mewl of pleasure was the only sound she could make as he kissed her hungrily.

She'd released a hungry beast, and she loved it.

"Lift your hips," he said against her lips.

She obeyed him without hesitation. He jerked her panties past her knees, then shoved his fingers inside her again. Brenna let her thighs fall open to give Eric more room. He pumped his fingers in and out of her pussy, pausing only to circle her clit with his thumb.

"You're so creamy." His hot breath flowed over her ear, sending another shiver through her body. "I love how wet you get for me."

Brenna reached between their bodies and wrapped her hand around his rapidly growing erection. "I love how hard you get for me." She squeezed his cock. "I need this inside me."

"I want to make you come first."

Since he insisted, she'd be crazy to deny him. Brenna stretched her arms over her head. "Then do it."

Eric removed her panties, pushed her legs wide open, and crawled between them. Brenna placed her feet flat on the floor and spread her thighs, giving him as much room as she could. For a moment, he simply sat on his knees, his hands on his thighs, and looked at her body. The intensity of his gaze, as if he wanted to feast on every part of her, made her clit start to throb again. She rotated her hips to try and ease the ache.

"Touch me, Eric."

He shook his head. "You first. I want to watch you rub your clit."

He didn't have to tell her twice. Desperate for release, Brenna placed two fingers of her right hand on her pussy. She gathered up the moisture from her body and spread it over her clit. A groan slipped past her lips when she touched her swollen flesh.

"Oh, yeah," Eric whispered. "I love to watch you do that. Rub it harder. Make yourself come."

Brenna increased the movement of her fingers. Knowing Eric watched her every move made her feelings even stronger. Just a bit longer…

Eric pulled her hand away from her body.

Brenna's breath hitched as her orgasm faded. "Wha—"

He raised her hand to his mouth and licked away her juices.

Brenna's body jerked and her clit throbbed. "Why did you stop me?"

"I wasn't ready for you to come."

She tried to sneak her left hand between her thighs. He captured it before she could reach her destination.

"Eric, touch me. Please!"

Holding both her wrists in one hand, he brushed his thumb across her clit in the barest of caresses. Brenna bit her lower lip and raised her hips completely off the floor. "More!"

A devilish grin tweaked the corners of his mouth. "Greedy little thing, aren't you?"

"Eric, don't tease me."

"*You* teased *me*. I should have the right to pay you back."

Eric slowly circled her clit. Each pass of his thumb over the sensitive tissue made Brenna want to cry out in frustration. She wanted—*needed*—to come. "Eric!"

The pressure of his thumb increased as he slid two fingers inside her again. Brenna drew in a sharp breath. It felt so good…

She gasped when Eric's other thumb slipped past her anus. She'd been so involved with her feelings, she hadn't realized he'd released her wrists.

"Relax," he whispered. "I want to play a little."

Brenna enjoyed anal play, but she had to be mentally ready for it. She took a breath and blew it out slowly to help her relax.

"That's the way." Eric pushed one thumb inside her ass. He continued to caress her clit with his other thumb while he pumped his fingers into her pussy. Brenna rotated her hips to his movements, establishing a rhythm with him. Each time she shifted drove all the digits farther inside her.

She purred with pleasure.

"Touch your breasts," Eric demanded softly.

Cupping her breasts, Brenna squeezed and pushed them together several moments before rubbing her fingertips over her nipples. Eric's eyes flared with desire. That look spurred her to continue. She plucked at her nipples until they were hard, rosy points.

The combination of her hands and Eric's on her body sent Brenna over the top. She cried out as her climax washed over her.

The tremors were still coursing through her body when Eric rolled her to her stomach. She wasn't allowed a nice, slow descent from the heavens. Instead, Eric pulled her to her knees and jammed his cock into her.

"Oh, God, Eric!"

"Oh, yeah. Take it all, babe."

Brenna closed her eyes tightly and bit her bottom lip to keep from crying out again. Eric held onto her hips as he rammed into her pussy again and again. Her ears rang with the sound of her pounding heart and his flesh slapping against her. Despite just having a powerful orgasm, the heat quickly pooled low in her belly.

Brenna moaned when he pushed his thumb inside her ass again.

"I haven't fucked you here in a long time."

Thinking of that hard cock inside her ass made her shiver with anticipation.

"How about it? Will you let me do that, babe?"

The climax shimmied down her spine and between her legs. Brenna arched her back as her clit pulsed and contractions gripped Eric's cock.

"Oh, yeah, that's it. I love when your pussy grabs my cock. Yeah. *Yeah!*"

His fingers dug into her hips. He pushed his cock all the way inside her and released an animalistic grunt. He thrust once, twice, three times, then remained still.

Her heartbeat throbbed in her temples. Eric still gripped her hips, and she had the fleeting thought that there would be light bruises on her skin tomorrow. She didn't care.

"God, babe," he said huskily. "That was… God."

Chuckling at his inability to speak, Brenna moved forward until his cock eased out of her. She heard an audible sucking sound, as if her body didn't want to release him. Stretching out on her stomach, she sighed tiredly and closed her eyes. Sleep definitely wouldn't be a problem tonight.

Light kisses up her spine tickled her. She turned her head and smiled at Eric as he lay beside her.

"That was incredible," he said softly.

"Yes it was." She touched his lips, and he kissed her fingertips. "You wanted anal sex."

Eric bent his elbow and rested his head on his arm. "I wanted *everything* with you tonight."

"So why didn't you?"

"For one, you didn't say yes. For another, when you came and your pussy clenched around my cock, I couldn't hold back coming too." He rubbed her back in small circles. "I'm not the least bit disappointed."

"I am."

Eric frowned slightly. "Why?"

"We didn't have dessert."

He rolled to his back and laughed out loud. Grinning, Brenna propped up on her elbows. "I made chocolate mousse, and I had a lot of ideas on how we could play with it."

Laughter still shone in his eyes when he looked at her again. "That certainly sounds interesting. We'll play with it tomorrow. How's that?"

"Deal."

Eric cradled the back of her head and pulled her closer for a deep kiss. She'd been gone for three days, overseeing a lighting project at a new casino in Reno. He couldn't believe how much he'd missed her. He'd missed the sex, yes, but he'd also missed *her*. He'd missed her smile, the way her eyes crinkled at the corners when she laughed, the scent of her lavender soap in his bathroom. He'd missed sharing meals, and waking up with her in his arms.

"I'm glad you're home," he whispered.

"Me too."

"You don't have to leave again right away, do you?"

She bit her bottom lip. Eric knew that telling action meant she didn't want to say what she was about to say. "Wednesday."

He hadn't known she would leave again so soon. He tried to be understanding about her many out-of-town trips because he knew how much she loved her job. At times, though, it was hard to be patient. "How long will you be gone this time?"

"I'm not sure, exactly, but it should only be a few days. It's the same job, Eric. It's almost finished and I need to be there to make sure everything works."

"I know you do. It's just…" He ran his thumb over her cheek. "It's getting harder to be away from you."

"For me too."

She leaned forward and kissed him. "After this trip, I won't have to leave again until I go to Athens."

"But you'll be gone several weeks then, right?"

"Yes," she said softly. "Setting up for the Olympic ceremonies will take several weeks. Plus, I have to be there for the actual opening ceremony."

Eric sat up, one knee bent and one leg flat on the floor. "I'm very proud of you, Brenna, but sometimes I wish you weren't so damned good at what you do."

"You could go with me."

"To Reno?"

"No. To Athens." The thought must have just occurred to her for her eyes lit up with excitement. She scrambled up to her knees and grabbed his hands. "Oh, Eric, that's a wonderful idea! Say you'll go with me. Penny can run everything while you're gone, can't she?"

"Penny's run things while I was gone for a couple of days. You're talking *weeks*, Brenna. You know how busy my office is. I don't think that would be fair to her."

Brenna twitched her mouth back and forth. "What if you came over for, say, a week after the Olympics start? Ooh, Eric, that would work. We could watch some of the games, sightsee, go out for romantic dinners, make love every chance we get." She squeezed his hands. "Please say you'll go."

He couldn't possibly say no when it obviously meant so much to her.

And it was the perfect lead-in for his proposal.

"I think it'd be great to see Athens with you. It would be a great place for a honeymoon."

Brenna clapped her hands. "Oh, we'll have soooo much fun. I already have dozens of brochures. We can…" Her voice trailed off and the laughter quickly disappeared from her eyes. "Honeymoon?"

If she hadn't looked so shocked, Eric would've laughed. "Yeah, honeymoon. As in the place where two people go after they get married."

She sat down, hard. Eric couldn't resist dropping a kiss on her parted lips before he grasped his jacket he'd tossed on the loveseat upon his arrival. Reaching inside one of the front pockets, he withdrew the blue ring box.

Glittering tears filled her eyes when he looked at her again. One tear fell down her cheek. He wiped it away before he opened the box and held it up for her to see the ring.

"I love you, Brenna Marie West, and I want to spend the rest of my life with you. Will you marry me?"

More tears fell from her eyes as she nodded. Eric removed the ring from the box and slipped it on the third finger of her left hand. Brenna moved her hand and wiggled her fingers.

"It's beautiful, Eric," she said, her voice raspy. "And it fits perfectly."

"I would've bought a bigger diamond, but—"

She touched his lips with one fingertip. "No, this is perfect. It's absolutely perfect." Cupping his face in her hands, she kissed him tenderly. "*You're* absolutely perfect."

"Funny, I feel the same way about you."

Eric kissed her while lowering her back to the floor. The kisses continued as he moved between her legs. Brenna wrapped her arms around his neck, her legs around his waist. Still kissing her, Eric slowly slid his cock inside her.

He didn't hurry toward a climax. He didn't increase the speed of his thrusts. This was a time for tenderness, a gentle buildup to completion.

A time for love.

Brenna's choppy breathing told Eric of her rapidly approaching orgasm. Hooking his arms beneath her knees, he drove deeper into her. Still maintaining the slow, steady rhythm, he circled his hips while thrusting to give Brenna the greatest stimulation on her clit.

"Come for me, babe," he whispered into her ear. "I want to feel you come again."

He'd barely uttered the words when her body tightened and he felt the contractions deep inside her. She arched her neck. Unable to resist that tempting flesh, Eric lightly bit it as he continued to thrust. No more than a few moments passed when Brenna trembled and the contractions once again gripped his cock. Her second orgasm sent him over the edge with her.

Heart pounding, lungs burning, Eric lay still on top of Brenna. When he finally gathered enough strength to raise up on his elbows, he kissed her softly.

"I don't think I can do this every time you're gone for three days."

Brenna chuckled. "Me either."

"Sore?"

"A little. But it's a good sore."

"*Definitely* a good sore." Her eyes looked drowsy, as if she could fall asleep in seconds. He pushed her damp hair back from her forehead and kissed it. "How about if we get some sleep? I want you to be all rested tomorrow for my surprise."

The drowsy look instantly left her eyes. "Surprise? What is it?"

"If I tell you now, it won't be a surprise."

"Eric—"

He stopped her objection with a kiss. "Sleep now, surprise tomorrow."

Chapter Five

Eric moved his head to get the bright light out of his eyes. As consciousness slowly seeped into his brain, he realized it was the sunlight streaming through the east window. After three tries, he managed to open his eyes and look at the clock. A few minutes before ten. He rarely slept this late. But then, he rarely had all the…activity he'd had last night.

Three times in the living room hadn't been enough. Once they went to bed and Eric had drawn Brenna into his arms, once he'd felt her nude body against his, he'd wanted her as much as before they'd ever made love.

She'd felt the same as he, and had decided to be in charge again. His little temptress had ordered him to lie on his back in the middle of the bed. Her warm mouth had quickly perked his "friend" back up so she could climb on top of it. Eric had laid on his back, his arms beside his head, while she rode him to another climax.

Seeing her back arched, her head back, her breasts thrust forward while she came, was so incredibly sexy.

His sex life with Brenna was more exciting, more passionate, than he'd ever imagined. Finding a woman so free, so willing to try anything he wanted, made him feel very lucky.

It also made him feel very horny.

Thinking about her passion sent blood rushing to his cock, despite everything they'd done last night. He turned to his side and reached for her. Her side of the bed was empty.

The smell of coffee drifted to his nostrils. Eric looked toward the door. Brenna stood in the doorway, sipping from a large mug. She wore a floor-length, black silky robe. A mischievous smile touched her lips.

"Want a taste of my…" She shifted her leg, giving him a glimpse of a creamy thigh. "…coffee?"

The sight of that thigh turned him hard instantly. Eric sat up and stuffed his pillow behind his back. "A taste of your…coffee sounds delicious."

Brenna sauntered toward the bed. The way she walked made him think of a cat on the prowl.

Eric bit back a groan as even more blood rushed into his cock.

She sat on the bed, facing him, and held out her mug to him. "Rich blend, with a dash of cream."

"Just the way I like it." Eric accepted the mug and took a healthy sip. "You're good at giving me things the way I like them."

"So are you." Leaning forward, she kissed him softly. "Last night was incredible."

"Yes, it was. What do you think about a repeat today?"

"We'd probably have to stay in bed all day."

"I have nowhere else to go."

"Then I think it's an excellent idea."

Eric cradled her neck in his hand, intent on pulling her to him for another longer kiss. The ringing telephone stopped him. He frowned at the offending instrument.

"There are times when I really hate the telephone."

Brenna touched his chest. Her fingers felt warm on his skin. "The machine will get it."

At that moment, Brenna's boss" voice came over the answering machine. "Brenna, call me ASAP. There's been a change of plans for the casino in Reno."

Biting her lower lip, Brenna looked from the machine to Eric and back again. He could feel her frustration. She wanted to be with him, but she had an obligation to her client. He sighed to himself while his erection deflated. "Call her back, babe."

She combed her fingers through his chest hair. "I want to concentrate on *you*. I'll call her later."

"Call her *now*. It sounded important. I'll just sit here and be horny."

She kissed him quickly before reaching for the telephone. Eric sipped his coffee and listened to Brenna's end of the conversation.

"Hi, Carey, what's up...He did? When?" She glanced at Eric and fiddled with the lapels of her robe. That nervous gesture told him he wouldn't like whatever her boss was saying. "Yeah, I can bump it up a bit... *Today*?" Another glance. "Well, yes, I have plans for today. Eric is here and... Oh." More fiddling with her lapels. Eric would've grinned at her unconscious movement if he hadn't been so disappointed. He wanted to show Brenna the house today. From her end of the conversation, it sounded like she'd be flying off again before either of them wanted her to leave.

"I'll check on flights and call you back… I'll tell him. Bye."

Brenna slowly hung up the receiver, not looking at him. "Carey sends her best."

"Carey sends an apology for taking you away from me so soon."

"That too." She scooted closer to him, sitting on her heels. "The wife wants some changes. Since she's the one with the money, hubby does whatever she wants. I have to go back."

"Today?"

Brenna nodded. "I'm sorry," she said softly. "I really wanted to spend the whole weekend with you."

She looked sad, and guilty. Eric refused to let her feel either way. He cupped her face in his hands and gave her a long, deep kiss. "Check on your flight. I'll cook breakfast while you get ready."

Brenna wrapped her arms around his neck and kissed him again. "You're wonderful, do you know that?"

"Yeah, I'm a prince. Now get off this bed before I change my mind and ravish you."

* * * * *

Brenna held tightly to Eric's arm as they walked into Sea-Tac Airport. She didn't want to let him go. She'd had so little time with him lately, hopping all over the United States for her company instead of being with the man she loved. This weekend was supposed to be for *them*, not for a too-rich-for-her-own-good casino owner in Reno.

She already had her electronic ticket and boarding pass, so they bypassed the ticket counters. She walked slowly toward the security gate, trying to postpone her leaving as long as possible.

Ten feet from the gate, Eric pulled her to the side, away from the crowd making their way through security. Brenna went willingly into his arms and clutched him tightly.

"Be a good girl," he whispered.

"I will."

She pushed her hands into his hair. The movement made the diamond in her ring sparkle. She'd hoped they could start making wedding plans today. They hadn't even had the chance to set a date. "I'll miss you."

"I'll miss you, too." Eric pulled back and looked into her eyes. "This is it, right? No more out-of-town trips until you leave for Athens?"

"This is it, I promise. Carey's guaranteed I'll stay here at the office and plan future projects until it's time to leave for Athens."

"Good, because we have a lot of things to talk about."

"Like my surprise I didn't get?"

"That's one thing, yes."

"And setting a wedding date?"

"That's another thing." He ran his hands up and down her sides. "Keith will probably be here by the time you get back. I want you to have plenty of time to get to know him. He's a good friend."

Eric had told her about his friend coming for a visit while they lay in bed last night. She'd heard a lot of stories about the famous foreign correspondent in the year she'd been with Eric and was eager to meet him. "You two need some time for yourselves without me anyway, so you can talk about old girlfriends and stuff like that."

Eric grinned. "Us talking about old girlfriends and stuff like that won't make you jealous."

"Well, maybe a little. Just don't have too much fun without me."

"Never."

With tears burning her eyes, she reluctantly hugged and kissed Eric once more, then stepped up to the security entrance. She passed through, picked up her large tote from the belt, and waved to Eric before turning the corner to head for her gate.

Stuffing his hands in the pockets of his slacks, Eric watched Brenna until she disappeared from sight. He missed her already.

Man, I've got it bad.

The intensity of his feelings always surprised Eric. He never would have believed he could care so much about a woman as he did about Brenna. There'd been other lovers in his life, other women he'd loved. What he'd felt for them was nothing compared to what he felt for Brenna. Spending the rest of his life without her wasn't even a remote possibility.

He hadn't planned to spend his Saturday at the office, but with Brenna gone, Eric had no reason not to get some work done.

He stepped out of the airport into the bright spring sunshine. Halfway to his car, his cell phone rang. Eric pulled it from his jacket pocket and flipped it open.

"This is Eric."

"This is Keith."

Eric smiled. "Hey, man, what's up?"

"I'm flying into Sea-Tac tomorrow. Can you still pick me up?"

"Tomorrow? What happened to Atlanta, Dallas, and all those other stops you had to make that I can't remember?"

"Change of plans. I'm tired, my friend. I need some rest. I want to do absolutely nothing for the next week except sleep late, eat good food, read, have sex with several gorgeous women, relaxing stuff like that."

Eric unlocked his car and slipped behind the driver's wheel. "I suppose you want me to set you up with those gorgeous women, right?"

"Hey, what are friends for?"

"I threw away my little black book when I started dating Brenna."

"Does she have a sister?"

"Nope. Only child."

"Cousin? Best friend? Not-so-best friend? Hell, I'm not picky. Do you have any idea how long it's been since I've been laid?"

Eric found that hard to believe. Not only was Keith what women called "a hunk", he had an exciting, adrenaline-pumping job. "You? The famous foreign correspondent? Don't you have a girl in every port?"

"Hardly. Sweaty guys wearing fatigues who spend a lot of time in foxholes aren't exactly my idea of possible lovers."

Eric laughed. "I'll see what I can do. I wouldn't want you to suffer too much while you're here."

"If Brenna is as great as you've told me, you could share her with your best friend."

"Sorry, friend. Brenna is off-limits."

"Damn. And here I thought I could convince you to try a little *ménage a trois*, like we did in college."

"What time does your plane land?"

"Talk about changing the subject fast. Got a pen and paper?"

"Yeah," Eric said, reaching for the small clipboard he kept on his dash. "Go ahead."

Eric scribbled down Keith's flight information. "Got it." He tossed the clipboard on the passenger seat. "So, what do you want to do first when you get here?"

"This will probably sound boring to you, but I want to have a great meal, preferably home-cooked, and relax."

"I can handle that. I just happen to be a great cook."

"My mouth is watering already. See you tomorrow."

Eric closed his cell phone and laid it on the seat next to the clipboard. It'd be great to see his friend again. Keith had been to Seattle once almost a year ago, right after Eric had started seeing Brenna. She'd been out of town working, so she'd never had the chance to meet him.

He hadn't seen Keith again until they managed to hook up in Chicago when Eric went there for a broker's convention six months ago. They'd fallen right back into a routine, as if they saw each other every few days instead of every few months.

Part of that routine included talking about women and sex. Keith had tried to talk him into picking up a couple of gals for the night. Eric had flatly refused. He loved Brenna and had no intention of ever cheating on her. It wasn't like college, where they were both unattached and could have sex with a different gal every night.

Or even sex with the same gal for one night.

Rubbing his upper lip, Eric thought about Keith's joke regarding a *ménage* with Brenna. At least, he assumed Keith had been joking.

Of course his friend had been joking. Eric had spoken on the phone and e-mailed back and forth with Keith many times, so his friend knew how much Brenna meant to him. That thing in college with Keith's current fling hadn't been serious because Keith hadn't been serious about the girl. This was totally different. Eric loved Brenna.

Part of the love he felt for Brenna meant wanting to please her in every way possible. Brenna was a very sensual woman who loved sex, and loved it frequently. Having two men make love to her at the same time would certainly give her pleasure.

Eric drummed his fingers on the steering wheel. *Can I do it? Can I share Brenna with another man, even if he is my best friend? Can I watch Keith touch, kiss, fuck, the woman I love?*

Shaking his head, Eric chuckled while starting his car. *Keith was teasing. We're both thirty years old and beyond college pranks.*

Still, the idea grew in his mind on the drive from Sea-Tac to Olympia. Brenna was always willing to do whatever Eric suggested, and she came up with some great ideas herself. He couldn't think of a sexual position or act they hadn't tried. They'd made love in every room of her house and his condo. They'd made love at both their workplaces, and in both vehicles. This would be something new, something different.

Something to please his woman.

What a wild wedding present.

Eric grinned as a plan began to formulate. Yeah, it just might work…

Chapter Six

Eric chuckled as he watched Keith collapse on the couch. "How can you be tired? You just spent four hours sitting on an airplane."

"I just spent four hours sitting on an airplane. That's why I'm tired." Keith let his head fall back to rest on the couch. "Getting on a plane is harder some days than others."

"You log a lot of air miles."

"*Too* many." He tilted his head and looked at Eric. "I'm too young for burnout."

"After a week off, you'll be itching to get back to work."

"Maybe." He rubbed one hand over his face. "Don't mind me. I've just spent the last two months in the Middle East seeing things I wish I hadn't seen. I'll be all better after a drink and something to eat."

"Let's go in the kitchen. I'll fix us that drink, then start dinner."

A spark of excitement lit Keith's eyes. "Food? *Real* food? Something I don't have to order off a menu?"

"No menus. Everything in this house is the chef's choice."

"I can live with that." He struggled to stand. "Lead the way."

In the kitchen, Eric gestured for Keith to sit on a stool at the center island. "You still drink bourbon?"

"That'll work."

Eric glanced at his friend often while preparing their drinks. Despite his tan and sun-streaked hair, Keith did look tired, and older than his thirty years. The e-mails Eric had received from Keith lately told him his friend had been in Europe and Asia practically full-time for almost six months. Getting only a short time at home every few weeks had to be tiring.

"You want to talk about those things you wish you hadn't seen?"

"No."

That "no" didn't sound very convincing to Eric. "Seeing people who have so little makes you appreciate how lucky you are, doesn't it?"

"Yeah," Keith said softly.

Eric set Keith's drink in front of him. He watched his friend raise the glass to his mouth and drain half of it.

Keith returned the glass to the bar. "Good bourbon."

"Thanks." Without asking, Eric added another shot to Keith's glass.

"It's the kids, you know?" Staring into the amber liquid, Keith rolled the glass between his palms. Silently, Eric sipped his own drink, giving his friend the chance to talk at his own pace.

"They have nothing, Eric. No running water, no electricity, very little to wear, almost nothing to eat. God, just looking at them hurts. I wanted to pack up every one of them and bring them home with me."

"Tugged at your heart, huh?"

"Big time." Keith took another sip of his bourbon. "I never thought of myself as the dad type. Seeing those kids…"

"Seeing those kids made you realize there's more to life than hopping around the world."

"Yeah." Keith cleared his throat. "We're getting way too serious here. I'm supposed to be on vacation."

Eric believed his friend needed to talk more about what he'd experienced, but pushing Keith wasn't the way to get him to open up. "Okay, no more serious stuff."

"Good." Keith sipped his drink. "So, where's Brenna? I'm eager to meet her."

"She's in Reno. Her company is installing the outside lighting of a new casino."

"Sounds like she travels almost as much as me. Do you ever go with her?"

"Not so far. But I will go to Athens in August. Her company is doing some of the lighting at the Olympics. She's in charge of the lighting at the opening ceremonies."

"I'm impressed. She must be good."

"Her company's been steadily growing. Sometimes I wish it wasn't so successful."

"She's gone a lot?"

Eric nodded. "More often than I like. But I knew what she did when we got together, and I try to be supportive."

"It's hard to be supportive when you're alone in your bed."

"True. I like it much better when she's in my bed with me." Eric drained his glass and set it on the bar. "Are you hungry?"

"Starving."

"Then I'd better get busy."

Eric washed his hands, then crossed the floor to the refrigerator. He removed lettuce, tomatoes, cucumbers, celery, and radishes. Carrying them back to the island, he set them on the bar in front of Keith. "You can make the salad while I start the steaks."

"Hey, I'm a guest."

"Guest, hell. Get busy. Wash your hands first."

"Nag, nag, nag. You sound like my mother." Keith walked to the sink and washed his hands while Eric added a cutting board, large bowl, and knife to the bar. Leaning against the counter, Keith dried his hands with a paper towel. "Nice place."

"Thanks. I like it."

"How come you and Brenna don't live together?"

"We practically do. Half of my clothes are at her house and half of hers are here." Eric laid two thick T-bones on a broiler pan. "We just never made it official." He chose seasoning salt and pepper from a cabinet and proceeded to sprinkle them over the meat. "That's gonna change soon. I proposed to her last night."

Keith smiled. "Hey, that's great. When's the big event?"

"We didn't get the chance to set a date before she had to leave. That's our first priority when she gets back."

"I envy you, man," Keith said softly while walking back to his stool. "I don't even have *dates*, much less anything more serious."

"You were always the one who didn't want to get married, who wanted to play the field and see the world."

"The world is a big place to see alone." Keith picked up a cucumber and started to peel it. "So, are you gonna help me while I'm here?"

Eric paused while sliding the pan of steaks under the broiler. "Help you?"

"You said you threw away your little black book, but surely you know some single women. You and Brenna could go out with me and Kate."

"Kate?"

"I've always liked the name Kate."

Eric chuckled and closed the oven door. "Kate works."

"Okay, so you and Brenna could double date with me and Kate. A nice night out, dinner, dancing, a good bottle of wine, then back to her place for some...you know."

"You're sure she'll want to...you know?"

"Absolutely. I'll charm her so thoroughly, she won't be able to resist me."

"Of course." Struggling not to laugh, Eric leaned against the cabinet and crossed his arms over his chest.

"So, Kate and I will go back to her place. And if you and Brenna want to tag along, we could have a *real* party." Keith waggled his eyebrows and grinned.

Eric didn't return the grin. His friend's joke was too close to what might actually happen to be funny.

The amusement quickly faded from Keith's face. "Hey, man, I'm shitting you. I'm not trying to horn in on your lady."

"What if I want you to?"

Keith's mouth slackened and he dropped the tomato he held. He had to do a fast juggling act to keep it from falling to the floor. "You want to run that by me again?"

Eric walked to the bar and stood facing Keith. "I know you were joking when you mentioned the *ménage* with Brenna, but I've been considering it. It might be a good idea."

"Are you serious?"

"Yeah, I am. Brenna is a very passionate woman. I think she'd really enjoy it."

"Whoa." Keith laid down the tomato and knife. "We haven't done anything like that since college, and then only once."

"Didn't you like it?"

"Well, yeah. It was wild." A crooked grin touched Keith's mouth. "*Naomi* was wild. She wore out both of us and could've taken more." He rubbed his upper lip. "I haven't exactly been celibate since then, despite the dry spell lately, but I think that was the best sex I've ever had. It was certainly the most...intense."

"So you're willing? Consider it a wedding present for Brenna."

Keith laughed. "It'd be a hell of a wedding present." Picking up the tomato again, he began to slice it. "You sure she'll be okay with it?"

Eric walked back to the stove and turned the steaks before he answered Keith. "I think she'll be apprehensive at first, then curious, then very turned on."

"Very turned on is good." Keith scraped the tomatoes into the bowl and picked up the stalk of celery. "So, do you have this all planned out?"

"I have some ideas…"

* * * * *

Brenna waved at Eric as he pulled up to the curb. With the tight security at Sea-Tac, Eric couldn't come inside the terminal and wait for her at the luggage carousel. Luckily, the weather was still beautiful, so it hadn't bothered Brenna to stand outside the terminal and wait for her ride.

He met her at the trunk. After a quick hello kiss, he opened the trunk and placed her suitcase inside. "How did it go?"

"Good."

"Did you please the wife?"

"Finally." Brenna walked with Eric to the passenger side and waited while he opened the door for her. "She's actually a tightwad. After I told her how much all the changes she wanted would cost, she was willing to back off a bit and leave everything to the 'experts'."

"I knew you'd win her over."

Brenna watched Eric shut her door and jog around the front of his car. God, he was gorgeous. He wore tight faded jeans and a gray polo almost the same color as his eyes. She'd casually mentioned three months ago how much she liked longer hair on a man. He'd been letting it grow ever since, until soft waves now covered his ears and touched his neck. The longer length looked so good on him.

Everything about him looked good. She could hardly wait to get him alone and tear off his clothes.

Eric slid into the driver's seat, cupped her neck, and drew her toward him for a deep kiss. "Welcome back," he said with a smile.

Brenna touched his cheek and let her fingers glide over his lips. "I'm glad to be back."

After checking his side mirror, Eric pulled into the traffic leaving Sea-Tac. "Do you want to go to your house first, or straight to my place? Keith can't wait to meet you."

"Why is it I've never met Keith? You two have been friends for over ten years."

"He's only been here once since you and I have been together. You were out of town working."

"Oh." Brenna didn't doubt that. She'd been out of town working a lot lately. That would change once she and Eric were married. She'd been training new people, and they were just about ready to test their wings. As soon as Brenna knew they could handle the load, she'd tell Carey she wanted less time on the road and more time at the company working on the initial planning stage so she could stay in Olympia with her husband.

Husband. She did love the sound of that word.

Brenna laid her hand on Eric's leg. "I suppose Keith is expecting us right away."

"He knew what time your plane landed, and he knows the time it takes to get from the airport to my place." Eric glanced at her. "Why?"

Brenna drew little circles high up on Eric's thigh with one fingertip. "Well, you mentioned going to my place first. You could…welcome me home in a very special way before we meet Keith."

Eric raised her hand from his thigh and kissed her palm. "Trust me. I will definitely welcome you home in a very special way before the night is over."

Chapter Seven

Brenna almost choked on her sip of wine. Keith had been telling stories all through dinner about his and Eric's college days, and some of the crazy things they had done.

"You know," Eric said as he leaned back in his chair, "I don't think Brenna really needs to hear all the sordid details of my past."

"You leave him alone. This is fun. Go ahead, Keith."

Keith looked from Brenna to Eric and back again. "I don't like the look in his eyes, Brenna. I think I'm about to get in major trouble here."

"He wouldn't dare hurt you in front of me."

"Don't be too sure about that," Eric growled.

Keith opened his mouth to speak again, but stopped when the telephone rang. He grinned. "Saved by the bell."

"Just hold whatever you were going to say until I get back." Eric laid his napkin next to his plate and stood. "I'll take that in the living room. Excuse me."

Once he left the room, Brenna picked up her wineglass and took another sip. This was the first time she'd been alone with Keith. He seemed like a great guy. He was certainly easy to look at with his tall, muscular frame, broad shoulders, and sun-streaked light brown hair.

He was also affectionate. When Eric had introduced them, he'd lifted her off the floor in a tight hug. A man's hug told a lot about him. She could tell by the way he squeezed her that he'd be very attentive to a woman.

If she wasn't so crazy in love with Eric, she'd definitely be interested in dating Keith.

"Would you like more wine, Brenna?" Keith asked, touching the bottle of white zinfandel.

"Yes please." She held up her glass and let Keith refill it. "The dinner was wonderful. Eric didn't tell me you're such a great cook."

"He didn't know. I've been a slug for the last three days. Either Eric's cooked, or we've eaten out." Keith set the wine bottle back on the table. "It's usually been Eric cooking. Having real meals I haven't ordered off a menu has been great. But I decided I should do something other than be a slug, so made a trip to the grocery store while he went to the airport. I'm afraid I'm not much of a baker, though, so no fancy dessert."

"After this wonderful meal, I don't have room for dessert." She propped her elbows on the table and held her glass in both hands. "You've done a lot of talking about Eric, but very little about yourself. Your job must be so exciting. Where do you go next?"

"Back to the Middle East. I'll fly out of Sea-Tac to New York Saturday, then on from there."

She wondered at the flat tone of his voice. She thought he'd be excited to get back in the middle of all the action. "You don't exactly sound enthusiastic about it. Being a foreign correspondent sounds absolutely fascinating."

"I love my job, I do, but I'm just… I was really tired. I needed these few days off. Eric's been a great friend. He's pretty much let me do whatever I've wanted to, which has included a lot of sleeping and reading."

"Then you must have needed to sleep. I firmly believe your body tells you what you need."

Keith tilted his head. "Eric has been bragging about how intelligent you are. Looks like he wasn't simply bragging."

Warmth flooded her cheeks. Receiving a compliment always embarrassed her. Brenna quickly turned the conversation a different direction. "Tell me more about Eric's college days."

Picking up his wineglass, Keith leaned back in his chair. "I don't think I should talk about my friend behind his back. How about if we talk about you?"

Brenna shrugged. "There's nothing exciting about me."

His gaze dipped to her breasts for a second. "I disagree with that."

Knowing Keith was teasing her with that wicked look in his eyes, Brenna shook one finger at him. "Coming on to your best friend's girl is not allowed." She sipped her wine. "C'mon, be brave. Eric is a gorgeous guy. I"ll bet he didn't lack for dates, did he?"

Keith chuckled. "Well, I don't know how 'gorgeous' he is since he isn't my type, but no, he didn't lack for dates."

"Did he have a steady girlfriend?"

Keith shook his head. "No. He never dated anyone for more than a few weeks. That hasn't changed over the years. I've known him a long time, and he never stayed involved with one woman for very long…until you. He really loves you, Brenna."

"I love him, too, more than I ever thought I could love a man."

"I like the sound of that," Eric said as he walked back into the dining room. He kissed Brenna's lips softly before returning to his chair.

Keith set his glass on the table with a *thump*. "If you two are gonna get all mushy, I'm outta here."

"You're just jealous "'cause I got the girl first." He kissed Brenna again. "Brenna's a lot of fun when we're mushy."

"I'll bet she is."

"Okay, guys, that's enough. You both sound like you're flirting with me."

"*Moi?*" Keith asked, wide-eyed. "I would never flirt with my best friend's girl. Besides, you told me I couldn't."

"I think it's time to change the subject." Brenna stood and began to gather up the dirty dishes. "Would anyone like coffee?"

"Sounds good," Eric said as he also stood. "If you'll start the coffee, I'll get dessert."

"Dessert? But Keith said he didn't make any."

"He didn't. I did." He looked directly into her eyes. "I made chocolate mousse."

Eric watched Brenna's eyes widen, then narrow seductively. He knew the mention of the creamy dessert would affect her. They hadn't had the chance to eat the mousse she'd made Friday, or the chance to play with it during lovemaking. They would do both tonight.

He and Keith had plans for that chocolate mousse later. Eric had prepared a double batch to be sure they had enough.

Eric dished up their dessert while Brenna started coffee. Keith winked when Eric set the dish in front of him. They'd talked at length about Brenna's sexual likes and dislikes. Eric had been open with Keith, telling him intimate details about Brenna's body. This evening was for her, to give her as much pleasure as possible. The more Keith knew about what Brenna liked, the more he could please her.

And if he and Keith had fun along the way, that would be even better.

* * * * *

Brenna stretched out on her stomach and sighed from pleasure. She hated sleeping in hotel beds whenever she went out of town. They were never as comfortable as her own bed. And they definitely weren't as comfortable as Eric's.

Sighing deeply, Brenna snuggled her head into the pillow. While she loved sleeping in her queen-sized bed, she especially loved sleeping in Eric's decadent king-sized one. She'd gone right from his decadent huge bathtub to the middle of his bed without bothering with any type of clothing.

She saw no need to put on any clothing when it would be removed as soon as Eric came to bed.

"Mmm, I do love that view."

Smiling to herself, Brenna wiggled her butt at Eric. She let out a squeak of surprise when he swatted one cheek. Holding her wounded flesh, she turned to her side. "What are you doing?"

"Paddling that luscious ass," he said with a grin as he rubbed his hands together. "It felt really good. Roll back to your stomach so I can do it again."

"I don't think so."

"Aw, c'mon. Let me have some fun." He kissed the side of her knee, then slid his tongue up the outside of her thigh. "I promise I'll make it feel *really* good."

Brenna had no doubt about that. Everything Eric did to her felt really good. They'd never tried any kind of bondage or S&M, but she'd thought about it. She doubted if there was anything to do with sex that she hadn't thought about.

She rolled back to her stomach.

She heard his belt buckle being loosened. The rustle of clothing made her shift on the bed as her clit began to throb in anticipation.

"Lift your ass," he rasped.

Heart pounding, Brenna did as he ordered.

"Pump it."

Again, she did as he ordered, slowly pumping her hips up and down.

"Reach back and pull your cheeks apart."

Brenna didn't think she could wait one more moment to feel his hands on her. "Eric, touch me."

"I will, I promise. Just do what I want."

Blood surged in his cock when Brenna spread her legs, lifted her ass high in the air, and pulled her cheeks apart, exposing her puckered anus. He licked his lips and swallowed hard. It'd been much too long since he'd had his cock buried inside her ass. He planned to remedy that tonight, with Keith's help.

Catching a movement in the corner of his eye, Eric looked toward the door. He'd left it partly open when he came in the bedroom. Keith quietly entered the room. Already naked, he walked to the end of the bed. One look at Brenna's ass and exposed pussy and his cock began to harden. He glanced at Eric and nodded, indicating he was ready.

Eric dropped a kiss on each cheek, then one on Brenna's anus. She shifted on the bed and he heard her catch her breath.

"Do you like that?" he whispered against the sensitive flesh.

"Yes."

Starting at the top of her cleft, Eric licked down to her clit. He wiggled his tongue over it, smiling to himself when it peeked out from the feminine lips as if seeking more. He gave it another moment of his attention before running his tongue back to her anus. He dipped his tongue inside her, once, twice, three times.

"God, Eric, that feels so good."

"I want to fuck you here."

"Yes, yes, but please lick me more first."

Eric looked up and motioned to his friend. Keith bent over and touched Brenna's ankle with the tip of his tongue. Eric watched him slowly begin to work his way up Brenna's leg for a moment before returning to his pleasant task.

He knew the moment Brenna realized something was different. She'd been lying with her face buried in her arms, writhing beneath his tongue, when she suddenly stiffened.

"Eric?"

He glanced at Keith and grinned. "Yeah?"

She cleared her throat. "I feel... How are you doing that?"

"Doing what, sweetheart?"

"Your tongue is...back there, but it's also on my leg."

Keith switched to her other leg while Eric spoke. "I don't know what you mean, Brenna."

Jerking away from them, Brenna sat up and scrambled around to face them. Eyes wide, her gaze traveled from one to the other, finally landing on Keith's face. *"What are you doing?"*

"Licking your leg."

Her gaze swung to Eric. "What's going on? Why is Keith in here..." She glanced at Keith's groin, but quickly looked back at Eric. "...naked?"

"We want to give you a wedding present. One night of incredible passion and pleasure."

"What?" she said weakly.

Eric tugged on her arms, which she had wrapped across her breasts. At the same time, Keith climbed up on the bed and took her ankles. She kicked at his hands. "Eric, I don't want this!"

"Don't you? Haven't you ever imagined two men making love to you at the same time?"

The pink climbing into her cheeks answered his question. He would never force Brenna to do something that would make her uncomfortable, but he knew she'd enjoy herself if she'd just let go.

"I'd never ask you to do something you didn't want to do, Brenna, but I know you'll like this. We'll make *sure* you like it." He caressed her chin with this thumb. "Let us love you, babe," Eric whispered before kissing her softly.

Keith took her ankles again. This time, she didn't pull away.

Chapter Eight

Two men at the same time. Yes, Brenna had fantasized about it…more than once. What woman wouldn't dream of having two men who wanted nothing except to please her? But she'd never expected it to ever happen, especially after she became involved with Eric. What they shared in bed was amazing. He was all the man, all the lover, she'd ever need.

Yet she couldn't deny the thought of both of them making love to her at the same time was incredibly exciting.

Keith gently tugged on her ankles. Brenna's curiosity got the best of her. She wanted to know what they'd planned to do to her. After an instant of resistance, Brenna took a breath and let him pull her until she lay on her back.

Eric leaned over her, his face close. The hot look in his eyes made Brenna swallow. "We're going to make you feel *so* good, babe. All you have to do is relax and enjoy it."

Brenna nodded. Part of her still wasn't sure about this. Part of her was intrigued and becoming more and more aroused.

Keith began licking her ankle again. He circled the delicate bone with his tongue until it was thoroughly wet. Then he blew on it. The combination of his warm breath on her damp skin sent goose bumps scattering over her body. Brenna moaned softly and closed her eyes.

Eric cupped her left breast and rubbed his thumb over her nipple. "No, don't close your eyes, babe. Watch what he's doing to you."

Opening her eyes again, Brenna propped up on her elbows. She looked from Eric's hand on her breast to Keith's mouth on her leg. She'd soon have four hands and two mouths on her at the same time. And two cocks inside her. Her gaze shifted to Keith's groin. Very impressive. His cock wasn't quite as thick as Eric's, but every bit as long. From the stories Eric had told her about Keith's love affairs, she had no doubt Keith knew how to use it, too.

Brenna gasped when Eric closed his mouth over her nipple. He rolled his tongue around the peak, then suckled hard. He'd told her to keep her eyes open, but the strong sensation made her eyelids too heavy. Brenna's eyes drifted closed and she sighed in pleasure.

Her eyes popped open again when she felt a warm tongue on the inside of her right knee. Keith was drawing closer and closer to her center. If she wanted to stop this before it went any further, before none of them would be *able* to stop, she had to do it now.

Brenna lay back, stretched her arms over her head, and spread her legs.

Keith moved up her body and started suckling her other nipple. Brenna almost complained for she desperately needed one of them to pay attention to her pussy, but their mouths felt too good. She loved having her nipples sucked, licked, nipped. Nothing turned her on faster than Eric playing with her nipples. She laid her hands on their heads to hold them even closer to her breasts.

A gentle hand on her stomach made Brenna catch her breath. Another hand slid low on her abdomen. She couldn't tell which touch belonged to which man. Not knowing made it even more arousing. She arched her back and spread her legs a bit farther.

One fingertip dipped inside her navel. One fingertip ruffled her pubic hair. Brenna raised her head, trying to see who was doing what to her. She couldn't see over their heads.

Right now, she didn't care who was doing what, as long as one of them speeded up this whole process.

Keith's suckling became harder. Eric kissed his way up her chest and neck to her jaw. He nipped the lobe, then darted his tongue inside her ear. It all felt wonderful, but she needed more. Brenna was ready to shout for *someone* to rub her clit.

Two fingers pushed inside her, and Brenna moaned loudly.

"That's Keith touching your pussy," Eric whispered in her ear. "It makes me crazy to see another man's hands on you." He shifted, rubbing his hard cock against her side. "God, I need to fuck you."

"Then do it. Please."

"No. Not yet. Not until you come." He clasped her breast firmly. "I want to watch Keith make you come."

Brenna looked into Keith's eyes as he raised his head from her breast. They were a startling blue, made even more startling by the fierce desire in them. Holding her gaze, he pushed his fingers higher inside her and pressed her G-spot. Little curls of sensation shot down her legs to her toes, then quickly climbed back up her legs to between her thighs. She spread her legs another inch and shifted her hips, trying to draw Keith's fingers even farther inside her.

She was so hot, one little whisk across her clit would be all she'd need to climax.

Unfortunately, Keith didn't seem to be in any hurry to locate that needy part of her anatomy. He returned his mouth to her breast and continued to pump his fingers in and out of her wet pussy. Brenna had no problem telling Eric what she wanted sexually. She wasn't sure how to do the same with Keith.

He lifted his head and gazed into her eyes again. "What do you want me to do, Brenna?"

It was no wonder these two were such good friends. They were both psychic.

"Do you want this?" he asked. He located her clit and brushed it with his thumb.

"Yes!" She raised her hips off the bed. "Oh, yes. More, please."

"Like this?" Keith pressed his thumb against her. "Or like this?" He drew a small circle over it.

"Like that. Oh, yessss!"

It took four whisks, not just one. Brenna cried out when the orgasm galloped through her body.

Eric loved watching Brenna's face as she experienced a climax. She'd scrunch her eyes shut and bite her lower lip, so he never doubted when the feeling took over her body. Knowing she had received pleasure made him feel almost as good as when he had his own orgasm.

He wanted her to have more. A lot more.

Lifting her torso, he moved behind Brenna and leaned against the headboard. He tugged her up a bit farther so she lay on his chest. Covering her breasts with his hands, he began slowly massaging them and looked at his friend.

"Lick her pussy."

"With pleasure," Keith said, smiling devilishly.

Eric plucked at Brenna's nipples as Keith moved between her legs, slipped his hands beneath her buttocks, and lifted her to his mouth. Eric could only see the top of his friend's head, but Brenna's moans and movement let him know exactly what Keith was doing to her. Brenna loved having her pussy licked, and Eric loved doing it. She tasted so good. And her scent! Her musky, feminine scent drove him crazy with desire.

Eric shifted, rubbing his hard cock against her back. He didn't think he'd ever had such a massive erection. He felt as if he'd explode if he didn't get inside her soon. If he lifted her just a bit, he could slip inside that luscious pussy while Keith licked her clit…

Why not? Eric thought. It would give Brenna even more stimulation if he was inside her while Keith licked her. But Keith might be uncomfortable having his mouth so close to Eric's cock.

"Hey, Keith."

"I'm busy," he mumbled, his mouth still close to Brenna.

Eric would've laughed if he wasn't so turned on. "I'm gonna slip inside her. Okay?"

That made Keith raise his head. Looking at Eric's face, he wiped Brenna's juices from his chin. Eric could see understanding flare in Keith's eyes as he realized what Eric meant. "Sure," he said softly.

Eric wrapped his hands under Brenna's thighs and lifted her enough to slide his cock into her. He drew in a sharp breath to keep from groaning. Her pussy was so wet and hot. He slowly lowered her back to his lap until he was completely buried.

Brenna leaned against his chest, her head resting on his shoulder. "I love the feel of you inside me."

"So do I." Cradling her breasts once more, he massaged them firmly as he flexed his hips.

Eric watched Keith lower his head between Brenna's legs again. Brenna jerked, then relaxed and sighed. He wanted to thrust, he *needed* to thrust. Instead, he remained still and played with her breasts, trying not to think about his friend's tongue so close to his balls.

This is for Brenna. Get your mind back where it's supposed to be.

Where it should be was making sure Brenna had more orgasms…at least three more.

Three orgasms would be easy for her. A year ago when they first started dating, it wouldn't have been possible.

They'd made love after their third date. Their first time together hadn't exactly been earth-shattering. Brenna had ended up in tears and Eric felt frustrated because he couldn't please her. He'd done everything he could to arouse her—long, deep, wet kisses, lots of attention to her breasts and nipples, a slow exploration of her wet pussy. She'd been aroused. Eric never doubted that. She'd clung tightly to him and moaned while he fucked her, so he knew she'd enjoyed the feeling of him inside her. Still, he'd experienced a climax and she hadn't.

That's when Brenna had told him she always had problems achieving an orgasm with a man. She'd loved everything he'd done to and with her. It wasn't his fault; it was hers. There had to be something physically wrong with her. She became aroused, but couldn't finish.

Eric didn't believe that, and had told her so. He'd asked her if she came when she masturbated. She'd blushed profusely, which answered his question without the need of words.

Brenna had no physical problems. She was a healthy, vivacious, passionate woman. She just needed a man who would take the time to arouse her, to make sure she was truly ready to make love. Even if Eric suffered bouts of frustration while helping her find satisfaction, she would be worth it.

Frustration had never entered the picture. After many minutes of kissing and foreplay, which included stopping and starting the stimulation several times, Brenna had come for the first time with a man inside her when they'd made love two days later. She'd cried afterward in his arms. This time, they'd been happy tears.

Eric's memories came to a halt when he felt Brenna shudder. He wrapped his arms tightly across her breasts and held her while she rode out her climax.

Brenna lay still, wrapped in Eric's arms and with Keith still gently licking her pussy, and willed her heart to slow down. Wow. No other word better described the intense orgasm she'd experienced.

She felt Eric's soft kiss on the top of her head. His arms loosened and his hands caressed her breasts. "Feel good?" he whispered.

"Oh, yes. Very good."

He rolled both her hard nipples between his thumbs and forefingers. "Want more?"

Brenna looked at Keith kneeling on the bed between her legs, his cock hard and his balls tight. Eric's erection throbbed inside her. Both of them had put aside their needs to please her. Now it was their turn.

"Yes, I want more. Keith, move back a bit."

Once Keith had done as she requested, Brenna lifted herself away from Eric. She turned on her hands and knees and took his shaft in her hand. "I want to suck on you while Keith fucks me."

Chapter Nine

Eric closed his eyes in bliss when Brenna's warm mouth engulfed his cock. She took him all the way to his balls, then slowly drew her mouth back to the tip. She circled the tip with her tongue, then covered the entire head with her lips and sucked.

Oh, she did that *so* good. Eric placed his hands on the sides of her face. Pumping his hips, he began to fuck her mouth.

A few moments of this would make him come long before he'd planned to. He wanted this night to be for Brenna and her enjoyment. Although by the way she was devouring him, it appeared she was enjoying herself just fine.

Eric looked past Brenna. Keith sat on his knees, watching Brenna's mouth. "Looks good," he said.

"It feels even better."

Still watching Brenna's mouth, Keith slipped his hand between her thighs. She arched her back. Eric felt the vibrations of her purr against his cock. Whatever Keith was doing between her legs, she must like it.

Brenna released him and glanced over her shoulder at Keith. "Inside me," she whispered.

Eric could tell by the movement of Keith's arm that he'd inserted his fingers in Brenna's pussy. That, and the way Brenna moved her hips from side to side.

"She's really wet," Keith said.

Eric had to swallow before he could speak because Brenna had once again taken him into her mouth. "The more you play with her, the wetter she gets."

"Mmm, nice." He moved behind her, grasped her hips, and thrust. "*Very* nice." he groaned.

Keith held her hips while he continued to thrust into her. Eric wished he could see Keith fucking Brenna...see her swollen feminine lips grip Keith's shaft as he moved it in and out of her wet pussy.

The thought sent another surge of blood through his body.

If he pulled away from Brenna, he *could* watch. The temptation to do so evaporated when Brenna slid her mouth to his balls again. He was being selfish, but her mouth felt too good right now to pull away.

Sweat beaded Keith's face and chest as he thrust several more times, then stopped, closed his eyes, and took a breath. Keith must be as close to a climax as he.

Despite not wanting to stop Brenna, Eric knew he had to. If he didn't, he wouldn't be able to hold back much longer.

His good intentions flew out of his head when Brenna pushed one finger up his ass. That did it. Eric tightened his hold on her face and began pumping again. Keith resumed his thrusting into her pussy. The feel of Brenna's warm lips and tongue, plus the knowledge that his best friend was fucking her, sent Eric over the edge. He groaned loudly and shot his seed into Brenna's mouth.

Eric had barely drawn a breath after his climax when Keith gripped Brenna's hips tightly and moaned.

A final swipe of her tongue caught the last drop of semen on the tip of Eric's penis. Brenna grinned up at him. She loved it when she made him lose control.

"Get that damn grin off your face," Eric said with a frown. "I wasn't supposed to come yet."

"I don't know why not." Brenna shifted, and Keith pulled out of her with a soft squishing sound. "I'm not the only one who's allowed to come."

"This evening is for *you*, not us."

"I thought it was for *all* of us." Brenna reclined on the bed and propped up on one elbow. From her angle, she could see both men perfectly. Their cocks were relaxed, but nowhere near soft. "Surely you two aren't *completely* finished for the night."

"Hardly," Keith said.

"I didn't think so." She looked from Eric to Keith and back again. "You two planned this whole thing. What's next?"

"What's next, Eric," Keith asked as he lay next to Brenna and started rubbing her nipple with his fingertips, "besides recuperation?"

"I think it's time for the chocolate mousse."

"Great idea. I'll get it."

Brenna watched Keith leave the room. She couldn't help noticing he had a bottom almost as nice as Eric's.

Turning back to the man she loved, she ran her hand up his damp thigh. "I have a question."

"What?"

"Earlier, when you were inside me and Keith had his mouth on me, were you... I mean, his mouth was right *there* next to you. Didn't that bother you?"

Eric shook his head. "It would've bothered Keith more than me and he was fine with it."

"Did he ever...touch you?"

"Yeah, a couple of times."

"Did it excite you?" She continued to caress his thigh, enjoying the sensation of his hair-dusted skin against her palm. "Would you like this night to be more? Would you like to turn this threesome into a *real* threesome?"

He hesitated, which told Brenna he didn't want to answer her. "Are you afraid I'll think badly of you if you admit the idea of sex with Keith isn't repulsive?"

"No. I know you wouldn't think badly of me. And yeah, knowing Keith's tongue was right there by my balls was exciting. But this evening is for *you* and what pleases *you*, not me."

Brenna smiled. "Thank you," she said softly.

"For what?"

"For loving me. Not every man would be willing to share his woman with another man."

Eric laid his hand on top of hers. "Not every man loves his woman as much as I love you."

A comment that romantic deserved a kiss. Brenna rose to her knees next to Eric. Cradling his face in her hands, she kissed him gently.

The gentle kiss soon turned more passionate as tongues came into play. Eric's hands roamed over her back and buttocks while Brenna held his face and kissed him over and over. She stroked his lower lip with her tongue, then slipped it into his mouth. His breathing deepened, his hold on her tightened. A quick peek at his groin showed her he was quickly becoming hard again.

Brenna slid one hand down his torso and wrapped it around his penis. "Are you ready for more?"

"Definitely."

"Uh, should I go back out?" Keith asked.

"No," Eric said. "We aren't through with Brenna yet."

She looked at Keith over her shoulder. He stood at the end of the bed, holding a bowl of chocolate mousse. Her imagination ran wild with the things they could do with that mousse. Despite having two powerful orgasms mere minutes ago, her clit began to throb.

Keith walked to the side of the bed and set the bowl on the nightstand. "Do you want to pull back that fancy bedspread of yours, Eric?"

"Hey, I gave him this fancy bedspread!" Brenna said, her voice playfully indignant.

Keith grinned. "If you don't want chocolate on it, I suggest we pull it off."

A shiver ran up her spine at Keith's words. She and Eric had fed each other finger foods during sex. They'd shared wine from the same glass. Ideas had run rampant through her mind about more playful acts with food, including chocolate mousse. She'd fantasized many times about painting Eric's body with chocolate and licking it off, then having him do the same to her.

She'd get to fulfill her fantasy tonight.

Eric squeezed her buttocks. "I'll take care of it, babe."

Brenna scrambled off the bed. From the opposite side, Eric grabbed everything but the blue fitted sheet and pillows and tossed it off the end of the bed. Facing her again, he pointed toward the mattress.

"Lie down, Brenna."

She looked at the two men standing on the other side of the bed from her. They were both tall, well built, handsome, and aroused. They both looked ready to pounce on her.

That shiver skittered up her spine again.

Crawling to the middle of the bed, Brenna lay on her back and waited for what the guys had planned next.

Keith picked up the bowl and rounded the bed to her right side. He sat beside her, resting one knee on the bed. Looking into her eyes, he drew his index finger through the mousse. The scent of chocolate teased her nose.

"So, where should I start, Brenna?" Keith touched her right nipple, leaving a dime-sized spot of mousse. "Here?" He dipped his finger again and left another spot of mousse between her breasts. "Or here?" One more dip, one more spot close to her navel. "Or maybe here?"

By the time he'd placed the fourth spot of mousse, Brenna was writhing on the bed.

Eric lay next to her. He swiped his tongue across her nipple and removed the mousse. The spot between her breasts came off next. As he licked off the spot near her navel, Keith dabbed another one at the top of her thigh. Over and over, he placed dots of mousse on Brenna's skin. Each spot of mousse Keith left, Eric slowly removed with his tongue.

Foreplay was one thing, but this was pure torture.

Keith held the bowl out to Eric. "My turn."

"Once more for me first." With one finger, Eric spread mousse over Brenna's lips. He kissed her, his tongue swiping the chocolate from her lips before dipping deep inside her mouth.

Brenna melted. She did so love the way Eric kissed. His kisses made her feel cherished and loved and beautiful.

And so hot.

Eric sat up and took the bowl from Keith. "*Now* it's your turn."

Closing her eyes, Brenna concentrated on the subtle touch of Eric's finger as he painted her with mousse. Each gentle brush sent an arrow of sensation to between her legs. Several moments passed before she felt Keith's tongue following Eric's path. Brenna bit her bottom lip to keep from crying out. They'd touched her on practically every inch of her torso, except for where she needed to be touched the most.

Brenna opened her eyes again when she felt Eric's fingers glide through her pubic hair. She spread her legs wider and lifted her hips.

Eric collected more mousse and spread it over her clit and feminine lips. Keith followed with his tongue, lapping up the sweet chocolate along with her juices. He darted his tongue inside her, then tickled her clit. He paused only long enough for Eric to spread more chocolate before starting all over again.

The orgasm started at the base of her spine and quickly flowed through her entire body. Brenna couldn't hold back her cry as pleasure gripped her. She closed her eyes, bit her bottom lip, and rode out the wave.

The sight of two very aroused men greeted her when she managed to open her eyes again.

Eric sat on her left side, Keith on her right. They were both touching her softly, rubbing their hands up her thighs, over her stomach, across her breasts. Instead of arousing her again, their touch soothed her, brought her back down from the heavens.

"You okay?" Eric asked gently.

Brenna nodded.

"You aren't ready to quit, are you?"

She gazed from one erection to the other. "It's obvious you two aren't."

"So that means we get to play a while longer." He picked up the bowl of mousse from the bed. "Your turn."

Oh, my. Where do I begin? She couldn't decide which man to start on first. The obvious solution was to take care of both at the same time.

"On your knees, guys."

Chapter Ten

Brenna sat on her heels and watched Eric and Keith scoot on their knees until they were a couple of feet apart. She shook her head. "Closer together, guys, and turn a little toward each other."

Once they'd moved the way she'd instructed, Brenna picked up the bowl of mousse. She set the bowl back on the bed between the two men as she thought about what she wanted to do. Scooping up a generous amount of mousse into her hands, she began to spread it over both their cocks and balls at the same time. A noticeable increase in their breathing urged Brenna to use even more of the creamy dessert on them. She dipped her fingers again and added additional mousse to their skin.

Chocolate-covered erections. Yum.

Brenna smiled to herself, then leaned forward and gave a single lick to Eric's head. He inhaled sharply. She ran her tongue down to the base on one side, gathering up mousse along the way. She made the return journey up the other side.

When she reached the head again, she withdrew her mouth from Eric and shifted to Keith.

Eric inhaled even deeper when her tongue touched Keith's cock. Brenna shifted a bit so she could see Eric's eyes as she took Keith's head past her lips. He was staring intently at her mouth. Deciding to give him a little show, she drew back so just the end of her tongue touched Keith's cock. She circled it slowly, then licked the slit. She repeated the action again and again, until Eric's chest rose and fell rapidly.

Brenna drew back and examined what she'd done. They definitely needed more chocolate. She spread additional mousse on their cocks and started all over again with Eric. She concentrated on his head, knowing that's where he was the most sensitive.

When he began to pump his hips, she released him. "Uh-uh. You have to stay still."

The expression in his eyes was a combination of lust and warning. "You're playing with fire, Brenna."

"I like playing with fire."

She turned back to Keith. She licked all the mousse from his head before slowly sliding her tongue down the underside to his balls. After giving them her thorough attention, she dragged her tongue back up his shaft.

"God, that's good," Keith moaned.

"It looks good, too," Eric rasped.

With her mouth still on Keith, Brenna looked at Eric. Despite a generous amount of mousse still on his cock, Eric wrapped his right hand around it and started stroking it. That's when Brenna knew she had him.

She did so love making him lose control.

"Do you like watching me lick on Keith?"

"Yeah." Eric's voice sounded deep and guttural. "Take him all the way down your throat this time."

Brenna engulfed Keith's cock to his balls. He groaned loudly, and so did Eric.

Out of the corner of her eye, Brenna saw Eric open the drawer in the nightstand. She knew that's where he kept the lubricant.

There was no doubt he'd reached his limit.

She returned to sucking on Keith, but listened for the subtle sounds of Eric's movements. The drawer shut. A flip top opened. Then silence.

Keith cradled her jaws and began pumping his hips. His breathing deepened. Assuming he was close to a climax, Brenna took him farther into her mouth.

Eric's slick fingers touched her anus.

"On your knees, babe."

Without taking her mouth off Keith, Brenna shifted until she was on her knees, her bottom in the air.

"You know what I want to do," he said as he pressed one finger inside her ass.

Brenna couldn't say anything since her mouth was occupied. To tell him she did know what he wanted and she agreed, she wiggled her hips.

Another finger joined the first. Brenna inhaled sharply. Oh, yes, it had definitely been too long since they'd had anal sex. Brenna cupped

Keith's balls and sucked harder on him as Eric pumped his fingers inside her ass. He withdrew, pushed, withdrew.

She expected him to remove his fingers and push his cock inside her. She was surprised to feel him slide into her pussy instead.

"Mmm, babe, you're nice and wet. This feels *really* good."

"So does this." Keith rotated his hips. "I'm close to coming, Brenna. Do you want to stop?"

She released him long enough to say, "No."

"Thank God."

Brenna took Keith back in her mouth and he began pumping again. Eric speeded up also, until his groin slapped her buttocks with every thrust. It felt so good, but Brenna needed more. Reaching between her legs, she rubbed her clit in time to Eric's movements.

Keith shuddered and moaned. His warm, salty semen filled her mouth. He tasted different than Eric…not unpleasant, but different. She swallowed greedily and rubbed her clit harder. So close. She was so close…

Eric gripped her hips and slammed his cock into her as he pushed his fingers hard up her ass. Brenna released Keith and cried out when another orgasm snaked through her body. Resting her forehead on the bed, she shivered through the contractions.

Eric tilted his head back and gulped in oxygen. He hadn't had such a powerful orgasm in… He couldn't remember when he'd had such a powerful orgasm. Something about playing with that gorgeous ass of Brenna's turned him into an animal.

Luckily, she seemed to like it as much as he.

He looked at Keith sprawled on his back on the bed. Keith's eyes were closed and he was breathing deeply. His entire body was covered with sweat. Eric sympathized. Exhaustion was going to overtake him at any moment.

At least temporarily.

Gently, he withdrew from Brenna's body. She collapsed on the bed. Eric lay beside her and drew her into his arms.

"You okay?" he asked, kissing her cheek.

Brenna nodded. "I think so." He saw her throat work as she swallowed. "Whew. That was wild."

"Did you like it?"

"How could I *not* like it? I had two gorgeous guys wanting nothing but to please me."

"Did I hear someone call me gorgeous?" Keith asked, his eyes still closed.

Brenna grinned and waved her hand. "You have a fan right here, Keith."

He opened his eyes and smiled devilishly. "I aim to please."

"You aimed *really* good." She looked at Eric. "You too."

Eric kissed her softly. "How about something to drink?"

"That sounds wonderful."

"I'll get it," Keith said. "That is, if my legs will work."

"There's tea in the refrigerator in that blue pitcher."

Keith nodded. It took him two tries to be able to stand, but he finally managed to wobble from the room.

Once he'd left, Eric drew Brenna tighter against him. Her body felt warm and damp, and limp as an overcooked noodle. "So, are you really all right?"

"I'm terrific." She ran her hands up his chest and over his shoulders. "What made you decide to do this, to…share me with Keith?"

"I wanted to drive you crazy with desire."

"It worked." She dropped a kiss in the center of his chest. "It's been incredible, but…"

Eric tilted up her chin. "But?"

"I just want *you*, Eric. You're everything I've ever wanted in a man, a lover. You satisfy me completely. I don't need anyone else."

Her words made him realize all over again why he'd fallen so deeply in love with her. How could he help loving a woman who cared so much for him? "I don't need anyone else either."

"That's good, because I'm not as generous as you. If you think I'm going to bring a girlfriend into our bed, you're very much mistaken."

Eric chuckled. "I can live with that." He kissed her softly. "But for tonight, we're going to play, all right?"

Brenna's eyebrows drew together. "For tonight? Aren't we done?"

He shook his head. "Not yet."

"Eric, I've had four orgasms. I can't do any more."

"Oh, I think you can."

"But you're..." She lowered her gaze and gestured at his flaccid penis.

"You know how fast I can get hard. And I doubt if Keith will have any problem either."

Keith came back into the room carrying three glasses of iced tea on a tray. He handed one to each of them and sat back on the bed with his own glass. "So, did you talk about me while I was gone?"

"In detail," Eric said.

"What did you decide?"

"That we'll drink our tea and rest a bit before we try some double penetration."

Brenna still looked confused. "We already did that."

"I'm not talking about using your mouth this time, Brenna."

Her eyes widened. "Surely you aren't talking about... Both of you? At the same time?"

Keith smiled wickedly. "I like the sound of that."

"Wait a minute! Don't I get a say in this?"

"Nope."

"Eric, that isn't even physically possible."

"We watch porn movies, Brenna. You know it's physically possible."

"She watches porn movies with you?" Keith asked Eric.

"Yeah."

Keith turned to Brenna. "Are you sure you don't have a sister?"

"I'm an only child." Brenna blew out a breath and pushed her hair back from her face. "Eric, I don't think that's a good idea. I mean, you guys are both pretty...well endowed. There can't be that much...room in there."

"Drink your tea and we'll find out."

"What if I don't want to do that?"

"If you hate it, we'll stop, but we're going to try it."

What a time for the macho to come out in him. "Eric—"

"Drink your tea, Brenna," he commanded softly.

Brenna obeyed that command and took a large sip of the peach-flavored tea. Both of them at the same time. *No way* could she do that.

Or could she?

Chapter Eleven

She looked at Eric's groin. Well, it was obvious *he* liked the idea. A glance at Keith's groin showed her he was quickly becoming aroused again. These two guys certainly recuperated fast.

Goody.

This is a night that will never be repeated. Go for it, Brenna. If you don't like it, Eric promised they'll stop.

She rose to her knees and moved closer to the man she loved. She ran her hands through his hair, then kissed him. "So let's find out."

A moment later, she found herself sandwiched between two hard, male bodies. All of them were on their knees. Eric kissed her deeply while fondling her breasts. Keith licked and bit her neck and shoulders while pumping his fingers into her pussy and his thumb into her ass. The smell of sex overwhelmed the scent of chocolate, making Brenna's head swim and her blood race.

She couldn't believe another orgasm built so quickly. It was *there*, ready to break with just a little more stimulation.

"Pinch my nipples," she whispered to Eric.

He rolled them between his thumbs and forefingers. Brenna bit her lower lip and arched her back, trying to get Keith's fingers deeper inside her. She gasped when his thumb wiggled inside her.

"Yes, like that, Keith. More. Harder, Eric. Pinch my nipples *harder.*"

As if they had some preconceived signal, they both released her at the same time. Brenna crashed back to earth, her orgasm fading like a puff of smoke. Tears of frustration flooded her eyes. "Why did you stop?"

"Because I want you to come with me inside your ass," Eric said fiercely.

"Eric—"

He cut off her protest with a hard kiss. "Patience, my love. Keith, lie down."

Taking Brenna's hand, Keith drew her on top of him as he lay on his back. His erection pressed into her stomach. Needing to get back to that level of sensation where she'd been only moments ago, Brenna wrapped her hand around his cock and impaled herself. She groaned, and so did Keith.

"Yesssss." Closing her eyes, Brenna braced her hands on his chest and began moving up and down. Keith lay still at first, his hands gripping her hips. Then he began to meet her thrusts. Oh, yes. That delicious friction, the slide of hot, hard flesh into her wet sheath. Nothing felt better than this.

"God, that looks good," Eric growled. "Move faster, babe."

Brenna picked up the pace. Keith joined her, rotating his hips as he pumped into her.

She stopped when Eric slid one hand over her buttocks.

"Don't stop, Brenna. I want to watch you fuck him."

She looked at Eric over her shoulder. He stroked his cock as he stared at the spot where she and Keith were joined.

When he raised his gaze to her face, Brenna gasped. She'd never seen such a wild gleam in his eyes.

"Bend over, Brenna," he ordered.

Brenna swallowed. She liked anal sex with Eric, but double penetration was something she'd never experienced. She couldn't help feeling a bit apprehensive, even while the idea excited her. Taking a breath, she released it slowly before reclining on Keith's body.

Keith gripped her legs behind her knees and tugged them farther forward. "Relax, Brenna. You know Eric would never hurt you."

"Yes, I know that," she whispered.

Wrapping his arms around her, Keith pulled her closer to his chest. The position left her completely open for her lover.

The touch of Eric's cool, slick fingers on her anus made Brenna swallow again. One finger entered her, then another. Keith shifted, driving his cock into her pussy again. He pulled halfway out, and Eric pressed his fingers forward. They repeated the action over and over. Brenna's breathing quickened as desire flared up inside her again.

Eric removed his fingers. A moment passed while Keith slowly thrust into her, then Brenna felt the head of Eric's cock against her. She tensed at first, as she always did. She took a deep breath and released it to help her relax.

"That's the way," Keith whispered into her ear. "Think about how good you're gonna feel."

Eric pressed harder, and his head slipped past her anus. Keith stilled. Again Eric pressed, withdrew, pressed farther. The fourth time he pushed forward, she could feel his groin against her buttocks. He was completely inside her.

Brenna moaned.

"My God, babe, that feels good." He pumped slowly several times. "I've been wanting to fuck this beautiful ass for weeks."

Keith gripped her waist. "I'm gonna move, Brenna. Okay?"

Unable to speak with her heart pounding so hard, she nodded.

Keith lifted his hips as Eric drew back. They repeated their actions of a few moments ago—one of them pulling back as the other one pushed inside her. Brenna buried her face in Keith's neck, not sure if she could stand so much sensation at once.

They picked up speed, the depth and intensity of their thrusts increasing. Brenna could do nothing but lie on top of Keith and accept whatever they did.

She never would have believed double penetration could feel so good.

Clutching Keith's upper arms, Brenna spread her legs as far as she could. Keith growled loudly. His grip on her waist tightened. Sweat poured off his face and upper body. The intense heat in his eyes signaled his rapidly approaching climax.

He growled once more and shuddered beneath her. Brenna could feel the pulsations of his release deep inside her. Her own climax began to build again.

It crested when Eric jammed his cock into her ass, all the way to his balls.

Brenna screamed.

She never screamed. She'd never passed out from having an orgasm, either, but Brenna would swear she blacked out for a moment. When she could concentrate again, she realized she was incredibly sore.

And very well satisfied.

She groaned as Eric pulled out of her. With his help, she rose from Keith's body and collapsed on her stomach. Her hair hung over her face, obscuring her vision. She sincerely hoped nothing drastic happened the rest of the night, for she wouldn't be able to move to save herself.

"Wow," Keith muttered, his voice sounding breathless.

"I second that," Eric said.

Brenna said nothing. She couldn't get her tongue to work.

Eric slid his hand slowly over her back. "You okay, sweetheart?"

She managed to nod, but that was the best she could do.

Eric had the nerve to chuckle. "It's usually me who's wiped out after sex, not you."

Using every ounce of strength she could muster, Brenna pushed her hair back from her face and glared at Eric. "Don't gloat."

He grinned.

"Well, I am definitely wiped out," Keith said as he propped himself up on one elbow. "And I desperately need a shower."

"Me too," Brenna said, "but I can't get to the bathroom. I'll just have to stay sweaty until tomorrow morning."

"I'll let you and Eric work that out." Keith leaned over and dropped a soft kiss on Brenna's cheek. "That was incredible. Thank you."

Brenna smiled. "Thank *you*."

After Keith left the room, closing the door behind him, Brenna rolled to her back. Eric lay resting on the pile of pillows. His hair was mussed, his body moist with sweat. His eyes were at half-mast, as if holding them open required a great effort.

He was so gorgeous.

"Any objections to me waiting until tomorrow morning to shower?" Brenna asked.

"If you think I'm able to make these legs work to stand in the shower, you're very much mistaken."

"So we'll shower together in the morning."

"Deal." He levered himself off the pillows. "Let's pull up the covers and get some sleep."

It took only a few moments for them to turn off the lights and snuggle together under the covers. Brenna lay in the circle of Eric's arms, her head resting on his shoulder. Despite the soreness between her legs, she felt utterly content.

"Tomorrow morning," Eric said, gently stroking her hair, "I'll show you my surprise."

Brenna tilted her head so she could see his face. "That's right, I never got my surprise. What is it?"

"You'll find out tomorrow."

"Don't I even get a hint?"

"Nope. Not even a hint."

She slid her hand down his body and wrapped it around his soft cock. Eric burst out laughing.

"That won't work, sweetheart. My poor little friend is completely used up."

Brenna giggled. "It was worth a try."

Eric kissed her. "Tomorrow. I promise you'll like it."

Chapter Twelve

"Can I open my eyes yet?" Brenna asked for the fifth time since they'd started this drive.

"Not yet," Eric said for the fifth time since they'd started this drive. "Have a little patience, sweetheart."

Patience wasn't Brenna's strongest point, not when it came to surprises. She'd always shaken the packages under the Christmas tree, trying to figure out what they held. Folding her arms over her stomach, she slumped in the seat.

Keith chuckled from the backseat. "Shut up, Keith," she growled.

"Hey, I didn't say a word."

"I heard that chuckle. You're enjoying this, aren't you?"

"Immensely."

Once again, Brenna understood why Eric and Keith were such good friends. They could be brothers, they were so much alike. Teasing must be at the top of the list of what they enjoyed.

"As long as I have to keep my eyes closed, I might as well take a nap."

"If you think you can, go ahead."

"Eric McFarland, you know very well I can't take a nap now!"

His chuckle made her want to punch him.

"I don't understand how you can be so mean to me when I was so good to you last night."

"*You're* the one who had five orgasms."

"You had three!"

"Yeah, I did." He slid his hand over her upper thigh. "That last one was wild."

"I'm game for a repeat," Keith said. "Maybe we could trade places next time, Eric."

A delicious shiver ran through her body at the thought, but she refused to show any excitement to Eric. Besides, what happened last night was a one-time thing. She released an aggravated huff. "There you two go again, making plans without asking me what *I* want."

Eric slipped his hand between her legs and cupped her mound. "I didn't hear any complaints last night."

"If you'll recall, my mouth was occupied a lot of the time last night, so I *couldn't* talk."

"Oh, man," Keith groaned, "I'm getting a hard-on."

"Yeah, and Brenna's getting wet," Eric said, sliding his fingers farther between her legs.

"Hey, Brenna, wanna fool around in the backseat?"

"Not while I'm driving down I-5, Keith," Eric said.

"You're a party pooper, my friend."

Brenna chuckled at their banter. Only really good friends could joke about what the three of them had experienced. It had been wild and wonderful, and she'd enjoyed it thoroughly. But it wouldn't happen again, despite Keith's teasing offer that she join him in the backseat. One *ménage a trois* in her lifetime was enough. She only wanted Eric.

From the motion of the car, Brenna could tell they'd turned. Eric slowed, then stopped. "We're here. Open your eyes, sweetheart."

Brenna did. She looked out the windshield at the beautiful Tudor house she'd fallen in love with a year ago. Not understanding why they were sitting in the driveway of someone else's house, Brenna looked at Eric. He was smiling.

"What's going on?"

"That's your wedding present," he said softly.

It took several moments for his words to sink in. He couldn't possibly mean… "Wedding present?" she whispered.

Eric nodded. "It came on the market Friday. I've already made an offer to the owners and they accepted it. All that's left is the paperwork."

Brenna remained still, not quite believing the words coming out of Eric's mouth. This beautiful house, the one she'd dreamed about despite loving the small one she'd finally bought, was about to be theirs? "Eric, are you teasing me? This is really mean if you're teasing me."

He shook his head. "I wouldn't tease about something I know is so important to you."

"We can go inside?"

"The owners went to visit some friends in Eastern Washington. Penny's inside, ready to give us a tour."

Tears welled up in her eyes. She didn't know what she'd ever done to deserve a man who loved her so much. "I don't believe you did this."

"Believe it." He took one of her hands, raised it to his mouth, and kissed her palm. "Let's go look at our house."

Her mind still a jumble, Brenna let Eric help her from his car and lead her toward the front door. Keith walked next to her, his hands loose at his sides.

"How much land comes with the house, Eric?" he asked.

"Three acres."

"Great view of the water."

"The view from the backyard is even better. We'll be able to see Mount Rainier on a clear day."

They walked through the front entrance. The foyer was cool, but well lit with natural light from the window above the front door. Brenna looked around with wide eyes. She couldn't believe this gorgeous house would belong to her and Eric in a short while. A wide, curving staircase directly in front of them led upstairs. To the left, she could see the large living room, complete with a rock fireplace that took up a huge portion of one wall. Two steps led down to the den on the right.

She wanted to see every inch of it.

"I thought I heard someone drive up."

Eric turned at the sound of Penny's voice. She came through the kitchen door at the end of the hall, a smile on her face. "Hey, Pen. Ready to give us a tour?"

"You bet." She smiled at Brenna. "Surprised?"

"Shocked is a better word."

"It's a beautiful house, and in perfect condition."

Eric chuckled. "You don't have to give us the sales pitch, Penny. It's a done deal."

Keith cleared his throat. Loudly. "Aren't you going to introduce us, Eric?"

Eric watched Penny's gaze shift to Keith. Her eyes widened in what he'd call appreciation...or downright lust. He understood that. Keith wasn't his type, but Eric knew Keith was a handsome guy.

Turning his attention to Keith, he saw the same look of appreciation and lust in his friend's eyes. Eric understood that, too. While he and Penny were only very good friends, he recognized her beauty. She wore a blue sweater and matching slacks that showed off her voluptuous figure. With her natural long blonde hair, large breasts, full hips, and killer legs, she drew the attention of many men.

"Keith, this is Penny Sorenson, my best agent. Penny, Keith Dillard, my best bud from college."

Penny stepped forward and offered her hand. "It's a pleasure, Keith."

Keith took her hand. "For me, too." Instead of shaking it, he lifted it to his mouth and kissed the back.

Eric could see Penny's eyes go all unfocused. Fighting a grin, he looked at Brenna. She was biting her lower lip and her eyes sparkled with laughter.

"I'm gonna show Brenna the kitchen," Eric said, although he doubted if Penny or Keith heard him. "You two get acquainted."

Neither of them said anything; they just stared at each other. Eric took Brenna's hand and led her into the kitchen. Once inside the room, they both started laughing.

"Did you see the way he looked at her?" Brenna asked.

"Yeah, the same way she looked at him. I wouldn't have been surprised if they'd started tearing each other's clothes off right there in the foyer."

"There were definitely sparks in the air."

Keith stuck his head around the swinging door. "Hey, Eric, Penny invited me out for coffee. She said the keys are on the cabinet by the stove, and lock up when you leave."

"Sure, no problem. We'll wait for you."

"Uh, you don't have to do that. Penny will give me a ride back to your place. Later." He grinned. "Maybe *much* later."

"Do you mean you've already recuperated from last night?" Brenna asked.

"I'm a fast healer."

"Be careful with her, man," Eric said. "She's a special lady."

"I knew that the moment I saw her." He waved. "Bye."

Once he'd left, Eric turned his attention back to Brenna. She stood in the middle of the kitchen, looking around the spacious room with such happiness on her face, it almost took his breath. "You like it?"

"I *love* it. Oh, Eric, it's perfect. Are these cabinets ash?"

"I think that's what Penny said. We could've gotten all the information from her if she hadn't run off with Keith."

"We'll get all the information later. Right now, I just want to absorb everything. Is the rest of the house as wonderful as the kitchen?"

He nodded. "Wait until you see the master bedroom. It has an incredible view of the mountain and inlet."

That sultry, sexy look he loved filled her eyes. "Master bedroom, hmm? Are you referring to an…initiation?"

He wasn't, but now that she mentioned it… "Aren't you still sore?"

"Like Keith, I'm a fast healer."

"It'd be rude to make out in the bedroom until the house is ours."

She sauntered toward him. "We wouldn't use their bed. That *would* be rude."

"So you're suggesting, maybe the carpet?"

"Or the wall."

Eric grinned. "I do love the way you think."

Brenna returned his grin. "I'll race you up the stairs."

The End

About the author:

Lynn LaFleur was born and raised in a small town in Texas close to the Dallas/Fort Worth area. Writing has been in her blood since she was eight years old and wrote her first "story" for an English assignment.

Besides writing at every possible moment, Lynn loves reading, sewing, gardening, and learning new things on the computer. (She is determined to master Paint Shop Pro and Photoshop!) After living in various places on the West Coast for 21 years, she is back in Texas, 17 miles from her hometown.

Lynn would love to hear from her readers about her writing, her books, the look of her website...whatever! Comments, praise, and criticism all equally welcome.

Lynn welcomes mail from readers. You can write to her c/o Ellora's Cave Publishing at 1056 Home Ave. Akron, Oh 44310-3502.

Also by Lynn LaFleur:

Ellora's Cavemen: Legendary Tails I (Anthology)
Enchanted Rogues (Anthology)
Happy Birthday, Baby
Holiday Heat (Anthology)

Saving Sarah

Michele R. Bardsley

Chapter One

"Raped?" Therapist Annie Miller stared at the man on the other side of her desk. "How long ago?"

"Almost a year." He ran restless fingers through his shaggy blond hair. He looked exhausted, but more than that, he looked like he was skirting the edge of hopelessness.

Oh no. She would have none of that.

"Two weeks after our anniversary, in April last year. I had to attend one of those inane business cocktail parties and she didn't want to go. I always check the locks, the windows, but I was late, in a hurry. And she never remembers to do that stuff. We lived in a safe neighborhood." He rubbed his face with both hands as if doing so would scrub away his self-recrimination.

"Have you and she had sexual intercourse?"

"No. Sometimes I do oral for her, but I've never asked or expected her to reciprocate. I won't lie, Ms. Miller. I miss making love to my wife. She used to be fearless, you know?" He shook his head. "I love Sarah more than my next breath, but she's slipping away from me."

Annie picked up the folder on her desk and opened it. "I'm not sure what I can do for you, Ben. Sarah should be the one sitting in that chair."

"She's been to doctors, therapists, psychologists, and shit...even a voodoo priestess. She knows something is wrong and she's tried to fix it, but she can't. She's been lost to me ever since those bastards—" His fists clenched. He took a deep breath and settled into the leather wingback. "The rapists were caught and they were put into prison for life. She had a scare earlier this year when one of them escaped. He was shot and killed by police—on Valentine's Day. Can you believe it? That asshole died on a day that celebrates romance and love. Ironic as hell."

"Indeed." Annie looked at the desk, assessing its neatness, trying not to focus on the personal tragedy that had unfolded for her on that day as well.

"They can't ever hurt her again, but every time I touch her...she sees them." Despair rimmed his gaze. "In her heart, she knows it's me, but in her head—it's like her mind keeps playing the same movie over and over again. They didn't just violate her body. They murdered her soul."

"I've heard enough, dear boy." She stood and tossed the folder to the desk. "There is a place that might help your wife recover, but you have to agree to the terms. It's an unusual therapy."

His wary gaze assessed the business card she handed to him. "Dunley's Beach Resort?" He frowned. "This is a clinic?"

"No. It's a beach resort."

Annie rounded the desk and stood in front of Ben Slatterly, leaning a hip against her desk. "You must send Sarah to the resort alone for five days. After two days have passed, you will join her. When you arrive, you will be asked to participate in her...sessions. Do this without doubt or hesitation or judgment."

"What the hell are we talking about?"

"Healing, Ben. And one last chance to save your wife."

* * * * *

After Ben left the office, Annie pressed a button under her desk and watched the far wall slide open. She crossed the room briskly, intently, and the moment she cleared the entryway, the door swished shut behind her. The room was small, lit only by special-made candles of sage, rosemary, cinnamon and other herbs and spices. On one wall was her altar to the Goddess. It was made from driftwood, carved with intricate signs and pictographs; it had been passed down from mother to daughter since the 1700s, when her family once lived in a town named Salem and her ancestor had swung from the gallows, branded a servant of Satan.

The people of Salem had not been the first to condemn and kill one of her family members for witchcraft. There had been others, including the greedy priests of the Inquisition in the 1400s. Annie had always been amazed at the fortitude and determination of her ancestors to pass the knowledge and wisdom of ancient times down through the ages. In each generation, her family's magic matured and strengthened and, with Annie, the gifts bestowed were great, indeed. The Goddess had blessed her beyond measure...and given her a solitary, sometimes too heavy, burden.

She turned to the wall opposite the altar. From ceiling to floor, every inch of space was covered by a wooden shelving system that looked much like post office mailboxes. Each space was one foot by one foot, doorless, labeled by last name, and all held boxes made of rosewood.

The one she wanted was easy to find, and she plucked it from its slot and opened the lid. Inside was a vial of ashes, a rolled vellum paper, and a gold locket.

"Dunley."

He appeared in the blink of an eye, floating a few inches above the floor, his form as see-through as a dusty window. He was tall and handsome with longish brown hair and soulful brown eyes. Annie smiled. Dunley was not as tender as his gaze and lazy stance indicated.

"How are you, Dunley?"

"Limbo is lovely this time of year."

She laughed. "It is time to earn your freedom."

He straightened, a bright hope flaring in his eyes. "You will give the locket to my mother? And release my ashes?"

"Yes. If you succeed with the task I give you."

"Have I failed you yet?"

"Only once."

"Annie—"

She shook her head, refusing the memories that threatened. "You were sent here, to me, for redemption. You were given the choice—"

"Hell or slave to your whims?"

"There is no such thing as hell."

"But there is Limbo, isn't there? And it is worse than fire and brimstone." He shook his head, sighed. "I never meant to hurt your daughter, Annie."

"She chose her own path. I do not blame you for her attempted suicide. She is not why you are here."

"I know." He looked uncertain then shrugged, as if he had nothing to lose by speaking his thoughts. "How is Titania?"

"She has not yet recovered."

"How much time has passed?"

"Almost two months." Annie swallowed the knot of grief threatening to choke her. She tried not to remember Dunley's callousness toward her daughter, the way he'd scorned the college student's affections. When Dunley's soul was given to her, he confessed that he'd been drinking heavily and rammed his car into a tree at ninety miles an hour. Both he and his passenger were killed instantly.

The day Dunley died — Titania slit her wrists.

Annie believed that it wasn't so much Dunley's sudden death, but the fact that his passenger and new lover had been Titania's best friend, Miranda. The deaths of two people she loved, and their double betrayal, was more than Ti's sensitive soul could bear.

Because Dunley had earned his redemption by helping others these past two months, he had also earned Annie's forgiveness. She had refused to tell him anything about Ti...until now. "She is well cared for at the institute. She will eat, she will sit in the sunshine, and she will allow me to hug her goodbye. But she doesn't speak — she doesn't look at me. She is empty inside. My daughter is the one who truly knows the bounds of hell."

An uncomfortable silence fell between them. When Dunley looked as if he might apologize — as he had done since the day his soul was sent to her — Annie turned to the altar and started preparations for Dunley's temporary transformation.

With her magic, he'd be able to solidify, or turn invisible but only for three days. If he did his task well, Sarah Slatterly would find healing and hope. Then Annie would release her daughter's former lover into the Light and maybe, just maybe, Titania would begin her own journey back to the living.

"You have three days, Dunley. Help Ben Slatterly save his wife...and you'll save yourself as well."

Chapter Two

Sarah Slatterly trudged up the beach to the weather-beaten steps of the Victorian three-story house. A crooked sign above the door proclaimed "Dunley's Beach Resort". She dropped her suitcases; they thunked to the porch. Turning, she watched the dinghy row out to the yacht that had transported her to the tiny island off the California coast.

Ben had given her this retreat for their tenth anniversary. When she thought about the way they had celebrated their last nine anniversaries...a smile ghosted her lips. She loved him so much, but no matter how many times she tried to recapture their lovemaking, she panicked. The idea of sucking his cock or of letting it ram into her...no!

Calm down.

Breathe in.

Breathe out.

Sarah sucked in a few more relaxing breaths, then picked up her suitcases and entered the house turned beach resort. To her right was a staircase, in front of her a long hallway, and to the left a small check-in counter. Her gaze continued left and spotted a nook with three floor-to-ceiling windows. She noted the two pear-green loveseats facing each other and the oblong cherrywood table between them. That seating area offered the only furniture — or any other objects — in the lobby. It was sparse, clean, and smelled strongly of lemon with teasing hints of cinnamon. She loved the simplicity of it all.

A big black woman behind the check-in counter waited for her. Her bright white smile was cheerful and reached the twinkling brown of her eyes. Her corn-rowed hair framed an apple-cheeked face with a brownie-dark complexion. A beautiful pink dress artfully draped her girth. She moved with an ease and grace that spoke of a woman comfortable with her size and with herself.

"Welcome, Sarah," she said, her voice tinged with an accent Sarah could only guess at. Jamaican, maybe? "We've been waiting for you."

Instantly comfortable, Sarah approached the counter and once again dropped her suitcases. "It's so quiet here. And beautiful."

"Just what a soul needs, isn't it?" The woman held out an oversized gold key. "My name is Rowena. Please call me if you need anything."

"Thank you, Rowena." Sarah took the key, and laughed. "I don't suppose there really is a Dunley, is there?"

"Oh yes. He's hangin' around somewhere. You'll meet him soon enough."

Sarah felt a strange excitement whisper through her, but she pushed it away. She didn't care to meet Dunley or any other man for that matter. The only one she trusted was Ben and even he paid the price for the terror that lived inside her.

"Leave your bags, miss. Our bellboy will take them up." Rowena made shooing motions. "You go on to your room and enjoy the refreshments and the view. Take a nap."

Sarah smiled, grasping the cold metal in her fist. Sleep was not her friend, and hadn't been for the last year, but she would try. For Ben, and to honor his gift to her, she would try.

Room 30 was on the third floor. Actually, Room 30 *was* the third floor. Sarah closed the door behind her and wandered around the simple but beautiful suite. The floor was the same weather-beaten blue-tinted wood that made up the inside and outside of the house.

To the left, there was a teeny kitchenette with a mini-fridge, microwave, and coffeepot. Next to the single counter was the dining area. The small round table and two chairs made from the familiar blue wood sat on top of a yellow rag carpet. On the table, cheese, crackers and fruit were arranged on a plain white plate. A bottle of merlot chilled in a bucket, or she could choose the tea service that included packets of her favorite flavored tea. On the other side of the kitchen was the bathroom. She glanced inside and was delighted to discover a stand-up glass shower and a huge tub with jets. A long marble counter held the sink and a basketful of complimentary lotions, shampoos, conditioners and more. She'd have to go through that later. The decoration reflected the blues and yellows of the main room.

She turned and wandered to the right, pausing to take it all in. The large sitting area had a couch, two wingbacks — pear-green in color — and the same kind of oblong table she'd noticed in the lobby. Two yellow throws draped the couch, which faced two huge French doors that opened onto a deck. She crossed to the windows, peered outside, and smiled. The deck overlooked the quiet, surging ocean. In its rectangular space she saw only a comfy chaise lounge and a single table perfect for one glass of wine and one paperback.

Sighing in contentment, she moved from the windows and looked at the one section of the room she'd saved for last. The distressed yellow dresser sat in its own nook. On the far wall, huge bookshelves stuffed with books marched nearly the entire length. Her gaze bounced to the nightstand that matched the color and design of the dresser. On it sat a slender lamp shaped like an opening flower.

Finally Sarah allowed her gaze to rest on the four-poster bed. It was made from deep, rich wood, the same color and texture as the coffee table. Curtains of gauzy white drifted from the ceiling and surrounded the bed—a blushing bride hiding behind her veil. The material offered thin protection from prying eyes. Sarah inhaled a deep breath and dipped inside, and found herself in a plush heaven of thick comforters, endless pillows, and the promise of sleep most divine.

After the rape, she and Ben had moved from their house—from the house they had spent years scraping and saving for—and into the guesthouse owned by Ben's boss. She was protected there. The house was far enough away from the mansion to offer privacy, but close enough to be included in the bi-hourly patrols by Security and their mean-ass dogs. The tiny house had a state-of-the-art alarm system and three guns stored in easy-to-get locations. She knew how to fire a gun now. Guns used to scare her. Their ugliness, their weight, their noise…she used to hate everything about them, but no longer.

She couldn't sleep in their new bed, either, and spent restless nights on the couch. Ben slept in a sleeping bag on the floor rather than seek the comfort of bed without her. He had sold the other bed—the one where…*no, best not to think about it.* He had sold all of their furniture. He had tried, in every way possible, to disconnect her from old memories so that she could rebuild her life.

"Quit my job, cut my hair, learned self-defense." Nothing fixed the hole inside her. She was empty, a shell of her former self, and helpless to do anything about it.

Sarah crawled into the huge bed, settled against the pillows, and waited for the usual terror to snake through her. Oh God, to sleep in a bed again. *To make love to Ben again.*

Fifteen minutes passed, then half an hour. She realized she felt more at peace in this bed, at this resort, on this island than she'd felt at any time in the past year. Giddy with the prospect of sleeping in a real bed, she scooted off, got rid of all her clothes, cracked open the French doors, and jumped on the soft bedding, rolling on it and, God help her, giggling.

Soon, Sarah lay on her bed naked, and luxuriated in the warm breeze blowing in through the open windows. The gentle wind felt like fingers caressing her skin. She stretched, lifted her breasts as if to an invisible lover and sighed when her nipples puckered, aching to be touched, to be kissed.

Safe.

Her eyes drifted shut.

Hands on her breasts, cupping and molding. Lips on her throat, trailing to the dimple at its base, a soft kiss to mark the place. Tongue trailing a hot, wet line down to the juncture of her thighs.

Safe.

The tender weight of man on top of her, lifting her arms over her head, while another grabbed her wrists and pulled her long hair. The one between her legs grabbing and pushing, ugly laughter echoing as he forced open her legs and ripped off her panties. The hair-pulling jerk leaning down to bite her breast...no! No! No!

SAFE!

The terrifying images disappeared.

Sarah floated...rising and moving as if carried by an ocean swell...in this dream, she lay upon yards and yards of white material, warm and cozy, in a place lit by candles. The coverlet she lay upon was softer than a cloud. "Safe," she murmured.

Her body felt flushed and needy. She stretched, the material beneath her nude body stroking her sensitized flesh like tiny fingers. *Oh yes.* It had been too long since she'd felt the hot, insistent need for touch, for sex. Heat filled her and her pussy grew wet as aching need crept through her.

She rolled onto her stomach and rubbed her puckered nipples against the wonderful cloth. Tiny lightning strikes zapped her all the way to her cunt. It pulsed, greedy for its pleasure, and grew wetter still. Her legs spread and her hips pumped, but swiping her clit against the comforter wasn't doing much.

"Ben..."

Sarah wanted satisfaction, but feared turning her fantasy into one that included a man. To her sorrow, not even imagining having sex with Ben helped her find satisfaction. The few times she'd allowed him oral sex, she had orgasmed, but somehow it lacked the joy she used to feel when she made love to her husband.

She turned onto her back, tears in her eyes, and clenched her fists.

"Sarah." A man with long brown hair, brown eyes, and a long, rangy, very naked body appeared next to her.

Her breath stalled. Her heart flipped. Her horrified gaze was drawn down, down, down, until she saw his...smiley face boxers.

She couldn't help but grin at the ridiculous underwear. The fear pounding through her faded, just a little.

"My name is Dunley."

"*You* own this place?"

"In a manner of speaking." His smile was tender. "No fear, Sarah. You are safe."

"Am I... I thought I was...dreaming. Or-or fantasizing."

"You are."

Her fear dissolved completely and a strange sense of contentment surrounded her. She felt...wonderfully...drugged.

"May I kiss you?"

Memories flickered, stealing through her lethargy. "Ben."

"Ben loves you. He wants you like I want you." Dunley stretched beside her so close she felt the heat of his body, but he didn't touch her. "One kiss, sweet Sarah." He bent to her ear and whispered, "This is a fantasy. Your fantasy. You can have anyone you want and do anything you want."

The idea fluttered in her mind then took root. *A dream*. In a dream, nothing was forbidden and nothing was real.

"One kiss," she offered.

His lips were warm and tasted like cinnamon sugar. His fingers hovered above her hip, not touching, but waiting, wanting. His tongue parted her lips and dipped inside. Heat exploded inside her stomach, spiraling down to her pussy. Her heart stalled then tha-thumped in a staccato rhythm that stole her breath.

"Please..."

Dunley withdrew and looked at her, his left eyebrow quirked. "Please what?"

"I-I don't know." Her gaze traveled down his firm body to the boxers and she knew, without a doubt, a delicious cock waited inside those silly shorts. She could see the way the material tented. His penis was hard and ready and she wondered how it would feel plunging into her wet heat.

Would it hurt? Would it tear her apart like the last penis had ripped at her? Bruising her tissues, making her bleed, oh but that was nothing, *nothing* compared to the battering of her anus when punishing her vagina hadn't been enough for the sick bastard.

Tears filled her eyes and her throat stung. She swallowed the unrelenting knot of sorrow as self-anger vibrated through her. She couldn't release herself from the past and move into the future with a light heart and a new hope. *Why? Goddamn it, why?*

"Sarah."

Her gaze sought Dunley's and in those chocolate depths, she saw desire, tenderness, and an offer of pleasure without pain.

"It's just a dream. Just a lovely dream that will bring you joy." Dunley dared to sweep two fingers across her cheek and down her neck. Two fingers became one as he stroked around her areola, circling and circling until the tip of his finger brushed her nipple.

"I want to taste you," he whispered. "Is that okay? One small taste."

Her nipple was a hard, aching point. She looked down at his circling finger and drew in a sharp breath. *Ben.* She hadn't let him touch her the way this dream man touched her. He deserved to be in her bed, the recipient of her desire, her love.

"Don't worry, Sarah. Ben will be yours again. And you will be his." Dunley lowered his head to her chest until his mouth was a kiss away from her nipple. He blew on it, and the swoosh of air tightened the peak even more.

"Taste it," she offered in a trembling voice.

His lips closed over the nipple. He suckled, his warm, wet tongue swirling against the sensitive flesh. A low moan rose from her throat as hot desire jabbed at her. Her hands wound into his soft hair and she pressed him closer, encouraging his gentle assault. "More," she said hoarsely. "Other one. Now."

Dunley obliged. He cupped her other breast and used his tongue to worship it. God, it felt good to have someone play with her breasts, suck and cajole her nipples into response. Her cunt felt slick and ready, its occasional pulse an invitation.

He lifted his head and looked at her. "You taste as sweet and fresh as a peach." His gaze flicked at the valley between her breasts and traveled to her navel before he again looked up at her. "I want to taste more of you. Please, Sarah."

Her heart thundered, a mixture of fear and sexual frenzy zipping down her spine. She wanted to feel his lips on her skin, the flick of his tongue on the pearls of sweat formed by her longing. All she could do was nod.

His lips pressed against her quivering stomach muscles and his tongue stroked a long, slow line to her navel. He encircled it then flicked inside it, making her giggle nervously. Ashamed at her schoolgirl reaction, she fisted her hands, but failed to stop squirming as the blissful sensations poured over her.

Sarah felt submerged in desire, hot and needy, and she wanted…she wanted to feel his penis slide into her, to show her how to like it again, how to come again with a dick pumping into her. *No more pain. No more fear. Just ecstasy…*

Her pussy convulsed, trembled. *Oh yes.* She wanted it again. Desired the pounding of flesh on flesh, to feel her slick, willing cunt joyfully penetrated by a thick cock, oh heavens…the smell and taste and feel of a man giving and taking pleasure. For the first time since—since *forever*, the idea of getting fucked didn't equate to rape.

It meant only rapture.

Dunley's hands coasted to her hips, his mouth following an invisible trail to the edge of her pussy. *Oh God.* He was so close to her clit. Just a few strokes of his tongue…maybe a slow suckling there, a nip of his teeth…

But he paused, and after a moment, she looked down to see why he waited.

"I'm not going to lie to you, Sarah. I want to be inside you. I want to feel you around me, taking me, moving with me. I want to give you pleasure." His gaze flickered with yearning. "Do you want my mouth? Or do you want my cock?"

Chapter Three

Your cock trembled on her lips, but Sarah felt frozen. If anyone's cock deserved pleasure from fucking her, it was Ben's. Dear, sweet, loving, patient Ben. Dream or fantasy, it didn't feel right to allow Dunley privileges denied to her husband.

"You shouldn't feel guilty, Sarah. I'm here to help you and to help him. Let me."

"How is...how does having sex with you, help me or Ben?"

"I'll show you." He rolled onto his back and wiggled off the boxers. His cock was just as beautiful as she had assumed. Circumcised, long, thick at the head, purple veins evidence of its straining hardness. She allowed herself the idea of feeling it slide inside her. Her breath hitched.

"This is a dream, remember?"

"It doesn't feel like one."

Another wave of strange contentment enveloped her. She relaxed, her eyes drooping, her body stretching as lust reasserted its hold on her.

"Get on top of me," said Dunley. "Take as much of my dick inside you as you want. Ride it the way you want. You're in control, Sarah."

Control. Power. Violence.

Wasn't that what every counselor she'd ever spoken to said time and again? *Rape isn't about sex, Sarah. It's about control and power over another person. It's an act of violence, as vicious and horrible as murder.* That's exactly how she felt, too, as if she'd been murdered, but her soulless body still walked around, unaware it was dead.

"Sarah?"

The drugged, happy feeling faded as familiar terror clawed at her. Her body shook with cold fear as she crawled on top of Dunley, her knees planted on either side of his thighs. She settled onto him, a few inches below his ball sac, and swallowed the knot of dread threatening to choke her.

"Why don't we pretend to have sex?" His voice was light, his body relaxed under her tense one, and his gaze filled with a tender desire that bespoke patience.

"What do you mean?"

"Stay where you are. Right there. And move like my cock is inside you, pleasuring you."

Unsure about this tactic, but relieved — and yes, disappointed — that she wasn't going to have his cock yet, she rose on her knees and hesitantly moved back and forth, as if she were riding him.

"I feel silly." Her gaze found his, and she smiled.

"Close your eyes. Pretend your hands are my hands. Pretend my cock is inside you and that your juicy cunt is plunging up and down on it."

She watched him wrap his hand around his shaft and stroke it. Seeing his strong hand pumping his hard cock made her pulse jump. It was sexy and beautiful to see him pleasure himself while watching her *pretend*. She licked her lips and allowed her eyes to drift closed. Slowly she moved her hips as her hands crept from her hips to her breasts.

He cups them, his fingers massaging the nipples, gently twisting…

Sarah increased her pace as she played with her tits, moaning as pleasure tumbled through her, spikes of joy radiating to her wet pussy.

His cock slides inside her. It doesn't hurt. It fills her slowly, it feels really good…

Her hips pumped hard now, memories of how she rode Ben this way, of how he grabbed her buttocks and thrust inside her, offering such wonderful, wonderful bliss. He loved to suck her nipples, too. Would watch her eyes go blind as she orgasmed, her pulsations so strong his penis would slip out. She'd rub her come on his thick shaft, her sensitive clit reaching for another orgasm…

One hand played with her nipples, trading off the pleasuring of each, while her other hand slid down to her primed pussy and rubbed the needy clit.

She fucks his cock, her movements frantic, the bliss rising…

She slipped one finger into her slick pussy, then two, and finger-fucked her own cunt while her palm massaged her clitoris. Dunley's moans made her tingle, made the edge of orgasm bloom into fierce joy.

She screamed as she came, her eyes opening so she could watch Dunley. He pleasured his cock with hard, fast strokes, his gaze steady on hers. Sweat dribbled down his neck, his eyes glazed with passion. Then he arched, his thighs tensed under her buttocks, and, as he groaned, seed shot from his cock onto his stomach.

Sarah trembled with her release, and with the knowledge she was one step closer to freeing herself from the demons that chained her to the past.

Suddenly exhausted, her eyes closed and she pitched forward.

She landed on the soft comfort of her bedding, already asleep, the fantasy of Dunley's lovemaking fading into the bright landscape of new dreams.

* * * * *

Annie entered the sterile room of her only daughter, Titania, and smiled with a cheer she did not feel. The old Titania would've hated this room with its unrelenting yellow and carefully placed pictures of flowers and rainbows. "Life is not rainbows, Mother," she would say with a look of humorous disdain.

"No, it's not rainbows, is it, baby?" She stroked the dark hair away from Ti's lovely, pale cheek and felt her heart break as the child she loved more than her next breath stared out the window, not seeing the rolling green lawn or blue-sky day.

Annie was too tired to chatter today. Usually she brushed then braided Ti's hair and filled the silence with small talk about everything—the weather, her job, the antics of their pets, any mundane, trivial thing that popped into her head. She sat next to her daughter and took her pale, cool hand.

"I'm letting Dunley go. He has my forgiveness and when he fulfills one last task, I will send him to the Light." She pressed Ti's hand to her cheek and closed her eyes. "You must forgive him, too. And Miranda. Let them go, baby. Let them go and come back to me." Tears fell, sliding between her daughter's too-still fingers. Annie took shuddering breaths, trying not to give in to the sorrow.

Ti's hand curved to cup Annie's cheek. Her eyes flew open and she found Titania looking at her, the vacant gaze shadowed with sadness.

"Titania?"

Annie's watched Ti's eyelids lower in one slow blink. Her head tilted, her eyes blinking fast now, then she stretched her arms above her head and yawned. It was like watching someone wake up after a good night's sleep. Annie kept still, holding her breath, afraid that a word or action would interfere with this unfolding miracle.

Titania licked her lips, turning her gaze to her mother, her lips quirked into the half-smile Annie hadn't seen in two months. "Hi, Mom."

* * * * *

When Sarah awoke, she raised her arms above her head and stretched, feeling refreshed and lighthearted. At some point, she had snuggled under the top comforter; she felt safe and warm in the cocoon of covers. Her eyes drifted open. The afternoon had given way to deep evening. She sat up and the bedspread slid off her shoulders, falling into her lap. Cool wind fluttered the curtains as it breezed inside and it seemed to swirl around her, stroking her naked flesh.

"Hmmm." Goose bumps pimpled her skin, her breasts aching as the peaks tightened. Her body's ardent response reminded her of the dream...the wonderful, terrible dream where she made love to the mysterious Dunley. *Well...sorta.* She somehow felt she'd been transported to another place, that what had happened had been surreal, yet *real*. Even before the rape, when nightmares had not been her sleep companions, she had never dreamed so clearly, so vividly. Her guilt for "cheating" on Ben might have been silly, but it was there, its sharp claws embedded in her conscience.

Shaking off her odd thoughts and the thick blanket, she slid out of bed and landed on a pair of white-cotton slippers. She blinked. On the top of the comfy houseshoes were gold-swirled initials, DBR. *Dunley's Beach Resort.* She looked at the end of the bed and confirmed her suspicion—a matching robe with the gold initials on the upper left corner. She glanced around. "Oh!"

Candles had been distributed throughout the room and on the deck. They were all lit and cast a lovely, romantic glow. She slipped on the shoes and the robe and walked to the tiny dining room table. The munchies she'd seen earlier had been exchanged. A bottle of Pinot Grigio chilled in a bucket of fresh ice. A round loaf of bread sat on an oversized white ceramic plate and next to it, on a yellow napkin, was a spoon. She lifted off the top piece of sourdough and grinned. A thick, hearty beef stew waited inside, its fragrant smell promising beef, carrots, onions, potatoes, and spices. For dessert, she'd been given strawberries and cream. As she gazed at the simple feast, her stomach rumbled and she realized she hadn't eaten since breakfast.

"This is heaven," she murmured, sitting down. She poured a glass of wine and ate, savoring the flavorful stew and nibbling around the edges of the "bowl".

After she finished, she refilled her wineglass and carried it and the strawberries and cream out to the deck. Candles had been lit here, too, along the rail, with a single tealight on the small table. It was too tiny for the plate of strawberries with the attached bowl of cream, so she put it on the floor next to the chaise.

At the rail, she scooted aside some of the votives and leaned on the wood, staring at the ocean. It was too dark to see the waves roll in, but she could hear the water rush the sand and the sucking sound of it receding. The moon was just a sliver of pale light, and the stars looked liked diamonds embedded in black velvet. Sarah laughed and shook her head. The sky looked like the ultimate jewelry store. Her gaze drifted to the diamond ring on her left hand.

"Ben." She thought of her husband, of his love for her. He'd been her rock, her anchor, her one true thing. After the rape, he'd suffered almost as much as she had. In some ways, she thought it had been worse for him because he couldn't get inside her head and help her carry the burden.

I should call him. She put her glass of wine on the table then went to the kitchen where she'd dropped her purse onto the counter. She noticed her suitcases had been delivered and stood near the door.

She opened her purse and pulled out the cell phone, hitting speed dial. Ben picked up on the first ring.

"Hey, honey," she said, her heart clenching. She missed him so much. "What's going on?"

"Just sitting around the living room moping because I can't be with you."

She grinned at the boyish longing in his voice. Had a man ever loved a woman the way Ben loved her? "You're the one who insisted I arrive on Wednesday. You'll be here Friday, right?"

"In the morning," he said. "How's it going with you? Anything...um, happen?"

I made love to a stranger in a dream and I wished he had been you.

"No, not really. I took an outrageously long nap," she paused, "on the bed."

She heard him suck in a breath. "God, baby. Did you have nightmares?"

"No. It was the most wonderful sleep I've ever had. This place is somehow… magical. It's wonderful here, Ben."

"I'm glad." He sounded glad, too, and did she sense his relief? Ben didn't like to be away from her. On days he went to work, he called every couple of hours to talk with her, to tell her he loved her. After a while, she realized he was worried, still, that she might commit suicide.

In the weeks after the rape, it had been a real possibility. She didn't want to live. She felt so soiled, so scarred, she took baths three or four times a day. She hadn't been able to get off the stench of those men, could not rub away her guilt that she had somehow invited their ugly attention. *If only I had double-checked the window locks before I went to bed. If only I had let Ben get the alarm system instead of complaining about the cost. If only I had gone with Ben to that stupid, inane cocktail party. If only…if only…if only…*

"Sarah?"

"I'm here."

"You okay?"

"Yes." She walked out to the deck, kicked off the slippers, and stretched out on the chaise. "I miss you. I had this weird—" *Damn it.* Telling Ben about her dream was a bad idea. She didn't want to hurt him by confessing she had a fantastic sexual experience with a phantom lover.

"Weird what?"

Shit, shit, shit. "Dream," she admitted.

"I thought you said you didn't have nightmares."

"That's why I called it a dream, Ben." The breeze wafted over the deck and she watched the tiny flames of the votives flicker and dance. She loosened the belt of her robe and allowed it to fall open. It seemed as though the wind had become her invisible lover. She enjoyed the way her skin prickled at its gentle assault. Her breasts felt heavy, aching, needy, and her nipples tightened to near-painful points.

"Hmmm." She settled deeper into the chaise and closed her eyes, enjoying the little gusts assailing her flesh. She'd tell Ben about the dream, but she would make him the star of it. "Do you want me to tell you about my dream?"

"Yes."

"Why don't you get comfortable?"

"I am comfortable. I'm sitting on the couch in my sweatshirt and jeans drinking a beer."

"I'm naked."

Chapter Four

"Naked?" Sarah heard Ben suck in a breath. "Sarah...what are you..." Another quick inhalation then, "Are you saying what I think you're saying?"

"In the dream, I was on yards and yards of white material, almost as soft and fluffy as a cloud. Candles were everywhere. It was romantic. It was safe." She sighed and let her hand drift from the valley between her breasts to her stomach. She stroked up again, encircling each distended nipple with a fingertip. She was reliving the dream — with one important change. "You were there. Waiting for me. Naked."

"Oh God. Hang on a sec." The phone clattered, presumably on the coffee table. She heard the zipper of his jeans, the soft plop of his sweatshirt, then Ben was on the line again, breathless. "I'm in my boxers. The ones you bought me Valentine's Day."

Two years ago. This year, they hadn't celebrated the holiday. Ben rented videos — all romantic comedies — and they tucked in, pretending everything between them was okay. But she knew that Ben, as well as she, had remembered other Valentine's Day celebrations, the silly ways they tried to surprise each other and the nights spent making love, renewing their vows and their passion. That, too, was the day the most vicious of her assailants had escaped, and hours later he was dead, shot by police.

Enough reliving the bad memories...it was time to create good ones.

"You kiss me," Sarah whispered. "Your lips are so soft, so sweet."

"I want to put my tongue in your mouth. To taste you."

"Do it, baby. Kiss me. Hmmm." Sarah swirled her tongue around her lips. "What do I taste like?"

"Cinnamon toast."

She laughed. "What?"

"Cinnamon and sugar, comfort and warmth. That's you, Sarah."

His description brought tears to her eyes. "I don't deserve you."

"Sshh. I'm kissing you."

In the last year, she and Ben had attempted to make love only a few times. It had been too painful, too difficult to open herself to him. The idea of vaginal penetration brought her to shuddering sobs. Her desire to be with Ben, to recreate the physical intimacy they had once shared, simply had not been stronger than the memories of that terrible night.

But today, after the dream with Dunley, she felt stronger, more alive and happy than she'd been in a long time. She felt defiant and willing and lustful. Maybe when Ben arrived on Friday they could begin again—one more time—and suture the deep cut in her soul with their love. For now, though, she could gift him with this...

"I feel your mouth on my breast, your tongue swirling around the nipple. It hardens and you suckle it. Oh Ben, that feels good." She shifted restlessly, almost feeling a male mouth on her tit, the wetness of a tongue, the touch of a strong hand. Her legs fell open and with one finger she stroked her clit. Her stomach quivered, sending a tender vibration into her pussy, making her thighs tremble.

"Touch your cock," she commanded softly. "Wrap your hand around it and pretend it's me. I wish I could suck it. Yes, oh yes. I want my lips on your hard dick, sucking and stroking and licking."

Ben moaned. She imagined his eyes closed, the phone cradled between his shoulder and cheek, as he reached into the heart-dotted silk shorts and wrapped his hand around his thick penis. He had a wonderful cock. It filled her, brought her to pleasure. She wanted to feel him inside her, plunging with swift, sure strokes...her pussy tightened at the image. She was already wet. She slid her finger through the slickness to dip inside.

"Sarah, you feel so good. What are you doing to me?"

"I'm kissing your neck. Nibbling that sensitive spot below your ear." She could almost feel his shudder. She pushed two fingers inside her cunt and slowly pierced herself. "Feel my tongue on your chest, baby. Kissing those flat, brown peaks and nipping at them with my teeth. But I can't wait to get back to that luscious cock. It's so big and so hard."

"It's been too long, Sarah." His breath hitched. "I don't know how much longer I can wait."

"What are you doing to me, Ben?"

"Sucking those gorgeous nipples. I love your breasts. Their shape, their weight, the way they feel in my hands. I kiss your neck, your stomach, your hips. My tongue slides down the inside of your thigh and I taste your beautiful cunt. You're sweet, baby. Like sipping nectar." His breathing was shallow, thready, and he groaned.

She knew he was stroking himself fast now. Fast and hard. She matched the same furious pace with her own strokes and felt the building of her orgasm, the jagged tendrils of pleasure too long denied.

"What do you want now, Sarah?"

She knew what he asked. How far could the fantasy go? Would pretending penetration bring back the memories? *Not this time.*

"Fuck me, Ben," she cried. "Put your cock inside me and fuck me."

"Yes, Sarah." He moaned, long and low, and she knew he was imagining that first deep plunge into her pussy. She could almost believe a man's penis slid inside her, filling her, taking deep strokes. It felt good. So good.

"Oh God, Sarah." He panted and moaned. "My dick's inside you. I'm fucking you. Hard. Plunging into that sweet little cunt. You're so tight. So wet."

Her hips arched off the chaise as she furiously rubbed her clit and reached for the stars. Pleasure exploded like a thousand fireworks, sparkling heat that burned and cleansed.

"Sarah! I'm coming. Oh God. I'm coming inside you." He groaned and the phone dropped away. In the daze of her own orgasm, she heard the sounds of her husband's bliss echo through the line, and smiled.

* * * * *

On Thursday morning, Annie stood in the chapel surveying her boxes of souls, her glance sliding to the one labeled "Miranda". It was no accident that Annie had claimed the souls of Miranda and Dunley. Dying while betraying another put both of them squarely into her area of work. She offered redemption to those lost in the place between alive and dead.

Some did nothing more than cause pain in their Earthly lives. Among them were the select few who enjoyed inflicting pain on their fellow human beings. These evil energies that had once been human souls turned into what was called "darkers". They went into Limbo and relived their heinous acts over and over again. Then there were others,

others who in genuine contrition sought forgiveness, who wanted to move into the Light. Dunley and Miranda had been two such souls.

Annie had never removed Miranda from Limbo. Her motto was "Harm none", but even the tenets of a white witch's faith could be tested. It was easier to face Dunley, who had at least not claimed to love Ti, than to release the girl who had been Ti's best friend since junior high. What was she supposed to say to the woman who'd been like her other daughter?

Annie pulled the box out of its slot. "Miranda."

She appeared in an instant, the slim, curly-haired girl Ti had loved so well. She wore a red T-shirt, a pair of faded jeans, and white Keds. She floated a few inches above the ground and looked more solid than most ghosts called to the chapel. She didn't hold the confused look of a soul who didn't understand what had happened to her or where she had been. She looked resolved and patient. She inclined her head. "Annie."

"Miranda." Annie inhaled a fortifying breath. "Ti has been unwell since your and Dunley's deaths. Today, for a few minutes, she came out of her self-imprisonment. She told me…she told me to get you and to ask you to tell me the truth."

"Is she okay?"

"No." Annie frowned at the resentment levied in her tone. She blew out a breath. "She collapsed after the car wreck. She just…she tried to kill herself."

"Oh God." Miranda's calm expression faltered. "She wants you to know the truth?"

"Yes. But I know it, don't I? You and Dunley betrayed her."

"No. No!"

"Souls with good intentions do not end up here. They go into the Light."

"Unless they don't want to go."

Annie frowned. "What? You were offered the Light?"

"Of course." Miranda floated around the room, looking at the boxes, the materials for potions, the beautifully carved altar. "Dunley was offered it, too. We both walked away from it. We both chose you."

"That's not possible."

"Choice isn't taken away after death, Annie." Miranda completed her circle. "If Ti wants me to tell you the truth, I will." She returned to the altar and passed her hand through a sage stick Annie used for cleansing the room before she performed a ceremony. "This is very important to you, isn't it? The tradition of passing your gift and your knowledge and your responsibility from mother to daughter...it's been that way for generations."

Annie nodded. "One mother, one daughter."

Miranda turned and faced Annie. "Tradition is to conceive young so that mothers have time to train their daughters. You can't marry. You're not supposed to have other children. It's such a burden."

"One we gladly bear. No daughter has ever turned away from her destiny, but always embraced it."

"I know." Miranda floated higher and sat as if she had a chair underneath her. "Ti loved you. She wanted to follow in your footsteps, but there was a problem. One she couldn't share with you."

"Infertility?" Annie laughed. "That's an impossibility with our knowledge and our magic."

"How many times we wanted to tell you...oh Annie. Ti is my soulmate. We fell in love in the seventh grade. We didn't understand it at the time, but later on, we did. Ti and I were in so much love. We lost our virginity to each other. But there was one thing I could not give her. A child."

Annie reeled as shock reverberated through her, so strong she felt her bones quake. "Chair," she gasped. One flew from its post near the door and caught her as she crumpled.

"Ti is almost twenty. Two years older than when you got pregnant with her. She wanted to follow the traditions. She knew she had to conceive and soon. But how?"

"Dunley?" She pressed a hand to her mouth then let it fall into her lap. "Oh my God." She struggled with the concept of Ti's sexuality, of how her love for Miranda must have battled with her desire to keep the centuries-long traditions of her family. "He told me...he'd dumped Ti. That he and you were...he lied. He told terrible, vicious lies. Why?"

"Because the truth would send us to the Light. It's one thing to have a choice and quite another to have a powerful witch cast you forward into the afterlife." Miranda grinned, her blue eyes twinkling. "He had to lie. To stay."

"Why would he want to stay? If he was just a...a sperm donor."

"It wasn't quite like that. Ti and I liked Dunley, and he liked us. We had fun together. We...well, I guess we loved each other. It wasn't the same as with me and Titania. The three of us..." Miranda waved as hand as if to conjure the right words. "Dunley and I wanted to protect Ti. I knew how she would react at our deaths. She's got an unshakeable innate strength, but she's also fragile."

"What about the accident?" Annie stood, but her knees wobbled, and she sat down again.

"I don't know. Dunley and I haven't been able to figure it out. It was almost as if something wanted us to crash. The brakes failed. Then the wheel got jerked out of his hand..." Miranda shrugged. "We didn't go into the Light because we wanted to help Ti move on in this life. But something evil was in the car that night. I felt it, in my chest, in my head, like a suffocating darkness. It went into Limbo with us, and hovered just beyond our perimeter, waiting."

Annie frowned, foreboding heavy in her stomach. "Waiting for what?"

"To leave." Miranda floated down until she sat across from Annie. "When you called Dunley, the presence left, too."

Oh God. A darker let loose on the Earth. Annie stood, strength flowing into her limbs as resolve steadied her shaky nerves. "We must get to work, Miranda. If we don't find the darker, he will use his energies to harm, maybe to kill. With each evil act, he will grow stronger."

Miranda paled, though it shouldn't have been possible given her ghostly complexion. "Dunley! You have to call him back. Now."

"No. His task is important and we don't need him to find the darker. I know what to do."

Chapter Five

"Take this, you bitch," he roared, stuffing his cock into her virginal ass. His companion laughed, but enjoying her defilement wasn't enough. While the man above her heaved and shoved, damaging tissues and ripping open her flesh, causing pain to spike up her spine and into her head, his fetid breath making her gag, the other guy managed to stick his dick into her mouth.

His mistake.

She bit it, her teeth ripping into the soft flesh.

His screams ended the rape, but started the beating. The hitting, punching, and kicking didn't last long. Bleeding and cursing and limping away, the second man couldn't afford to finish the job, and his buddy left with him, both of them believing they'd left her for dead.

Neither one of them had a gun, just raw nerve and good timing. She had fought, struggled, begged…it hadn't done any good, hadn't bought her any mercy. After they left, she stared at the ceiling, her eyes open and glassy, trying to fade from the physical world, beseeching God for death. Then Ben walked in, terror and panic in his voice as he shouted her name…

"Nooooooo!" Sarah struggled out of the covers and landed feet first on the floor, her heart pounding erratically. Sweat dripped down her neck and her body felt cold and clammy. She shoved herself into the robe at the end of the bed and hurried out to the deck, hoping the friendly breeze would clear away the nightmare.

She'd slept in. By the angle of the sun, she guessed it was past noon. She shivered, caught in the brutal memories she had mistakenly thought could be conquered. Her phone sex with Ben had given him hope…had given *her* hope. What would he say when he arrived tomorrow and found his wife as frigid as ever? Tears fell, but goddammit, she was tired of crying. She wiped away the moisture, but couldn't stop sobbing, and disgusted with herself, she turned and went inside.

Her tear-blurred gaze lit on the table. Brunch. It was like magic the way the food appeared without her ever seeing a single person. Hell, she hadn't left the room since she'd arrived yesterday. She'd slept more in the last twenty-four hours than she had in the last twelve months. But the nightmares had returned.

The contentment she'd owned since coming to the resort slipped away like sand clutched too tightly in a fist. The creeping depression she knew too well replaced it, the dark poison piercing her happiness like a scorpion sting.

The mango was juicy and sweet, the kiwi with an edge of tart. She ate mechanically, drinking the mimosa and nibbling the Danish with little enthusiasm. Feeling tired and weepy, she took a long, hot shower. She decided against makeup, pulled her hair into a ponytail, and dressed in knee-length summer dress the color of tangerines. She wandered aimlessly around the room, debating the merit of taking a walk on the beach. She didn't want to stay in the room, but she didn't want to leave it, either.

Knock. Knock. Knock.

Startled, Sarah whirled around and stared at the door, her heart stalling. "Oh crap." Shaking off her silly overreaction, she hurried to the door and cracked it open. "Yes?"

"I'm your tour guide, Mrs. Slatterly."

She opened the door wider and gasped. The man was tall and rangy, dressed in a pair of khaki shorts and an outrageous shirt sporting blue and red flowers. His shaggy brown hair was topped by a backward-worn blue baseball cap and his brown eyes twinkled with humor. He looked at her, his lips tilting into a familiar smile. "Hi! I'm Dunley."

* * * * *

The dark soul who'd escaped Limbo watched the one called Dunley. The night the darker left the mortal world, he carried his evil into the car with the handsome man and pretty, pretty woman. He wanted the woman, to hear her scream and beg, to give her the pain that brought him joy. But he had no hands to grab her, no cock to fuck her, no mouth to bite her tender flesh. In his rage, he used the last of his energy to increase the vehicle's speed, make the brakes fail, and wrench the wheel from the man's grasp.

When the car crashed into the tree, their souls left the bloodied and broken bodies, rising toward a place of light that repelled the darker. But they turned away from the horrible glow and he followed them, skirting the edge of the place known as Limbo, and waited.

Dunley was called and the darker followed, an invisible wisp of malevolence slithering out of the witch's lair and into the mortal world.

The darker looked at the woman and hissed in recognition. Her! Hate and hunger ravaged him. Alive. Alive when he was not. Still beautiful, the only scars left on her were invisible to the human eye. That pale, fragile beauty drew him before, made him watch her, follow her, wait for the perfect moment.

He floated near the ceiling, watching Dunley charm her. She laughed and nodded, then grabbed a large floppy hat. As they left the room, he remembered the pain he'd caused her and savored the memories of it. Hmmm. She had begged and screamed and fought. Pleasure shuddered through him. Oh yes. He would have the woman again. And this time…she would not escape her fate.

* * * * *

"I have a confession."

Sarah turned from watching the waves hit the beach to look at Dunley. She felt oddly at ease around him. He was the only man besides Ben that she felt comfortable enough to be alone with. The depression threatening her just minutes earlier drifting away like the clouds lazily moving through the sky above.

"Sins, Dunley?" She closed her eyes and dug her toes into the warm, wet sand. "I'm not a priest."

"I'm part of your anniversary gift."

Her eyes flew open and she stared at him. She had yet to figure out how she'd managed to have dream sex with a man she hadn't met. It boggled her mind. He was so charming, so kind. She hated to admit it, but there was a sexual awareness between them. She tried to quell the attraction because, damn it, Ben deserved better from her.

"The resort is a lovely place. I'm glad Ben arranged it."

Dunley's lopsided grin held a hint of embarrassment. "Not the resort, Sarah. Me."

"You?" She frowned. "What are you trying to say?"

He enfolded her hand into his own and lifted it, palm up, for a kiss. "I'm here to pleasure you. To give you what Ben wants to give you."

Her pulse leapt at the forbidden and tempting thought of having sex with Dunley. No. She snatched away her hand, anger zipping up her spine. "You're insane. Ben would never, never… God, I don't even know what to call it. He wouldn't rent a man for me."

"A husband who loves his wife wants only what is best for her."

"And that's you? Hah!" She turned and marched closer to the waves, sucking in a breath when the cold water surrounded her feet.

He followed, and when she looked over her shoulder to glare at him, he waved a piece of paper at her. "From Ben."

She whirled, snatched it out of his grasp, and opened it.

Dear Sarah,

I love you so much. This anniversary may be the most important one we ever celebrate. Please understand when I tell you that sending you to the resort is more than just a getaway.

I want you to have fun and to learn how to enjoy sex again. I've been promised that Dunley knows what he's doing and I trust that what unfolds between the two of you will only make our loving better. Remember, you are my life.

I will see you soon, baby. If all goes well, you will have the best weekend of your life.

Love always,

Ben

Sarah licked her dry lips, desire fluttering in her belly. Ben wanted her to—to fuck Dunley? Why? She pressed the note against her chest and closed her eyes. Did her husband think it was his fault she was frigid now? That if he couldn't rouse her desire, another man, a stranger, could? *It's true. You made love to Dunley, somehow, someway, in that dream…and you were able to imagine sex with Ben afterwards.*

"It doesn't feel right," she said, opening her eyes and looking at Dunley. "How can I sleep with you when I can't bear the touch of the man I love?"

"You will, Sarah." He brushed her cheek with a calloused thumb. "And when Ben arrives, you'll have us both."

Fear and desire clashed. Two men? No goddamned way. It would be too much like the rape. She heaved a breath, terror trapping the air in her lungs. Was Ben crazy? She sucked in calming breaths until her body stopped trembling. Her thoughts jumbled together, but one pushed to the forefront.

Ben and Dunley stretched out beside her, their hands stroking her flesh, their mouths kissing and suckling…

"Oh my God." Lust gathered, pushing thorny need into her cunt. Was it possible she was getting turned on by the scenario of fucking two men? After the rape…no, Sarah. Time to heal. Time to let go.

Could she find pleasure with Ben and Dunley together? If they would pamper and coddle and indulge her until she found only ecstasy…would that act replace the ugly memories of being tortured and hurt by two evil men? Would being taken in joy and in love by two beautiful, kindhearted lovers mean her salvation?

"Dunley…"

He slipped his hands under her dress, his fingers sliding up her thighs, lifting the dress until her thong underwear was revealed. His fingers looped under the band and drew them down. "I'm hard for you now," he said. "I want to take you from behind, okay? You'll feel me, but you won't see me. It's a good way to start. Remember, just say the word and I'll stop."

She'd lost the ability to speak. Her mind fogged with desire, its heat prickling her skin. God, she was so wet. It wasn't possible…shouldn't be possible…

"For you." Dunley produced a finger-shaped vibrator. It was pink, made of soft plastic, with spikes on the tip. "Control your pleasure." He winked. "Control me." He tucked it into his pocket. "When you're ready…"

He waited, demanding nothing. His tender patience released her from lingering doubts. Ben's note fluttered away in the wind as she let it go, and with it, her inhibitions.

Sarah unbuttoned the top of her dress. Her breasts were small, like grapefruits, and didn't need the annoying harness of a bra. Dunley's eyes darkened as he watched her reveal them, cup them, and offer them. "I love it when Ben plays with my breasts."

Leaning forward, he suckled the hardening nipple of the left tit, the pressure of his mouth, the swirl of his tongue, shooting fire down to her groin. She moaned, arching back to offer him more. He switched to her right breast, lavishing attention on the aching peak. "That feels good."

He sucked, kissed, licked for endless, wonderful moments...then he used his hands to knead the sweet flesh, pinching and tugging the nipples until Sarah panted and moaned and wiggled.

She needed something...something more...she looked down at Dunley, watched him pleasure her tits with hands and mouth. Her knees quaked, threatening to buckle. She pulled Dunley's head away from her chest, and stared at him, knowing her eyes had the glazed look of someone on the edge of orgasm. Her body shivered with terrible need.

Words wouldn't come so she lifted her dress, holding its edge, and got on her hands and knees. She offered her ass to him, her breathing reedy, her heart thumping fiercely, as she waited to feel his cock slid into her cunt. Smells of the ocean's brine, the sweet grasses in the dunes to her left, assailed her. The air smelled fresh and clean, the scents of hope and desire as heady as those of ocean. The sand was soft and warm under her palms and knees, nature's silky bedding.

She heard Dunley's shorts hit the beach, felt him kneel behind her. The thick length of his cock slid between her thighs and rubbed her sensitive clit. She swallowed the knot of cold fear lodged in her throat. *Go away, Fear. I'm tired of being scared.*

Dunley moved between her thighs, his cock sliding in and out to tease her pussy lips open, to bump the clit. Little waves of bliss rolled through her. Soon, she relaxed and simply enjoyed the pseudo-fucking. The sway of their bodies, the smack of flesh on flesh, oh yes. Joy shuddered through her, its heat melting away the cold terror that tried to hold her hostage.

He was waiting for her again, waiting for her permission.

"Take me," she said. "Please."

An eternity passed before she heard the tiny whirr of the vibrator. He bent over her, wrapped an arm around her stomach, and slipped the tiny pink device against her pussy, in the perfect spot along her clit. The heavenly vibrations kept her panic at bay when he edged the tip of his dick into her. It felt too good, too delicious to deny. Dunley pushed inside, inch by inch, until he filled her.

She breathed deeply, feeling the nearness of her orgasm. God, she was turned on. She bumped him with her ass, and he took the hint, starting a slow rhythm. His cock's tender pumping brought tears to her eyes. It felt good. Having a man's penis inside her felt good.

He increased the pace, his chest rubbing against her back, thinly protected by the dress. His groans made her pussy clench and pulsate. How he managed to rub the vibrator in the right spot and keep his perfect fuck rhythm was beyond her, but damned if she cared.

"Oh God. Yes. Yes!" Bliss threatened, spikes of pleasure piercing her, then she came, hard, her screams echoing down the beach. Her clit was too sensitive for the vibrator's ceaseless movements, but Dunley was merciless. He pounded into her now, his cock plunging into her come-slick cunt, and kept that vibrator rubbing and moving until another orgasm rolled through her.

Dunley dropped the vibrator and shoved away from her. She flipped to her back, still shuddering from the intensity of her orgasms, and watched him stroke his cock. His gaze held hers, dark with desire, glazed with passion. He stroked hard and fast, his hips moving, groans turning to cries as he came, his seed jetting out onto the wet sand.

Chapter Six

On Friday morning, Ben arrived at Dunley's Beach Resort. The weather-beaten Victorian three-story stirred a longing in him he couldn't name. It was quiet here. Only the wind greeted him, bringing along the smells of ocean and sweet grass. Freedom. Yes, it felt like freedom, standing on the porch as he stared at the waves lapping the shore and thought about Sarah. *This place feels just like Sarah.*

He entered the tidy, sparse lobby and saw a large, black woman tending the registration desk. Her wide smile was filled with perfect white teeth, and her brown eyes twinkled with mischief.

"Well, now, ain't you a pretty one?"

Her accent was faint...Jamaican? He placed the single bag onto the floor and leaned on the shining cherrywood counter. "So are you," he said, giving her a wink.

She laughed. "Oh you smooth, all right. Miss Sarah is waitin' for you. Told me to send you right on up." She passed him a big gold metal key. "Room Thirty. First door you see on the third floor."

"Thanks."

"Don't worry about your suitcase. The bellboy will take it up." She made shooing motions. "Go see your woman, Ben Slatterly."

* * * * *

"I can't do this." Sarah paced the floor, the white lace robe fluttering as she walked back and forth across the room. "He won't understand. Oh my God. What if—what if he hates me for..." She waved a hand. "You know."

She spun and faced Dunley who lounged, naked...really, really naked....on the bed. He flipped through a women's magazine, one of the many she'd brought with her thinking she'd need a distraction.

Hah!

"It says here that a man likes it when a woman sticks her tongue in his ear and breathes heavy." He looked at her with brows raised.

"Just for the record, tongues and heavy breathing are better enjoyed at cock level."

Sarah rounded the bed, snatched the magazine out of his hand, and tossed it to the floor. "My husband is on his way up here and I have to tell him I've had sex with you. You! When I haven't been able to—"

"Sarah!" Dunley pulled her onto his lap and held her by the waist. "Take a deep breath."

She sucked in a deep breath and blew it out.

"Have I told you that a cupless bra and matching thong are obscenely sexy?" He dipped a finger into robe and swiped her nipple. "Red is somehow so...sinful."

"Dunley, you are impossible."

"I know."

The key rattled in the lock, and Sarah nearly jumped out of her skin. She tried to clamber off Dunley, but his strong hands held her in place. She sat across his thighs, his cock nestled against her crotch, thick and hard and ready. He twitched it against her pussy, causing trembles of need. Then the door swung open and Ben entered, the grin on his face fading as his gaze took in Sarah and Dunley.

Sarah's throat closed, knotted with guilt and sorrow. "Ben. I can exp—"

"Join us, Ben." Dunley patted the bed. "I was just getting ready to make love to your wife."

Sarah felt the blood rush out of her face. "Stop it!"

"This is...the session Annie talked about?" Ben crossed the room, and Sarah wanted to smooth away the furrows in his brow, talk to him until the pain left his eyes.

"Yes, Ben. It's for her. It's all for Sarah."

"I understand."

He wouldn't look at her. Oh God. Ben was her one true thing and she'd betrayed him. Her body had betrayed him by allowing Dunley's touch, but not his. Her soul keened in wild grief.

"Should I go?" Ben asked.

"Why don't you get undressed and join us?" Dunley opened Sarah's robe, allowing it fall away from her shoulders. "She needs us both."

Ben took off the T-shirt then shucked off his jeans, socks, and shoes. Sarah watched, greedy to see his gorgeous, buff body. He was broad-shouldered, with muscular arms and legs and a washboard stomach. His cock was soft, the result of her betrayal no doubt, but still long, still beautiful. With his short blond hair and tall, muscled body, he was the opposite of Dunley in every way.

Dunley leaned forward, cupped her neck, and brought his lips to her ear. "This is difficult for him. No man wants to share his woman. He loves you so much." The tip of Dunley's tongue traced the shell of her ear. "What do you want to do?"

She wanted to show Ben how much she loved him. How much she needed him. How grateful she was for his love, his support, his devotion. He'd never given up on her. Not once.

"Ben." She heard the longing in her own voice. His name on her lips was laden with desire, and she knew he recognized the sounds of her need. His head snapped up, his gaze wide.

"Sarah?" He climbed on the bed, casting an unsure look at Dunley. "What do we do?"

She crawled off Dunley and into Ben's waiting arms. "I love you." She cried, sobs of sorrow and of joy racking her body. Her husband's arms closed around her and she felt his strength, the same strength that had kept her buoyed in a churning sea for so long.

"I want you," she whispered. She cupped his face, stared into his tearful blue eyes. "We can't go back, baby. I'm changed forever. So are you. And this—if we do this, it's something we can't change. I want you and I want Dunley. I want to feel again. I want to desire again." She kissed him, soft and gentle. "You are all that matters to me. I never, ever want to hurt you."

"I will do whatever it takes, Sarah," Ben said, as the tears in his eyes fell down his cheeks. "I love you. And that is the one thing that will never change."

He kissed her, a slow meeting of the lips that made Sarah's heart pound. He kissed her in the same way he had on their first date. The unsure movements of his mouth echoing that first kiss made her smile. Happiness curled through her.

She sighed into his mouth, suckling his bottom lip, tracing the upper one before spearing the seam. He tasted like mints. Like ocean. Like love. He groaned and she swallowed the sound, angling her head to taste more of him. His tongue danced with hers. They hadn't kissed like this since...never mind.

The past's sharp claws had been embedded in her soul too many months. One by one, she would pry them out so that her wounds would heal. And she would heal. This time, nothing and no one would drag her back into the monster's grasp.

Ben released her mouth and slid his lips along her jaw. Desire speared her, prickles of awareness driving a spike of heat into her groin. Her breathing shallowed as his mouth traveled along her collarbone, down the valley between her breasts, and slowly, too slowly, along the line of her right breast.

"Sarah," he murmured. His warm breath goose pimpled her skin. His tongue traced the areola then she felt his hesitant taste of her nipple. He licked and laved and she knew he wanted to show her the pleasure he'd once given to her. She arched her back and pressed his head against her chest.

His groan shuddered across her flesh as his lips clamped the nipple and suckled it into a taunt, aching peak. His other hand cupped her left breast, kneading it, two fingers pinching its hardening point.

"Let me love you," Sarah said, pushing on his shoulders.

As he lowered to the bed, she tossed off the robe. She looked at Ben. His eyes were glazed, his body trembling, and his cock growing and hardening. God, he was beautiful. Ben. Her Ben.

"I know what you need." She leaned forward and rubbed her nipples down his smooth chest, thrilling at his groans, his shudders. Her tongue lapped his flat brown nipples. She kissed the ridges of his stomach, swiped each hip with a wet kiss then...whoa. She took a deep breath, pushed aside the residual fear, and kissed the tip of his cock.

"Sarah?"

She looked at him, at the need he tried to hide, at the hope that glittered with his concern.

"It's okay," she whispered.

She suckled the tip, dipping into the tiny hole and was rewarded by a taste of pre-come. Her tongue swirled the ridge of his head again and again until his hands fisted the sheets and his thighs trembled. She slid her tongue down his shaft, peppering it with tiny kisses and quick licks. She cupped his balls, playing with them before lowering her mouth to each one, suckling and laving. Then she returned to his shaft, to the tip, and she put it into her mouth, slowly, inch by inch, until she'd taken it all.

"Sarah. Oh God."

Desire pounded an ancient rhythm, as strong as the fear, the memories threatening to overwhelm. *No. Please. It's good, so good. I can do this!*

She took Ben into her mouth again, all the way to the base. She loved giving him head. She used to do it all the time, used to surprise him with blowjobs at the oddest times, the weirdest places. It turned her on to fuck him with her mouth, to taste the essential maleness of him, to drink the cream of his desire.

They'd gone to an old movie house to see *Casablanca*. No one was in the tiny theatre. Only one person ran the ticket booth and candy counter. They were alone. Ben loved the old black-and-white film as much as she did and he tried to do Bogart all the time. He made her laugh with his bad impression of "Here's lookin' at you, kid."

She'd gotten on her knees, unzipped his jeans, and taken his sweet cock into her mouth, giving him a blowjob just as the film started. The music of the opening credits rose and fell, just as her lips and tongue rose and fell. He came into her mouth and she drank from him, licking every delicious drop from his trembling cock.

The memory was all she needed to beat back the terror. Like riding a bicycle. You never forget how to do it. Her mouth quivered with the familiarity of his cock sliding between her lips. Her tongue ravaged the hard length, licking, stroking. She took all of him as she went down again and again.

God, she was turned on. Her pussy was wet and needy, tight with an ache she wanted Ben to assuage. *Soon. Soon, Sarah, you'll be able to fuck him.*

His buttocks tensed and his hips lifted slightly as he came. She drank from his thrusting cock, swallowing his seed with a feminine satisfaction she hadn't felt in a while.

When his penis stopped its orgasmic quiver, she lifted her head and smiled at him. He rose on his elbows, tears once again in his eyes.

"That was amazing," said a male voice.

They both turned toward Dunley. Sarah had forgotten he was still on the bed. Her only thoughts had been of Ben, of his pleasure, and hers.

"I enjoyed it." A grin twisted his lips as he pointed at his straining cock. "But I still need a little something more."

"Dunley…" Sarah looked at Ben. Pleasuring her husband's cock had been a huge, huge step for her. But she knew making the next leap wasn't going to be easy. Could she stand a man's body hovering over hers? Fucking her pussy? Would it be too much like the rape? Or would those horrible memories finally go to the grave with the man who'd perpetrated the violence?

And two men? Her heart pounded as cold fear wound through her like an evil, slimy snake. She had to get through this. She was standing at the edge of the abyss and she knew it. This so-called therapy…it was her last chance. She had tried everything else…and it all failed.

Dunley patted the space between him and Ben. "C'mon, Sarah. Let's have some fun."

She turned from Dunley to stare at her husband. Would Ben enjoy this? Would it change their relationship for the better…or the worse? He nodded as if to reassure her that yes, he would share her with Dunley. Renewed desire rippled through her. Two men…

Ben sat up, leaned forward, and cupped her cheek, his thumb stroking her jawline. "Sweet Sarah." He brushed her lips with his. "Let us pleasure you."

Chapter Seven

Sarah lay between the two men, trembling in fearful anticipation. She and Ben had enjoyed many sexual adventures, but never a threesome. Would this experience truly be what she needed?

Dunley and Ben stretched out on either side of her. Dunley looked ready to devour her and Ben looked just as hungry, though she saw the uncertainty tingeing his gaze. Was he worried about her? Or about sharing her?

"What do you want, Sarah?" asked Dunley.

She licked her lips. *Here I go…* "I want you to play with my breasts."

"Which one of us?" asked Ben.

Sarah laughed. "Honey, I have two boobs and two men with two mouths. How about you each take one?"

Ben leaned forward and cupped her breast, suckling the soft peak and laving it to hardness with his tongue. Sarah's eyes drifted closed and she sighed against the lovely assault. Then she felt Dunley's hand on her other breast, cupping and kneading, then…oh yes, then his mouth encircled her nipple.

Heat flooded her as Dunley and Ben played with her breasts, their mouths warm and wet and hungry, their hands drifting down her rib cage, over her hip, down the inside of her thigh, then up again. She squirmed and moaned, arching up, offering her breasts as sacrifice, as penance.

Lust made her wet, made her slick and needy. She lifted her hips, a silent begging, then felt a hand slide into her curls. A finger diddled her clit, then parted the folds of her pussy and dipped inside.

"Oh God. Oh yes." She pumped against the teasing fingers, pressed against the palm cupping her pussy, and all the while Dunley and Ben loved on her breasts, their hands stroking, touching, burning. Both men pressed against her and she felt the thick lengths of their penises against her thighs.

"Sarah," Ben breathed in ear, his lips against her temple, his thumb and finger squeezed her hard nipple. "Baby, I want you."

"Take me," she whispered.

"Let's try something," said Dunley. "Sarah, get on top of Ben and I'll get on top of you."

Ben stretched out and she crawled onto her husband. Dunley grabbed something from the nightstand table, then kneeled at her and Ben's feet. She looked at him over her shoulder. "I'm not sure I can..." She swallowed the knot in her throat. "Are you going to..."

"Relax. All you have to do is say, 'Stop, Dunley'."

She nodded. Ben was ready for her, his cock hard and thick, his eyes glazed with passion. The whole experience had turned him on, not off, as she had feared. His pleasure was her pleasure. She lowered her pussy onto his cock and let her inner muscles stroke him.

As she stretched out over him, she whispered, "Fuck me."

He did as she asked, his smooth, long strokes filling her. Her clit trembled, her over-sensitized body reaching for release.

Then she felt the plastic tip of a lubricant tube inserted into her anus. She tensed as she felt the cold gel fill her. She and Ben had never had anal sex. The only time she'd ever had a penis in her ass was during the rape.

Panic threatened. She'd come too far, sacrificed too much, to allow terror to overwhelm her now. The only way to get over her fear, to beat back the darkness that haunted her, was to free her body, and her mind, from that horrible night. She relaxed, welcoming Dunley as he grasped her hips and worked his penis into her tight anus.

"Are you okay?" Ben kissed away her answer. His movements gentled and he kissed her again, his tongue matching the slow rhythm of his cock.

Her body tingled, rivulets of fire and need prickling through her. Dunley filled her ass with his cock and she trembled from fear, yes, but also from desire. The slow penetration of two dicks felt strange, but pleasurable. Together, they waited for her to assimilate the sensations. One gorgeous man below, the love of her life, and one gorgeous man above, the kind stranger who showed the way back to pleasure. "I'm ready, Dunley."

Dunley's slow rhythm matched Ben's. The movements and moans, the skin slick with sweat, and push of flesh on flesh overwhelmed her. Dunley offered a gentle domination, his warm hands cupping her ass as he penetrated her. Ben's hands curved around her hips, his penis sliding into her pussy with lustful precision.

Soon, lazy fucking wasn't enough. She wanted more...much more.

"Harder," she said.

Ben bucked under her, his cock pumping, and Dunley's grip tightened as he worked his dick in and out of her ass. She moved too, no longer passive in her desire. They all fucked each other, sweating and groaning. Her breasts scraped Ben's chest and her buttocks slapped against Dunley's hips.

Heat coiled low in her belly, arrowing to her core, blooming like a fire flower. "Oh God," she moaned. "More! Fuck me harder! Make me come!"

Their movements were frantic now, and the feel of Dunley's penis plowing her ass and Ben's cock fucking her pussy put her into orgasm overload. The pleasure rippled through her, a wave of blinding bliss that made her scream.

She had barely caught her breath when she felt Ben tense. He pushed deeply inside her, groaning his release as his seed spilled. She kissed him, still turned on, still enjoying Dunley's ass-fucking. Ben's dick slipped out of her pussy and rubbed along her clit.

"Baby..."

Sarah captured Ben's lips again, warring with his tongue, feeling the aching creep of another orgasm as her clit slid along the length of Ben's penis and her ass smacked against Dunley's hips. "Oh Ben," she whispered, as she moved against him, her clit throbbing, her second orgasm a few strokes away.

"I'm coming, Sarah," gasped Dunley. "Your ass is so tight, so sweet. Ooooohhhh."

As he came, his dick throbbing against her sensitive ass tissues, she came again, too, shuddering and joyful, collapsing onto Ben's chest.

* * * * *

In the ugly cheer of the institutional room, curled in a fetal position on the hard bed, Titiana Miller dreamed. It was the same dream...the surreal memory replayed of the last night she and Miranda and Dunley had been together. Ti and Miranda lived in an apartment off-campus and they hadn't been able to afford furniture, but it didn't matter. Nothing mattered except that Miranda loved her. And Dunley, too.

She'd come home from class to find the bare living room dotted with lit candles. On the floor she saw a checkered blanket, a picnic basket, and a chilled bottle of wine with three glasses.

Miranda stood by the window that looked into the street below and next to her, a tall, lean man with shaggy hair, dark eyes, and a sweet smile. When Dunley had come into their lives, Ti knew then, right then, Miranda had found the one they'd been looking for...the man who would give them a child.

Her lover, her best friend, her partner in parenthood crossed the room, tears in her eyes, and kissed Ti with passion and excitement. Ti discarded her backpack and purse, and returned that kiss. Miranda's mouth tasted sweet and minty, her tongue swirling with Ti's until the flames of lust licked at them...

"Let's make love," said Miranda, her happy gaze flickering with desire. She cupped Ti's breasts and brushed the nipples with her thumbs. Then her nimble fingers unbuttoned the Oxford shirt and reached around to unclasp the simple lace bra, as Ti eagerly shed the rest of her clothing. Miranda kissed her breasts, teasing the nipples to hardness, her hand drifted down Ti's stomach to the cunt already slick with need.

She didn't remember how she'd gotten onto the floor, didn't remember when Miranda or Dunley had gotten naked, too. It was as if she'd awakened in a beautiful fantasy. The three of them rolled around on the fuzzy blanket, kissing and touching and suckling until they were panting and groaning and sweat pearled their skin. She'd never been so turned on, so fulfilled, so joyful.

She'd lost her virginity with Miranda. They had penetrated each other with dildos and neither had ever had a male cock before Dunley. She liked fucking Dunley, but not even he could replace Miranda in her heart.

Miranda lay on her back and Ti crawled slowly up her beautiful body. She kissed her rounded hips, her trembling stomach, but didn't linger anywhere for long. She was too eager for Miranda's breasts, to taste the nipples, to sample and delight in the woman she loved.

Then Miranda flipped Ti to the side and she felt Dunley behind her, his hard cock nestled against her buttocks as he cupped her ass and kissed her shoulders. Miranda kissed her, her slim fingers dancing along Ti's rib cage, across her hip, down to her leg. Ti gasped as Miranda stroked her clit.

"Lift your leg," whispered Dunley.

She did, and he slid down, just a little, and worked his thick cock into her wet, tight pussy. She shuddered at the contact, awash in desire and lust, as Miranda cupped her breasts then gently pinched and twisted the nipples.

"Oh God," moaned Ti.

Ti loved the glazed look of Miranda's eyes. Her lover was close to orgasm. Ti lowered her lips to Miranda's sweet nipples and suckled, laved, teased.

"My beautiful ladies," said Dunley. "Let's fuck."

Miranda pressed close to Ti. Their breasts mashed and their clits rubbed against each other; Dunley wrapped his arms around Miranda's buttocks, and she wrapped hers around his, then both of them held on to Ti and fucked her.

The rhythm was perfect. Dunley's cock pumped into her, short, quick strokes that made her pussy pulsate. Miranda moved, too, her hard little nipples scraping Ti's breasts, her wet cunt sliding against Ti's.

Miranda moaned, increased her pace, and pressed closer still. "Oh God, baby. I'm going to come." She was frantic now, pumping her hips against Ti's, her eyes closed and her head thrown back. Watching Miranda's ecstasy increased Ti's pleasure. She felt the rolling wave of bliss already threatening…

Miranda cried out, her hips jerking against Ti's as she came. Ti's pussy throbbed, and the orgasm claimed her in a burst of pleasure so intense, she grabbed Miranda's hips and arched. They held each other, gasping and panting. Little waves of bliss still claimed them when Dunley plunged his cock deep and hard inside Ti and came, crying out as his seed spilled.

Afterwards, they kissed and fondled each other, relaxing in the love they had created. It had been a wonderful way to celebrate Valentine's Day.

Ti's eyes opened and she stared into the darkness of the room. She hadn't conceived that night. Her lovers were gone, her very heart had died, and she was still barren. If only a child had come of their union. Maybe then she would feel like she could go on without them.

"Miranda. Dunley. I miss you both so much."

She closed her eyes against the tears, the horrible wrenching ache of loss…then she opened them again.

Miranda floated at her side, her smile tender, her gaze filled grief. "We didn't want to go," she said. "I love you, baby. Nothing will change that."

"Miranda…" Ti sat up and stared at the apparition, her heart pounding. "Let me go with you and Dunley. My life isn't the same without you."

"No." She reached as if she wanted to touch Ti's face then clenched her fist. "This is the way things are, my love. We cannot change what has happened. You must heal and you must move on."

"I can't."

"Yes, you can. Your mother needs you, Ti. We need you."

Miranda floated closer and Ti wished they could touch each other. She missed making love to Miranda, missed tickling the backs of her knees, and brushing her soft hair before they went to bed at night.

"There's a darker loose," said Miranda. "The same one that caused my and Dunley's accident. Your mother thinks she can handle it on her own, but she can't. She needs your strength and your magic."

"A darker caused your accident?"

"An evil soul who went to Limbo with us. He escaped."

All the pain in Ti's soul wound through her, then a thin ribbon of heat, of anger pierced through the veil of her sorrow. Someone had taken away Dunley and Miranda. Something malicious had robbed them all of happiness. Purpose sharpened Ti's focus and burned away the tendrils of depression still clinging to her. Miranda was right. She couldn't spend the next fifty years in this yellow room with its fake rainbows, wishing for things to be different. Now that she knew some entity was responsible for killing her lovers, she no longer had to accept that it had just been an accident or a terrible quirk of fate.

"I'll help my mother," vowed Ti. "I'll make sure the son-of-a-bitch that stole your lives will pay."

"Not vengeance, dear one," said Miranda.

"No, not vengeance." Ti looked at her soulmate, and briefly despaired about the ghostly form of the woman who would soon leave her for the Light. "Justice."

Chapter Eight

Sarah awoke in the big bed with Ben's arm draping her waist, his soft snore tickling her ear. They had all drifted into a long afternoon nap, holding each other. She'd managed a peaceful, dreamless sleep and had not awakened with a pounding heart or sweaty fists clenching the sheets.

Dunley wasn't in bed. Her gaze traveled around the room until it reached the open balcony doors. She glimpsed him at the railing, staring at the ocean. The salty air blew through the curtains of open windows and she inhaled it. She wiggled out of Ben's arms, smiling when he resisted. She nearly laughed when he flopped over and pulled a pillow over his head like a schoolboy who'd been told to get out of bed.

She slipped on the robe that had been tossed to the floor and padded outside. She sensed Dunley's sadness, and knew his despondency had nothing to do with her or with the crazy sexfest in which they'd indulged.

"What happened?" she asked as she leaned on the rail next to him, her gaze tracing the waves as they rolled onto the beach.

"You passed out from sexual joy," he said, a smile in his voice.

Her gaze flicked to his profile. "Don't make light, Dunley. I know sorrow when I see it. I've lived in it for so long, it's like I can taste it. It's bitter after a while, bitter and vile."

"Indeed. The cup of life tastes much sweeter." He turned to her and pulled a wayward curl behind her ear. "I think you will be just fine, Sarah. And I'm glad. You are beautiful and kind and you love Ben with a fervor I have only witnessed once."

"In all your life—just once you've seen love?"

"Yes. And I was part of it for a while." He sighed, his lips cocking into a half-smile. "It's a long story with a bad ending."

"I have time."

"Time is a fickle thing. One day, it seems as if you have an abundance of it. The days stretch out before you, years of life just waiting to be lived. The next, your time on Earth is over—just as you were starting to discover the best parts."

Sarah grasped Dunley's hand, pricked by his suffering. It reminded her that in the last year, she had been so consumed by her own guilt and humiliation and anguish that she had fallen into complete selfishness. Everything had been about her—the long terror-filled nights, the lack of affection for Ben, the constant self-recrimination, the ugliness that she had inadvertently kept close so that she could keep everything else away. Including love. Including Ben.

Hot shame washed over her. She swallowed the knot lodged in her throat, refusing to give in to tears of reproach. She was determined to use the second chance she'd been given. First, she'd heal herself and second, she'd help heal others. And she'd start with Dunley.

"Tell me about it."

Dunley slipped his hand out of her grasp and returned to his vigil of the ocean. She leaned against the rail with him, watching twilight mesh with the churning sea. The sun dipped toward the endless water and left the sky ablaze in orange, purple, and deep blues.

"I loved two women who loved each other. It wasn't supposed to more than just an occasional ménage a trois. Hell, I had only meant to do an acquaintance a favor." He laughed, but the sound held no joy. "Calling it a favor makes it sound small and insignificant. They wanted a child. But I fell in love with them and they fell in love with me, but the truth was that they shared a deeper bond. Watching them made me believe in soulmates."

Sarah heard the wood railing groan as Dunley shifted his weight. She glanced at him and felt a deep pang of empathy at the look of longing etched on his face. "Did you leave them?"

"Not willingly. I would have stayed forever, you know. But it wasn't meant to be. I will miss being with them so much." He turned to Sarah and her heart clenched when she saw the sparkle of tears in Dunley's eyes. "I only wish I had been able to give them a child. There is no greater gift."

She cupped his cheek. "There are other kinds of gifts, Dunley. Like the one you've given to me and to Ben. We may not have our lives back yet, but we will. Because of you."

Taking her hand, he turned it up and kissed the center of her palm. "Then I will die a happy man."

* * * * *

The darker watched the one called Dunley smile at the woman. He wailed in silent rage, wanting to rend apart the light surrounding them. Light hurt the darker. Love was light, joy was light, sympathy was light.

He crowded into a dark corner of the room, away from the unbearable shimmer, and watched Dunley and the woman as they entered the room. The other man was awake now and he rolled to his side as Dunley and the girl crawled onto the bed.

Dunley pushed the robe off her shoulders and leaned down to suckle her nipples.

"Sarah," he whispered against her breasts.

Sarah. Yes. He remembered her. Beautiful. Succulent. Tight.

She scooted closer to the other man, moaning when he lifted her hair and kissed her neck. With one hand around the neck of Dunley and the other squeezing the ass of—

"Ben," she said, accepting his kiss.

Ben. Familiar, that name. He puzzled over it then remembered. She had said it during his playtime with her. She cried out for Ben, begging for his help, and later, for his forgiveness.

The darker stared as the three made love. They moved, and touched, and kissed. Sarah moaned and he savored the sounds, but he liked it better when she screamed.

Oh yes. Yessssss. She screamed and screamed and screamed until her voice gave out. She fought, too, and fought, until her arms and legs gave out. She had been the best of all the women he had taken.

And he would have her again...

* * * * *

Sarah moaned, her hands caressing the hard cocks and tense balls of the two men on either side of her. Dunley and Ben pleasured her breasts, their hot mouths and slick tongues on her flesh and her nipples. Tingling waves of heat engulfed her. Ben tugged her nipple between his teeth and she gasped at the sharp pleasure. *Oh yes.* God, she was turned on. Having two men cater to her appetites was mind-blowing.

Why had she been afraid? This whole experience was the ultimate in sexual satisfaction. But there was more than just physical enjoyment, there was tenderness and kindness. She reveled in her feelings for Dunley and Ben, and in their lovemaking.

She wanted more...she wanted both...and she knew exactly what to do.

"Ben..."

Ben and Dunley lifted their heads and looked at her, both of their gazes dark with desire and need. Her pulse jumped, and she licked her lips. They were both so damned yummy. *Which one first...which one...hmmm...*

"Remember when we went to Las Vegas? To that..." She blushed at the memory of what they did and felt another surge of heat in her pussy, "um, club?"

"Yes, baby. I definitely remember."

Dunley grinned. "Were you naughty in Las Vegas?"

"It was a swinger's club," said Ben. "But we didn't know it."

"And when you found out?" asked Dunley.

"There was an empty room with a big soft bed. We were so turned on...you wouldn't believe some of the things we saw." Sarah laughed softly. "But we weren't so horny we didn't consider just how many people had used the room and bed before us."

Ben grinned, and his hand coasted across her stomach, leaving streaks of tickly heat in his path. "So my beautiful wife took off her shirt and bra..."

"...and my gorgeous husband pulled down his jeans and boxers..."

They stared at each other, remembering the frenzy of that night, how letting people watch them make love made the whole experience sexier.

"Maybe you should show me," said Dunley.

"Sure," agreed Sarah. "But there'll be room for you between my legs." Her grin was wicked. "My pussy will need attention."

Dunley obeyed, taking his place between her legs, and waiting to see what Ben did. Ben found the lubricant and squirted some between Sarah's breasts. She already felt on the verge of orgasm. One lick from Dunley's tongue and she might be done for.

"Ready, love?"

Sarah squeezed her breasts together. Ben straddled her, leaning forward to hold onto the bed's headboard, and pushed his cock between the soft mounds. She loved it when Ben played with her breasts and nipples. It was as if her nipples held an electric connection to her cunt.

Sarah pinched her nipples, gasping at the zaps of bliss, and watched her husband's big cock fuck her breasts. "Yes, Ben. Oh baby. I love this. Do it, baby. Mmmm…"

He pumped faster, his grunts and groans increasing with his pace. Sarah knew he was close to orgasm, and she wanted to come with him. "Dunley," she begged, "please!"

She felt Dunley's warm mouth on her clit, suckling the sensitive nub.

Sarah pushed her breasts closer to tighten the gap, and twisted her nipples faster and harder. *Yes…oh yes!* Pleasure rose quickly and burst, a shower of sensations that made her pussy throb with exquisite release.

"Baby…" said Ben. "Oh God…Sarah!" He came, his hot seed spurting onto her breasts and neck, his dick throbbing and trembling between her sweat-slickened tits. He lifted a little, offering his cock, which she licked and sucked. God, he tasted good—sweet and salty and creamy.

"That was fun," said Dunley, poking his head around Ben's thigh. "How about a shower for three?"

* * * * *

"What do you mean we can't get to the island tonight?" asked Ti's mother. "It's an emergency!"

The grizzled old captain shook his head. "Can't go out in a storm, Annie. Winds are too high."

Ti put a restraining hand on her mother's shoulder. "If it's money, sir, we have plenty."

"Can't spend money if I'm dead." The captain tromped from his desk to the window and used a gnarled finger to point to the huge gray clouds crowding the skyline. "Gonna be a big one. I'll take you in the morning."

"We'll just find another boat," said Annie, rising from the rickety wooden chair and glancing with distaste around the shanty, the so-called "office" of Captain Solomon Dweedy.

"Won't find one."

He squinted and looked over Ti's shoulder. "Who's the ghost?"

"The ghost?" Shocked that a common mortal saw Miranda, Ti's jaw dropped. "You can see her?"

"Yep."

Miranda glided forward, exhibiting in death the same grace she had in life. "There's a darker loose on the island. People are in great danger." Miranda smiled, her pale hands held out in supplication.

"Darker, eh?" The captain nodded. "Why the hell didn't you say so?

Thunder cracked, startling Ti. *The storm...damn.* She looked at her mother and saw worry lurking in her gaze.

"Why can't Miranda warn Dunley?" Her lover had tried numerous times to contact Dunley to no avail. Strangely, Miranda could only manifest with Ti or Annie, but nowhere else.

"I don't know." Her mom frowned. "Something more is going on. One darker shouldn't affect magical currents this much."

"Strong evil," said the captain. He headed to the door, gesturing for them to follow. "No time to dawdle. Gotta get the boat prepared. Might beat the storm."

Ti's gaze strayed to the small window and she watched lightning zigzag to the sea. In good weather, in daylight, the trip to the private island took an hour. With rain, wind, waves, and the black of night—it would take much longer, if they made it at all. And when they arrived, what then? Even with all the preparations she'd helped her mother make, destroying a darker was damned near impossible.

Cold fear made her guts clench.

What if they were already too late?

Chapter Nine

Sarah snuggled into the soft bed and watched Ben and Dunley find and light candles around the room. Just as they had finished their shower, and making love yet again, the lights sputtered and died. Only then had they noticed that rain lashed at the house as thunder cracked and lightning jabbed the night sky.

Naked, as sexually sated as she'd ever been, her body aching in a delicious way, Sarah drowsed against the thick comforter. The storm didn't bother her. In fact, the sounds of the tempest created a strange lullaby.

"The main power source has been knocked out," said Dunley, "but the inn has a backup generator. I need to go outside and start it."

"By yourself?" asked Sarah, concern whipping through her. "It's too dangerous."

"Where is it?" asked Ben.

"About ten feet from the main house—in a well-protected shed. I have flashlights downstairs and I could walk around this island blindfolded and not get lost." Dunley's smile glinted in the flickering candlelight. "You don't have to worry about me. Get tucked in. I'll get the electricity working and bring up a batch of hot chocolate."

He sounded so confident, Sarah felt better. In truth, the idea of sipping hot chocolate while snuggled in this huge bed tempted her beyond reason. "With marshmallows?"

"Whipped cream and chocolate drizzle."

Ben finished lighting the last candle then stood and looked out the French doors. All was darkness; only the violent thrashings of the gale penetrated. "Are you sure you won't need help?"

"No, my friend." Dunley slipped out the door.

Sarah looked at Ben. "Do you think he knows he's naked?"

Ben laughed. "Maybe. I don't think he cares."

* * * * *

The darker followed Dunley through the hall, down the stairs, and outside into the full fury of the storm. When the man reached the shed, the darker entered with him. As the fool bumbled and cursed, the flashlight's beam bouncing across the interior of the shed, the darker searched for a way to stop him from returning to the house.

The big metal wrench gleamed like the Holy Grail.

I want it. I want it. I want it!

The wrench flew into the air.

Yes! Hit him! Hit him! Now!

If it had a mouth, it would've grinned with malice as the heavy tool slammed onto the human's head. If it had a voice, it would've have laughed as the man slumped to the cold concrete floor. If it had legs, it would've danced on the still form, kicking and smashing and crushing.

Victory!

Now, only one obstacle stood between him and Sarah. The darker turned to the house and swept toward it.

* * * * *

"What was that?" asked Ben, sitting up in the bed.

Sarah drifted in that sweet place between awake and asleep. Her husband's sudden movement jolted her awake. "Huh? What?"

He shook his head. "Sorry, baby. I guess the storm's making me jumpy."

"That's a switch." She chuckled. "If I'm not scared, you shouldn't be."

"I'm not scared," he protested, dropping a kiss onto her head. "Sarah…do you think everything will be okay?"

She'd never heard that kind of plaintive tone in Ben's voice. She tried to shake off the exhaustion, but only managed to open her eyes. "The storm will pass."

"No…with us."

With some groggy effort, she sat up and grasped Ben's face between her palms. "I love you more than any man—more than anything anywhere—on this planet. What happened this weekend has been incredible. It's been healing."

Ben stared at her intently and she wondered what he hoped to find in her gaze. He rubbed a thumb along her jaw. "You're you."

"Uh…yeah."

"It's just...you've been lost for so long."

"I know." Her heart clenched at the relief on his face. God, she had worried him too much. Trapped in her own pain, she'd been unable to reach out to him and only now had she begun to realize how much he had suffered, too. "I'm sorry, Ben. I'm sorry I wasn't—"

"All the bad things are behind us now."

She smiled sadly. "I don't think what happened to me will ever be gone from our lives. It's like trying to throw away your shadow." She kissed him. "But it's okay. I'm okay. I think I should go back to therapy. And after that, I want to help others who've been through the same thing. I mean, after I get to a place where I can do that."

Ben hugged her so hard she lost her breath. "I love you, Sarah."

"Does that mean you think it's a good idea?" she murmured into his shoulder.

He released her. "Yeah."

"Which part?"

"All of it."

"And what about Dunley? About our...about what we shared with him?"

"I like the way it pleased you." He smiled. "I liked the way it brought you back to me. If you're asking if I'm jealous, then yeah, I am. But if you're asking if I'm going to regret what we did, the answer is no." His lips brushed her temple. "You're mine. And just for the record, I have no plans to share you again."

He tucked her into the covers and in seconds, she felt sleepy. "C'mere."

"Dunley's been gone too long. I'm going to check on him."

"He's probably downstairs burning the hot chocolate," she murmured, feeling herself sink deeper into oblivion.

When Ben crept out, she barely heard the click of the door shutting.

* * * * *

The darker floated in the third-floor hallway, thinking. It felt stronger, more in control, alive. Hurting Dunley somehow helped make it that way. In the long mirror that hung in the hallway, it saw how it now formed a shadowy figure. Hands. It needed hands. Legs. Torso. Penis. Yes. It needed a penis.

Mouth? It felt lips and tongue and teeth. Every time it thought about what it wanted, what it needed, it got those things.

At the sound of the door creaking open, the darker ceased its attempts to create a solid shape and hid in the shadows.

It watched as Ben slowly shut the door and walked toward the staircase.

Look how Sarah's husband left her alone again. Just like before…yes, it had watched Ben leave her then, too, and had waited patiently for opportunity.

Just like he would this time.

Hah! The darker was meant to have the woman.

Hovering above the stairs, it followed Ben's progress. At the top of the second-floor staircase, it watched the man take the first step. It focused on the big bare feet.

Trip! Fall! Die!

Another step. And another.

Frustration welled in the darker. It focused on the feet again.

Trip! Fall! Die!

This time, it heard the crack of an ankle turned wrong, the surprised yelp of pain, and watched, gleeful, as the man rolled down the rest of the stairs and thumped to a stop at the bottom, lying pale and still.

Trip. Fall. Die.

Good.

* * * * *

"How far?" shouted Annie. The roar of the wind and the slap of water against the boat nearly drowned out her words. Crowded into a space meant for two people, the three—four if she counted the ghost— of them hunched together in the tiny space and peered out the windows. The cabin was stifling and hot, but it protected them from the storm.

Captain Dweedy shrugged, his attention on the gauges, and his grip tight on the wheel. "In fair weather, about fifteen minutes."

"And in foul weather?"

"Don't know."

Annie looked out the window and saw nothing but blackness. How the Captain knew his destination much less how far they were from it boggled the mind. "We waited too long."

"The preparations required time and perfection," soothed Ti. "Don't worry, Mom. We'll make it."

Annie took her daughter's hand and squeezed, taking comfort in the warmth and strength she found there. Again, her gaze sought the dark ahead, hoping to catch some glimmer of land or light. It was like looking into the gaping abyss of hell. If she and Ti did not arrive in time to catch the darker, that's exactly where Sarah, Ben, and Dunley would be—in hell.

"Is there any way to warn them?" She turned her beseeching gaze to Miranda. Annie knew a lot about the spirit realm, but surely Miranda knew more than she. She'd dwelled in Limbo long enough to figure out some ways around the so-called rules.

"I can't leave you or Ti. I don't know why."

"There is a greater force at work," said Annie. "We can't always know our purpose—or the purpose of others."

"Darkers serve no purpose." Ti's gaze burned with anger. "They're evil."

"Everything serves a purpose."

"Are you saying we shouldn't do anything? We should leave those poor souls to their fates?"

"Of course not!" Annie shook her head. "But we must take some comfort in the idea that we will arrive when we are needed—and that everything unfolding is necessary." Once again, she looked at Miranda. Fate or not, she could not abide the idea Sarah and Ben might get hurt. If only there was a way to tell someone on that island about the terrible danger. *If only…*

* * * * *

Sarah slept…and dreamed.

It was her wedding day. Under a rose-entwined arbor in a beautiful garden, she spoke vows with Ben. Her parents sat in the first row, tears glittering in their eyes. Birds twittered, a gentle breeze rustled the leaves, and the sweet scent of roses clung to the air.

The scene melted away.

Now, she stood in the kitchen of the house she loved and stirred the stew she'd made for dinner. This house. This beautiful, wonderful, perfect house. She and Ben had saved years for the down payment. It was the place where they would make babies and live out their dreams of wedded bliss.

The kitchen walls were butter yellow. She'd painted them herself, and put a cheerful rose border at the top. She loved roses. They reminded her of the day she married Ben. The best day of her life…

She hummed, stirring the stew, and thought about Ben.

"Sarah?"

She turned, surprised to see a dainty woman with curly brown hair and warm brown eyes looking at her.

"I'm sorry…do I know you?"

"You're in danger."

"What?"

"Tell Ben and Dunley…" The woman whirled around and stared at the wall behind her as if Satan might burst through it. The fear etched on the woman's face made Sarah's heart leap.

"What's wrong? Who's Dunley? Where's Ben?" Chills danced along her nape.

"Go, Sarah. Run. Run!"

The terrifying urgency in the woman's voice made Sarah drop the ladle and sprint toward the back door. She flung it open and ran out, dropping into a cold, black hole. "Help! Help me!"

Everything shifted, changed…

She lay on her bed, her breath caught in her throat, her heart hammering in her chest. Something had awakened her from a deep sleep. A noise. Foreboding crept through her…a deep ugly feeling lodged in her stomach…she removed the covers, her feet touching the floor…there, in the corner, a movement…no, a man…two men…

They pressed her to the bed, ripping at her shirt, grasping at her flesh…

She screamed…and screamed…and screamed…

Sarah awoke, screaming, her throat sore, her eyes blinded by tears. "Ben? Ben!"

Her gaze focused on the room around her. Candles had burned low. The storm still raged. Dunley had not returned. Ben was gone.

And something malicious and evil was in the room with her.

She felt its gaze, its hunger. She licked her dry lips and tried to calm her erratic heartbeat. Her first impulse was to run and to hide, but she knew it was futile. What hunted her from the shadows would find her, no matter how fast she ran or how well she hid. She stared at the darkness, waiting…

Chapter Ten

It slithered into the rim of light provided by the dying candles. Human-like, but fuzzy, like a smeared pencil sketch, the only discernable feature was the red glow of its eyes.

"Sarah," it lisped. "Sssssaaaarrraaahhh…"

She scooted backward until her back smacked against the huge wooden headboard. Her heart pounded fiercely and she felt chilled to the bones. Her hands clenched the comforter and for a moment, she wished she could toss it over her head and make the Boogey Man disappear.

"I want you, Sarah. You were good. So good."

Were good?

"That night, I shared you. I am generous. But tonight, I have you all to myself. Tonight, you will scream and beg…and bleed."

Sarah shivered against the cold, against the nausea threatening. Her stomach churned, her mind wild with fright. She remembered those same words, that same expression.

The man stood at the end of her bed, watching her struggle in the too strong grip of the one who held her. "Tonight, you will scream and beg…and bleed."

Her heart froze.

Impossible. Not him. It couldn't be him.

The creature shifted, melded, and solidified into the shape of man, but appeared sooty. Except for the eyes. The eyes looked at her with hunger, with malice.

He can touch me. Hurt me.

Its features, though malformed, looked familiar. This…this thing before her, dear God, she knew this tormenter.

"You." Her voice cracked on the single word. "No. No!"

"Yes. Yes. Yes." It grasped the footboard with ashy fingers. "Me. Hmmm? Remember our games? Such fun."

"Fuck you." The words held no courage, no fire. They were whispered, a frantic entreaty, a horrible hope wrapped in false bravery.

"Okay." It swept toward her, a wave of black, a thick blanket of evil that brought with it the smell of sulfur and the promise of retribution. Throwing the comforter at it, she was surprised to find it tangled in the coverlet.

Sarah wasted no time scrambling out of bed. "Ben! Dunley! Somebody help me!" She ran to the door and wrenched it open, but before she could step out into the hallway, the knob flew out of her hand and the door banged shut.

She grabbed the handle and pulled, her palms aching from the effort.

Then she felt its hands on her, wrenching her away, spiraling her toward the bed. No! She wouldn't be violated again. What could she do? Her gaze landed on the French doors. If she could make it out to the balcony, she could throw herself over the railing and free herself from the creature—and the world.

Somehow, she found the strength to push her thumbs into the red orbs. Her stomach roiled. It felt like puncturing Jell-O. The demon-man howled and released her, grabbing at its face.

Rolling off the bed, Sarah scrambled to her feet and fled, her only goal to reach the balcony railing.

I'm sorry, Ben. I love you.

* * * * *

When Dunley awoke, he found himself in his ghostly form. The spell was either at its end or had been broken when whatever—or whoever—had hit him. He hovered for a moment, considering his options. Usually when he was finished with one of Annie's charity cases, he returned to her and she shoved him into the box again. Except this time, she would give the locket to his mother and release him to the Light.

He looked down and saw the wrench. Had Ben, jealous about sharing his wife, followed him to the shed and bopped him with the heavy tool?

"Dunley!"

Whirling, he found Miranda staring at him. "How the hell did you get here?"

"Annie released me." She held up her hand. "No explanations, not now. Where are Ben and Sarah?"

"How do you—"

"Dunley, where are they?"

Miranda's urgency made him uneasy. "At the house. What's going on? Where are Ti and Annie?"

"They're just making landfall. I couldn't come to you while you were human. But when you returned to spirit, I finally connected." She waved at him. "We must check on Sarah and Ben. There's a darker loose."

"A darker!" He looked at the wrench again. Suddenly it made sense. "Oh my God."

They zoomed toward to the resort, two arrows of light in the darkness.

* * * * *

Ti and Annie struggled against the wind and rain, wading through the last three feet of churning water. The Captain rowed the dinghy back to his boat, his yellow slicker the only sliver of color in the roiling black sea.

"The house is dark," yelled Ti.

"The storm probably blew out the power," said Annie.

Ti nodded, but she knew the inn had a backup generator and it hadn't been turned on. Why not?

"Miranda and Dunley can't offer much protection." Annie readjusted the black satchel on her shoulder. "We must hurry."

Carrying her own satchel, Ti followed her mother up the beach, struggling through the wet sand and scratchy grass. The house was a dozen yards away—it might as well have been a million miles. Her heart thudded in dread. If the darker could harm mortals, it could harm spirits. Miranda and Dunley were in just as much trouble as Sarah and Ben.

The resort loomed ahead. She peered at the old Victorian house through the pelting rain. If she didn't know better, she'd think it was empty. Lightning flashed, and for a split second, she thought she saw a pale form lurching across the balcony, and watched as one pale leg was thrust over the railing.

Miranda?

No…not a ghost. A woman.

Ti grabbed her mother's arm and pointed up. Annie's gaze skittered to the top of the house. "Oh my God. It's Sarah."

"What's she doing?"

Annie didn't answer. Instead, she started to run, and so did Ti.

* * * * *

When Ben awoke, he stared through the pale faces of Dunley and a young woman he'd never seen before.

Through their faces?

"Jesus!" He rolled to his feet and almost vomited. His head throbbed to the beats of a thousand drums. He put his hands on his knees and breathed slowly. His right ankle hurt like a bitch, but he could walk on it.

"Are you okay, Ben?" asked Dunley.

"I fell down the stairs." He slowly straightened. "What the hell is wrong with you?"

"It's a long explanation, but the really short version is that we're ghosts."

"That's impossible! How did you…" His gaze slid toward the girl and he waved his hands. "*You know*…with me and Sarah?"

"I'll explain later."

"I'm Miranda," the woman said. "Where's your wife?"

"Upstairs, asleep. I was going to find Dunley and I swear something—" He shook his head then groaned as stars burst behind his eyes. "Shit that hurts. It felt like something knocked me down the stairs."

"We must check on Sarah," said Miranda.

Her insistent tone prickled the hairs on his nape. "What's going on?"

The rattle and bang of the front door bursting open startled Ben. He limped to the edge of the second-floor staircase and watched two drenched woman hurry toward the stairs. "Who the hell are you?"

One woman looked up, her expression grim.

"Annie?"

"Ben! You're okay. How's Sarah?"

Ben's heart tha-thumped and sweat pearled his brow. His mind couldn't process everything—Dunley was a ghost, Miranda, too, by the looks of it, Annie was here with another woman, both carrying big satchels, and everyone was concerned about Sarah.

The ghosts, or whatever they were, had disappeared, and Annie and her friend hurried toward him. Without another word, he hauled ass up the stairs to Room 30 and grabbed at the door handle. It was locked.

"Sarah!" He pounded on the door until his fists stung. "Sarah!"

"Move, Ben."

Annie sprinkled a yellow powder across the floor and muttered some words. Then she placed her palm out and commanded, "Open!"

The door wrenched off its hinges and flew backward, smacking the back wall so hard, it splintered.

She rushed inside, followed by the younger woman, and Ben followed. What met his gaze was more fantastic than ghosts and magic. Dunley and Miranda sparred with a dark figure that looked like a man with skin made of ashes.

He saw Annie and Ti kneel on the floor and pull items out of their bags. What the hell was going on? Frantic now, and so scared his body trembled, he sought his wife. Where was she? The bed was empty, the door to the bathroom was open and no one was in it, and the room held only the terrible battle.

"Sarah!" He ran to the open French doors, cursing the pain jolting up his leg from his injured ankle. "Sarah?" What had that monster tried to do to his wife? Had she escaped? But if she'd gone down the stairs, she would've found him. That left…no! He leaned over the balcony. "Sarah!"

The storm's frenzy was gone. The rain fell softly now, and the velvet black of the sky peeked through the gray clouds. He looked everywhere, around the balcony, above him, at all angles of the roof, and finally, at the sandy ground three stories below. Tears pricked his eyes. "Sarah!"

"Ben?"

Her voice came from the right. He leaned as far as he could over the railing, and saw her hands grasping the rain gutter that ran under the balcony and along this section of roof. "Hang on, baby! Just hang on!"

"I'm already doing that. Any other swell advice?"

He choked on the laughter. She sounded scared, but strong. Yes, she was strong, his Sarah. He clambered over the railing, his feet sliding on the tiles. "Shit!"

"Be careful!"

"Yes, dear." He crouched low, slowly stretching onto his belly. He inched toward the gutter, sweating and cursing, until his hands grabbed hers. "Thank God. Are you okay?"

"Almost."

He slid his arms down on hers, offering his strength, until his hands reached her armpits, and he pulled her up. She grabbed onto his arms and struggled upward, until her knees hit the roof. She slowly turned and sat, watching as he rolled over and did the same.

"Did it hurt you?"

"No. I-I jumped over the railing."

"What!"

"Ben, it was him. I don't know how, but it was him." She cuddled into his side. "I'd rather die than suffer at his hands again. But I didn't want to leave you. I didn't want to give up on my life. So I scrambled down the roof and…well, I managed to grab the gutter and hang on for dear life."

His heart nearly beat out of his chest. He'd almost lost her. Relief made him giddy. He fisted his hands in her hair and kissed her until they were breathless.

"You're naked," he said.

"You're almost naked. Those are nice boxers."

He chuckled. "My wife gave them to me. They light up in the dark."

"I can see that."

"We should go up. You wouldn't believe the crazy shit that's been going on around here."

They crawled to the balcony and climbed over, reaching the French doors in time to see Annie and the other woman blow blue smoke at the demon and chant in an ancient language. The creature writhed and shrieked…then it burst into a shower of red and black sparks, and disappeared.

Ben hugged his wife close, watching the drama unfold as if they were viewing a show at Disney World. None of this could be real. And even if it was, he wasn't yet ready to admit it.

* * * * *

"So mote it be," intoned Annie.

Ti looked at her mother. "So mote it be."

They were both sweaty, both trembling and aching from battling the darker, but it had been destroyed. No Limbo, no Light, and no Eternal Darkness for the evil thing—nonexistence was its punishment and for those it had hurt, their justice.

Annie held out her hands, and Ti's heart clenched. She knew what came next. The Releasing ceremony. The loves of her life would go to the Light, and she would be alone in this life until she met them in the next. Her heart filled with sorrow.

Miranda and Dunley floated to her, looking tired for people who were already dead. She smiled. "I will miss you. I love you both so much."

"We love you, babe," said Dunley, his ghostly fingers passing through her cheek.

"My love," murmured Miranda, brushing her lips against Ti's. Ti felt nothing, but the goodbye gesture brought tears to her eyes.

"What evil rent asunder, let the Light redeem," chanted Annie, waving a lit sage stick through the pentagram they had created with burning candles. "Let Love gather, heal, and mend, and what was meant to be, let be once again."

"Mother? Those aren't the—"

Light burst into the room, as if a huge spotlight had been aimed at Dunley and Miranda. It was so bright, Ti was forced to look away. The warmth and love she had felt at other Releasing ceremonies filtered through the room, wrapping all who were there in tenderness and understanding. At the same time this beautiful Love hugged her, grief struck raw blows. She fell to her knees and cried, her hands covering her face as she sobbed.

She felt arms around her and knew her mother tried to comfort her.

"Ti, open your eyes."

She obeyed her mother's voice and found herself staring into Miranda's eyes. On the other side was Dunley, his arms around her shoulders. Neither was an apparition, but real. Human. Alive. Breathing!

"It's impossible!"

She rose, and with her, Miranda and Dunley. They kissed and hugged and touched — arms, shoulders, hair. Ti laughed and cried and hiccupped.

"Mother! How did you do it?"

"I didn't. I offered a prayer and the Light made the choice. Obviously, you, Miranda and Dunley have more work to do on this plane."

Ti watched Annie cross the room and draw Ben and Sarah inside. Both looked stunned and awed. "I believe all of your paths crossed for a reason."

"The darker served its purpose," said Ti.

"Yes." Annie smiled. "Everything has a purpose."

"I know what to do," said Sarah, her voice soft, her gaze shiny with tears. "I know exactly what to do."

Epilogue

One Year Later
The Five Paths Healing Center
Formerly known as Dunley's Beach Resort

Sarah watched a very pregnant Ti carry a stack of thick white towels into the hallway. "Wait a minute, little mommy," she said, grabbing the stack. "No way are you going up those stairs."

"I'm pregnant, not useless," grumped the younger woman. "And you should talk, *little mommy*."

"I'm nine weeks, not nine months. Where's Miranda?"

"Talking to the woman who checked in last night."

"And Dunley?"

"He's in class showing the kids how to paint. I don't know why he gets to do that. He can't paint."

"It's finger painting, not recreating Van Gogh portraits." Sarah checked her clipboard for the day's tasks. All but one room were full and each room held a woman, some women with their children, and in one, a young man escaping from an abusive mother. The Five Paths Healing Center was a cost-free facility open to any and all suffering from emotional and physical trauma. People with wounded souls could recover on the island in peace and solitude. The Center offered free classes, exercise equipment, and therapy sessions. And when the person was ready to start into the world again, the Center gave him or her a stipend to help start a new life.

"Speaking of paint-splattered muscled men with wicked grins," said Ti.

"We weren't—" She felt Ben's arms around her as he whirled her around and smacked her with a big kiss. "Are you done painting the shed?"

"Work, work, work," he murmured. "I needed refreshment."

"Did you talk to Henry about the construction of the new beach house? You know we have a waiting list and I hate turning away people. Maybe I should—"

"Kiss your husband and chill out. You've gotten so bossy."

"Yeah, well, everyone agreed I would be a good manager."

"Yes, dear."

Ti giggled then waddled away. Sarah vaguely heard Rowena shooing the girl out of the check-out area, chiding her to go rest.

"You are beautiful."

"Thanks." She kissed him again and wrinkled her nose. "You smell like turpentine."

"No, that's my new cologne."

Sarah laughed, her heart so filled with joy, and her life so filled with purpose, she found herself dancing down hallways, singing in the shower, and laughing out loud for no reason other than she felt like it.

The front door swung open and Ben and Sarah turned. In the doorway was a young woman wearing a torn dress, a fading bruise on her cheek, and in her gaze an expression Sarah knew all too well

"Go on, baby. I'll meet you later for dinner."

Sarah put down her clipboard and hurried to the girl, wrapping her arms around her thin shoulders and urging her toward the stairs. "C'mon, sweetheart. We've been waiting for you."

The End

About the author:

Michele welcomes mail from readers. You can write to her c/o Ellora's Cave Publishing at 1056 Home Ave. Akron, Ohio 44310-3502.

Also by Michele R. Bardsley:

1-800-SEX4YOU
Life Without Raine
Lighthearted Lust (Anthology)
Shadows Present

Why an electronic book?

We live in the Information Age—an exciting time in the history of human civilization in which technology rules supreme and continues to progress in leaps and bounds every minute of every hour of every day. For a multitude of reasons, more and more avid literary fans are opting to purchase e-books instead of paperbacks. The question to those not yet initiated to the world of electronic reading is simply: *why?*

1. *Price.* An electronic title at Ellora's Cave Publishing and Cerridwen Press runs anywhere from 40-75% less than the cover price of the <u>exact same title</u> in paperback format. Why? Cold mathematics. It is less expensive to publish an e-book than it is to publish a paperback, so the savings are passed along to the consumer.

2. *Space.* Running out of room to house your paperback books? That is one worry you will never have with electronic novels. For a low one-time cost, you can purchase a handheld computer designed specifically for e-reading purposes. Many e-readers are larger than the average handheld, giving you plenty of screen room. Better yet, hundreds of titles can be stored within your new library—a single microchip. (Please note that Ellora's Cave and Cerridwen Press does not endorse any specific brands. You can check our website at www.ellorascave.com or

www.cerridwenpress.com for customer recommendations we make available to new consumers.)

3. *Mobility.* Because your new library now consists of only a microchip, your entire cache of books can be taken with you wherever you go.

4. *Personal preferences are accounted for.* Are the words you are currently reading too small? Too large? Too...**ANNOYING**? Paperback books cannot be modified according to personal preferences, but e-books can.

5. *Instant gratification.* Is it the middle of the night and all the bookstores are closed? Are you tired of waiting days—sometimes weeks—for online and offline bookstores to ship the novels you bought? Ellora's Cave Publishing sells instantaneous downloads 24 hours a day, 7 days a week, 365 days a year. Our e-book delivery system is 100% automated, meaning your order is filled as soon as you pay for it.

Those are a few of the top reasons why electronic novels are displacing paperbacks for many an avid reader. As always, Ellora's Cave and Cerridwen Press welcomes your questions and comments. We invite you to email us at service@ellorascave.com, service@cerridwenpress.com or write to us directly at: 1056 Home Ave. Akron OH 44310-3502.

COMING TO A BOOKSTORE NEAR YOU!

ELLORA'S CAVE
2005
BEST SELLING AUTHORS TOUR

NEED A MORE EXCITING
WAY TO PLAN YOUR DAY?

ELLORA'S
CAVEMEN

2006 CALENDAR

COMING THIS FALL

THE
ELLORA'S CAVE
LIBRARY

Stay up to date with Ellora's Cave Titles
in Print with our Quarterly Catalog.

TO RECIEVE A CATALOG,
SEND AN EMAIL WITH YOUR NAME
AND MAILING ADDRESS TO:

CATALOG@ELLORASCAVE.COM

OR SEND A LETTER OR POSTCARD
WITH YOUR MAILING ADDRESS TO:
CATALOG REQUEST
C/O ELLORA'S CAVE PUBLISHING, INC.
1337 COMMERCE DRIVE #13
STOW, OH 44224